QUEEN OF THE GODFORSAKEN

QUEEN OF THE GODFORSAKEN

a novel

MIX HART

thistledown press

Thistledown Press Ltd.
410 2nd Avenue North
Saskatoon, Saskatchewan, S7K 2C3
www.thistledownpress.com

Library and Archives Canada Cataloguing in Publication
Hart, Mix, 1966-, author
Queen of the godforsaken / Mix Hart.
Issued in print and electronic formats.
ISBN 978-1-77187-063-4 (paperback).–ISBN 978-1-77187-090-0 (html).–
ISBN 978-1-77187-091-7 (pdf)
I. Title.
PS8615.A7547Q44 2015   jC813'.6   C2015-905206-8
C2015-905984-4

Cover and book design by Stephanie Strain
Printed and bound in Canada

Canada Council   Conseil des Arts
for the Arts   du Canada

SASKATCHEWAN
ARTS BOARD

Canada

Thistledown Press gratefully acknowledges the financial assistance of the Canada Council for the Arts, the Saskatchewan Arts Board, and the Government of Canada for its publishing program.

To my parents, Sandra and John,
who gave me the childhood gift of freedom to run wild
through fields and forests.

ONE

We move in the sweaty heat of July, our St. Bernard Marx and I beside Dad in the cab of the U-Haul. My mom, Victoria, and George, our cat, follow begrudgingly in our Datsun extended cab pickup. The view from my window is like a trip to another planet. We leave behind shaggy, monstrous trees and moss-covered ground. As we cross through the Okanagan, the trees turn from cedar and fir to ponderosa pine. We drive on through the intimidating, towering peaks of the Rocky Mountains. Then everything changes as mountains melt into foothills and eventually dissolve completely. The few stunted trees gradually thin out and finally vanish. All that surrounds the truck for miles and miles is tall grass and land as flat as the ocean.

The windshield is plastered with oozing, yellow grasshopper corpses. My nose is dry inside. I miss the humidity already. Dad stops to pee freely at the roadside. I hold it in. There is nothing to hide behind in this desolate land, not even sagebrush. He climbs back into the truck, grabs my bottle of Diet Coke, and takes a giant swig . . . backwash. Somehow the road trip has burned his face; the contrast makes the colour of his hair look almost florescent orangey-blond. He hands the bottle back to me; now I have nothing to drink for the rest of the trip. I should have forced Victoria to switch vehicles in Calgary. I bet she's sweating buckets in the truck; she's wearing jeans.

My feet rest on the giant fur rug that is Marx. He's gone into some sort of depression down there. He hasn't moved since Drumheller. With my feet on his back, my knees are practically level with my boobs.

It's dusk when we finally arrive. The road to the farmhouse is dust tracks: soft, powdery, parallel trails that lead to a solitary vertical projection. It looks different than I remember, greyer, more depressing.

Dad stops the U-Haul. The engine cuts out. He walks his lanky body to the back, opens the rear door, and pulls down the ramp. He's insane. Two days on the road and no time to even take a pee first. Mom sits in the truck, her hands frozen to the steering wheel. Her golden-brown curls hang straight and dull, shocked by the prairie air. I open my door and coax Marx to follow me out. He whines, trembles, and refuses to move. I leave the passenger door open and walk past Victoria as she steps her skinny ass onto prairie soil for the first time.

The house stands tall, shabby, and silent. The porch door is open. I slip past my stunned family and walk, unnoticed, into the dark house. The air is heavy and malodorous, like opening a tomb. My instinct is to climb the wooden staircase towards the window at the landing. I recognize the railing, golden oak, like our banister back home. The stairs are covered in black topsoil. I stop in front of the window. I can't move. I can't even breathe. For miles and miles there is nothing but long grey grass. Blackflies buzz annoyingly all around my head, followed by mosquitoes. They've found life in a dead house.

The contrast is too great. "What have we done?" I ask the wind as it bangs against the window.

"Victoria, leave the cat alone and get over here and help your mother," says my father angrily. "Where is she? Lydia! Get out here, right now." I wipe my face with my sleeves and walk down the gritty stairs towards the door.

Dad pushes past me to Mom's still body. Her eyes are closed. She looks dead.

"What happened? Mary Jane?" he yells.

His hysteria is comical. I laughc into my hand. I highly doubt it's serious. Her collapse came first, after the tears over the gouge on the piano leg, followed by the back pain. The coma's new to me.

"What happened to Mom?" Victoria says, appearing bruised and battered. The claw marks on her face from George are still bleeding slightly and her perfect golden French braids have started to unravel.

"She's behind the piano. She won't move. Where's George?" I ask.

"I locked him in the bathroom," Victoria says.

Dad gently leads Mom past the stack of plastic-covered furniture to the back porch to sit on a bright orange chair left by a previous renter. "It's probably covered in lice, bedbugs, or something else disgusting," Mom says, her mascara smudged under both eyes. "Alexander, don't leave me here."

"Come on, girls. Help me set up the beds," Dad says.

Victoria, Dad, and I haul in four mattresses without incident and then the four bed frames. Mom and Dad's steel bars slide together and pinch my hand as we carry them in to their temporary placement in the living room. The first tears sting and then evaporate. Dad will lose it if I start to cry too.

"Lydia, get the broom, sweep the living room and dining room. We need one room clean for tonight, " Dad says.

"Where's the broom?"

His eyes tell me he hasn't got a clue. "It's in the back of the Datsun," Mom shouts from the back porch.

The hardwood is caked in topsoil. Sweeping does little. It only gets rid of the top layer. There are years of layers I cannot access. The furniture pile takes up most of the room anyway. It waits, stacked like Lego in covered plastic, until the floor is deemed clean enough. The floor needs a sandblaster.

Mom recovers enough to hobble past the living room entrance and out the front door just as the yard light surges on.

"Lydia, get out there and help your mother," Dad shouts.

"I'm sweeping. Why can't you do it? What are you doing up there anyway — are you in the can?" I yell.

"Now, Lydia!" he shouts in a tone that makes me think he might stomp downstairs and beat me with my own broom. The sweet, concerned Alex is only reserved for Mom.

The warm night air is foreign. It smells of hope — sweet clover, dry grass, and spicy sage. I can hardly see Mom but I hear her sniffles. She's standing deep in the back of the hollow van, unearthing sheets and pillowcases from a fridge-sized cardboard box.

"Can you hear them, Mom?"

"No. What?"

"The crickets. They sound amazing. They're singing loudly tonight. Come on out of the truck. You can hear them better."

"Not now. Can't you see I'm busy?" She thrusts a pile of sheets into my arms. I inhale their familiar clean scent. She tips the box over. "Do you see anything in there?" she says.

I shake my head. "No. It's empty."

"This just tops off the day. The fucking pillows have vanished," she says.

⚡

Dad and Marx are the first ones up. The image in the credenza mirror is unsettling. My face is a garden of freckles and whiteheads in full boom; my usually wavy hair is wheat stalk straight. How did that happen? I left Vancouver pale and zit free. I leave Mom and Victoria asleep on their mattresses and follow my father behind the house. He looks past the corral and garish silver trailer. Some renter hauled the ugly trailer onto the land to use as a makeshift barn. It's an assault to the eye, ruining what would otherwise be a pastoral view. Dad scans the land, our land, his hands inside his cut-offs and his face streaked with dirt from arranging furniture last night. He looks relaxed, contemplative, for the first time in months. I know, as tragic as it is for me, that he has come home.

The prairie is in his blood. His grandparents were German, living in Russia on the Black Sea. It was called Bessarabia back then. Bessarabia sounds so exotic. Just before the Russian revolution they immigrated to Canada. They bought a huge section of prairie on the South Saskatchewan River, our farm. Dad returned to the farm every summer of his boyhood. He knows everything about the land, his precious piece of prairie. He knows about the people and animals that came before us and he knows even more. He's dug deeper, beneath the topsoil to the fossils of ancient forests.

He points towards the pasture, "Our prairie as we know it, started to appear around ten thousand years ago. That's when grasslands started to replace the black spruce forests," he says, in his deep morning voice. I almost never hear it because coffee usually makes it go away before I get up.

"So all this grass used to be trees?" I say.

"Well, eventually. The forests covered the land after the glaciers melted," he says.

"Glaciers? Are we talking ice age?"

"Yes, yes we are."

"So, what was here? What kind of animals lived here?"

"Many, many different animals. It depended on the time. Giant bison and mammoth, big mammals," he says, adjusting his John Lennon glasses. He speaks with the confidence of an adored professor, always the teacher.

"What happened to them all?"

"No one knows. They died out, all of them, quite soon after the grasslands appeared, a mass extinction of nearly all mammals. The most recent expatriates are the grizzly bear and the bison."

"Why'd they leave?"

"Hunted into oblivion."

I am aware of each word in our conversation, our lone connection, me the eager student and he the enthusiastic historian. The morning sun ricochets off the silver trailer, searing my eyes. "There used to be a real barn. Wasn't there? Before the fire?" I say.

"Yes. Over . . . it stood where the trailer is now."

"It was pretty, I mean, architecturally attractive, wasn't it?"

"Yes it was. It matched the house, sided in white wooden shingles. It had a green roof too. It was big. A great big barn — huge hayloft." He laughs. "My grandparents had a barn cat — always had a litter of kittens up there."

"Wow. That must have been awesome. I'd love to play with kittens all summer."

"The problem was she'd have them all year, summer, winter. I remember taking the train out here for Christmas one year. My grandmother told me to go out to the barn, check out the new kittens. I climbed to the loft and found them — a pile of stiff, lifeless kittens. No mother."

"They were dead?"

"Dead, frozen."

"Where was the mom?"

"She'd left. Abandoned them, or was eaten by a coyote."

"That's horrible. It must have scarred you for life."

He laughs, a short, gravelly, morning laugh. "It took me a while to realize they were dead. I thought they were asleep, all huddled in a pile. But they were frozen solid. The land is always changing, Lydia, destruction, rebirth."

I scan the land, blotting out the trailer, trying to imagine it. It's got to be in the destructive phase right now. I can't think of anything new replacing all of the dead and gone.

I refer to my new bedroom as the tower. I am the unwilling resident, a prisoner for all intents. The worst of it is the smell, a godawful stench that rises from beneath the oak floorboards and permeates every inch of the room, including all of the clothes in my closet. Leaving my door open does little but expose me to an unattractive view: the brightly lit hall with its single hanging bulb illuminating dingy, faded urine-coloured walls.

"I can't sleep in here. What is that disgusting smell?" I shout.

"Chickenshit," Dad says, surfacing from behind the bathroom door and resting his naked shoulder against the doorframe. He folds his arms protectively across his skinny, nearly hairless chest, like he's cold from swimming. He's wearing jeans with the belt undone, the heavy buckle hanging from his hips. "This room was once an in-home chicken coop."

He's caught me off guard. "What are you talking about?"

"The house has sat empty since the last renters — the Zerebeskis," he says, then laughs. "They left behind a few parting gifts. Just be damn glad you're not sleeping in the basement like your mother and me. They had over forty cats down there — cat spray everywhere." He lifts his bony shoulder from the doorframe and walks down the stairs. His footsteps are undetectable except for the delayed moan each stair releases as he lifts his foot.

I never met the Zerebeskis. But I remember a couple of summers ago Mom freaked because Dad drove off half-cocked for Saskatchewan, all because of some phone call from the SPCA. I knew animals were involved, lots of them. But I thought they were just cattle. Dad has always had cattle on the land. The renters took care of them as part of the deal. But they always did a terrible job. Two years ago blackleg took out most of the herd. The year before it was a grass fire. Though I don't remember ever hearing anything about chickens.

"Hey Victoria, do you want to switch bedrooms? This one is even bigger than yours," I say loudly. Silence. I pull the crisp sheets under my chin. They smell like home: cedar chips and salty air. I breathe in their scented fibres.

"No way, the chickenshit is all yours," Victoria says.

Mom steps into the hall from the bathroom. The nape of her hair is wet. All that time I thought the folks were in the basement, they were actually in the bathroom. They must have been having one of their couple baths. She stands, not moving, in the yellow light. Why is she just standing there, looking at the floor? Move, Mother, move. She turns her head towards my open door and leans on the frame, just like Dad did a few minutes before. Her nose wrinkles up as she tries to stifle a laugh. She snorts instead, hanging her head, her shoulders trembling in laughter.

"What? What are you laughing at? Tell me, Mother!"

She shakes her head.

"I can't believe you find this dilapidated house funny. You can't leave me in here, Mom. All my clothes, everything stinks."

"I'll talk to your father about painting this room," she says, then turns to go down the staircase. Three steps moan then silence. I listen for the moan of more steps. I can't see her anymore but I know she's stopped on the landing. She must be looking out the window. It's a waste of time. The yard light shines too brightly, all you see are millions of moths fluttering beneath it. The prairie is blackened by its light.

The sound of running water wakes me. Mom is next to the old clawfoot tub in the bathroom. Her round bum sways as she scrubs the orange rust stains from the white enamel. She's squeezed into a pair of pants I've never seen before, plaid and made of stretch polyester. They make her rear look twice as wide as normal.

"Mom?" She doesn't hear me. "Mom? Can we go into Saskatoon today?" I say with more volume.

"No, Lydia. Can't you see I'm busy? I can't stand living like this anymore." Her voice is tight. She's either been crying or is about to start.

I slink past Mom's empty sewing room and into Victoria's bedroom. It's big, even bigger than mine. Her single bed looks ridiculously small and out of place stuffed in the corner of the sparsely furnished space. She sits on top of the unmade bed, drawing horses that look like cows. Her face is puffy and pink and her hair greasy. It has a sewer rat hue to it that blonde hair gets when it's wet. Not her usual coifed Miss Prissy Tits, as I used to refer to her, when she was still washing her hair.

"What's wrong with you?"

"Fuck off," she says and attempts to erase both mother and foal in gigantic scrubbing motions.

"Careful, you're going to rip the paper. Do you want to go somewhere with me?"

She looks up, her glassy eyes hopeful. "You're going to Saskatoon?"

I shake my head. "Nah, no one will take me. I'm just going to explore the pasture."

Her eyes sink back into her head. "No thanks, sounds boring."

"Nice cows," I say.

"Takes one to know one."

I unpack the worn, cracked leather cowboy boots that were Dad's when he was a kid. I spent my entire childhood trying to grow into Dad's sacred footwear. I slide my feet into their depths, push open the screen door, clomp down the wooden steps, and drag my feet through the tall, dry grass. They make a slick and crispy swish sound. I already know his answer so the slow walk is a waste of my time. I pause at the corral fence to watch Dad and evaluate his mood. He looks intense and in serious need of a haircut. How's he going to get a job at the university with hippie hair and cow-poo jeans? Rebel without a clue.

The morning sun has warmed all of the cow-pies that form the corral floor. Their sweet smell is pure Wild West. If I focus exclusively on the corral fence, made of long skinny tree posts, and the smell, the morning is romantic.

"I want the herd up to fifty head by fall," Dad says, as though I've been there all along, talking about cows. His bushy strawberry blond hair vibrates with each strike of the hammer.

"Dad? Can you take us into Saskatoon today? We just want to look around."

"No." I crawl through the fence, avoiding stepping in any fresh cow-pies. "Winter's coming. It's nothing like BC. They only have two seasons here: summer and winter, cold and hot, nothing in between. Lydia, do me a favour, hold onto the board. It has to be flush up against this one. I said flush."

"It is flush. I can't make it any flusher."

"Jesus! Tell your mother I need her help out here, immediately!" he says, his glasses nearly flying off the end of his nose.

"Go tell her yourself. I'm going for a drive!" I yell, once I'm safely near the back porch. He didn't even notice the boots.

Mom sits at the kitchen table with a mug of coffee, her hair curled around her forehead with tub-scrubbing sweat.

"Have you tasted this?" she says, holding up the mug full of black liquid.

"Your coffee? Why would I?"

"Don't. The bitterness overpowers everything," she says, referring to the well water.

"Where are the truck keys? Dad said I can practice driving in the fields."

Her forehead wrinkles in surprise.

Dad pops his head through the open driver's side window. "You're a brave crew," he laughs, stepping back in a hurry. The truck jerks forward. Marx whimpers.

"I've got whiplash," Victoria says.

I drown her out with manic laughter and then abrupt silence as I fall deeper into an unexpected hypnotic state.

The prairie grass folds before me, the blue sky matching the blue truck.

"Why do you think Dad caved? I never thought he'd let you drive."

"Dad wouldn't drive me anywhere, so I drove Dad crazy," I say and suddenly slam down the brake pedal. The grill is practically touching the nose of a big Hereford. She stares through the windshield with dark chocolate eyes, chewing on a wad of grass. Her gentle eyes frame a white blaze down the centre of her wide face. She doesn't flinch and neither do her thirty friends. I blast the horn. "Is there anything more wimpy than a Datsun horn?"

"No horn's going to move them," Victoria says and opens her door. She walks towards the herd, flailing her arms around and yelling, "Ya-Ya! Cha-Cha!" I follow her towards the entire herd. In the chaos of movement, I catch Victoria's wild eyes, then open my throat to release a savage call. We are warriors; fear our war cries. Marx's nervous whine is followed by an irritable bark. He's decided he wants out of the truck after all. I wave my arms in the Hereford's face like a demented angel from hell. The Hereford stops chewing and jerks her large, bony body around as her hooves scramble to find traction on the dusty trail. The entire herd follows, hooves clamouring, kicking up the scent of cow turd and fresh grass. The cattle vanish revealing an old wagon road, indentations etched into the grass by heavy wagon wheels.

"Why is there a road in the pasture?" Victoria says.

"Oh my God! We found it. We have to tell Dad. It's the Carleton Trail. Look at it, those aren't tire marks. This road is over 100 years old."

"Let's follow it."

"Roger that."

We hop back in the cab on either side of our big, smelly, slobbering brother. "The end is near," I say.

"What are you on about now?"

"The end of the pasture. Are you scared? What's beyond that gate, no one knows."

"It looks just like another pasture. Same as ours, whoopee," Victoria says.

"Maybe, maybe not. Alex says Louis Riel and Gabriel Dumont walked this very road to Batoche. They crossed over, went beyond the pasture, and look what happened to them — the North-West Rebellion. Things could get ugly on the other side. Who do you like the most? Louis or Gabriel?"

"I don't know," Victoria says. I let go of the wheel momentarily. "Lydia!"

"Sorry. Itchy pits."

"Well scratch them one at a time for God's sake, like a normal person."

"Normally I would but I tried Mom's leg wax on them — worse than death. It took off skin, so much skin. I thought I was going to die."

"Okay, enough. No more details. Just drive."

"The worst part was that I had all that goop stuck under my arms and no way to get it off."

"How'd you get it off?"

"I had no choice. I had to keep ripping it off. Look, I have no skin left."

"Gross — okay, I got it. Hands on the wheel," Victoria says.

"Can you smell that? The sweet smell is clover. The stink's canola. Stick your head out. Try it."

"All I smell is dog breath."

"Dad's favourite is Dumont. He was a warrior, liked to ambush the enemy. I like Louis' style. He was a true gentleman rebel, he liked a fair fight — like me."

"As if! You sound just like Dad. I thought we were trying to get away from him for a while."

"Prissy Tits. Just for that, I'm not taking you to the other side." I put on the brakes and turn the truck around.

"Like Dad would ever let you leave the pasture anyway," she says, hiding behind Marx.

The farm looks deserted as we approach. I am dying of thirst; I need something to take away the dry, dusty taste in my throat. The house is cool and dark inside, an unexpected but welcome escape from the prairie sun. Mom is waiting for us in the kitchen, in the same spot as when we left. Except this time she has a fly swatter in her hand instead of a mug of poison coffee. It's almost as though time stood still.

I place the keys on the kitchen table and open the fridge. Mom takes a break from fly swatting to watch me.

"How was it?" she says.

"Victoria has no imagination. God, there's nothing to drink around here," I say and close the fridge.

"Shut up, Alex!" Victoria shouts from the living room.

Mom slumps back in the chair. Her face is shockingly white in the window's light. She doesn't move or say anything. She just sits there in the sunbeam, bloody fly swatter in hand, eyes shut. If she'd ever step a toe outside, she might not look so deathly pale.

I climb up to chickenshit tower and flop down on my bed. It stinks, and it's not my armpits. The post-thrill of cattle herding is lost under the suffocating stench. I bury my face into my pillow and scream, "I hate it here and no one gives a flying fuck!"

⚡

At night, when the tower walls turn black, I can convince myself of almost anything. I pretend that I'm back home in Vancouver, though the trip is becoming more difficult. The sheets no longer smell like cedar and salty air; they smell of fresh latex paint. Mom and I finally painted my room Parisian Pink. My lungs burn from the fumes, but I don't complain. The fumes kill the chickenshit smell. After sunset the house's coffin-like silence submits to the sounds of the night. The night is loud, not urban noisy, jungle loud. First the crickets start chirping, a symphony of tiny legs, and as the sky darkens, the coyotes start up and Marx chimes in barking his low *woof-woof*. He drives the coyotes crazy. There are six or more that surround the house. Dad says they won't come close to Marx; they're only teasing him. I'm not convinced.

When the last of the coyotes yips its way across the pasture, the bed vibrates. It starts as an almost undetectable quiver and grows into a full on rumble — the train. The horn blows as it crosses our road, coming from the west, heading east. Not stopping, never stopping.

⚡

Victoria's empty bed is a complete mess. She's not made it once since we moved here. Mom is in the kitchen, wearing the polyester pants. She seems . . . I can't say happy. No, she's too weird for happy. I will say oddly animated. She swats this morning's flies with abandon, taking periodic sips from the coffee mug placed on the speckled Formica counter top. She slides gracefully on the battleship linoleum tiles in dirty slippers: dance of the dead flies.

21

"You're drinking that crap now?" I say. She ignores me. "Have you seen Victoria?" Mom points the tip of the blood-stained fly swatter towards the basement door.

It takes awhile for my eyes to adjust. The dark, unfinished wooden planks on the floor and walls soak up every last bit of natural light that squeezes in through two microscopic windows. Victoria is behind the massive furnace kneeling in front of an open pink plastic Barbie case. The large case holds past secrets to another world, a safe world of glamour and excitement. She holds up a naked, headless Ken doll.

"He's a keeper. Good thing you packed him," I say.

"He's the only guy we have with real hair. The rest have ugly plastic hair. Look under the clothes. His head's gotta be in there," she says.

I sit beside her on the cool wooden floor and rummage through the musty Barbie outfits until I locate a hard, round object. "Here's the handsome devil. Look, he's got Alex's 'do."

"Oh God, it's true. He needs a haircut. Bring me the scissors."

"No way. No one touches my mod-haired hottie."

"Where's the rest of his hair pieces? Didn't he come with a bunch of stick-on beards?"

"Yeah, he did. Beard, mutton chops, big stash — they were so cool. Damn, I lost them all."

"You used to stick the beard on his privates," Victoria says. She pulls down Ken's tight beach pants and flashes his smooth, androgynous crotch.

I laugh, "Maybe. You know how I feel about men with beards: el creep-o."

Victoria laughs, "No, I think it's because you're a perv."

"You're the perv. Get your mind off Ken's crotch for a minute and think of something we can do today. Something fun."

"We could catch a ride into town with the folks. Explore."

"Hicksville? Never. That place makes me sick. It's so depressing. It barely exists at the back of the Saskatoon phone book. A total of two pages are dedicated to its esteemed residents, and they're all related. There are way more Dycks than I'd ever want to know."

"You're right; they'll only torture us again. Dad will drive by the school in slow motion and park in the empty lot. We'll sit there, like a truck full of losers."

"We could go on another drive, " I say.

"The pasture's boring," she says.

"Batoche."

"What's there to do in Batoche?" she says.

"You know, the sight of the infamous battle — Louis Riel, Gabriel Dumont. Alex says it's like a town. There might be interesting guys there, or something."

Victoria hands me Ken's nude body. I pop on his head and slick his hair back to make him appear more sexy, sleek rather than seventies hairy beast.

"What about Dad? He'll never let you drive on the road," she says and wraps her arms around skinny legs, crossed at the ankle.

"He's not going to know. We're just exploring the pasture. Practicing my driving. Right?"

"I guess. It stinks down here," Victoria says, then closes the Barbie case.

"I know. I thought it was you. You didn't fart?" I say and reopen the case a crack to shove Ken inside.

"No! Get lost. It's coming from the furnace. Smells like something died in there."

"Let's check it out." I grip the heavy iron door handle.

Victoria jumps up and covers my hand with hers. "No — don't. Just leave it, please. If there's something in there, I don't want to know."

"Okay, for now. But I'm gonna open that door one of these days, and it might not be pretty," I say and release the handle while shaking off her cold clutch.

The truck bangs over rocks and dips into badger holes, heading straight for the barbed wire gate at the other end of the pasture. I stop and idle a few feet from the gate. Victoria, Marx, and I stare straight ahead through the windshield. No one moves. "Get the gate," I say.

"You talking to me?" Victoria says.

"No. Marx, you idiot."

"Get it yourself."

I turn my head to look across the cab at her upturned freckled nose, half hidden behind Marx's profile. "I'm driving. A cowboy never gets the gate. In the West, it's the ranch hand's job," I say.

"You made that up," Victoria says. She steps out and struts a surly ranch hand swagger towards the gate. "I hope you know where in the hell you're going," she shouts into my open window as I wobble the truck slowly past her.

"Alex says it's just up the river," I say once Victoria is back in her seat. I have a gnawing feeling in my gut as we leave the comfort of our land behind. All my Batoche tales, designed to scare Victoria, are starting to scare me. The place was a bloodbath.

The old wagon road follows the river's course for a while until the trail disappears underneath big rocks and skinny trees.

"It's too hot to walk." Victoria's face looks childlike next to Marx's, framed by two braids, her cheeks flushed pink with heat.

"There's got to be a concession at Batoche. It's for tourists." I lean over her lap and open the glove compartment. "Here's a dollar eighty, ninety, two dollars and fifteen cents. It should be enough to buy us each a pop. Come on," I say.

We walk along a cattle trail beside the river. Marx bounds towards the water and wades in to drink. I don't want him to step into the current. He might disappear from sight on one of those pretend sandbars that Dad warned us about. They appear to be a shallow place in the river but when you stand on them they collapse into a fierce undercurrent. Marx refuses to come to my calls. "Enter the river at your own risk, my boy," I shout then walk on. The trail leads through a few sparse poplars then climbs a low bank and onto pasture. Victoria stops and looks back longingly in the direction of the truck.

"Come on. Just think of how nice an ice cold pop will taste once we hit Batoche." Marx pushes past her, stops and shakes beside me. "Thanks, Marx — real nice. Now I'm hoping there aren't any cute guys in Batoche. I smell like dead fish."

We walk along the edge of the pasture overlooking the river. After a while, the pasture ends abruptly and we step from tall grass onto a wasteland of dirt, a field left in summer-fallow. Dust covers my sandals. A blade of dead grass slices my big toe. I pull out the grass as blood pools under my toenail.

Victoria stops. "I've got to go."

"Number one or two?"

"Does it matter?"

"Of course it matters. Here, take this." I pull a wad of tissue from my cut-offs.

"Gross. I can't use this. It's stuck together with petrified gum, for God's sake."

"Beggars shouldn't be choosers. You'll have to hold it until we hit the trees."

The land up ahead is shockingly different from the dead field. It is covered in a forest of lush deciduous trees. I wade through thigh-high wild grasses towards the trees where a small building is hidden. The flies won't leave me alone. There must be a dead animal or a fresh pile of poop around somewhere. The shack is empty inside except for a calendar on the wall. Five round-faced dark-eyed babies dressed identically look out from the picture, eagerly awaiting their bowls of identical mush.

"What is this place?" Victoria's hot breath moves the sticky hair over my ear.

"It's French, *juillet*. Look at that date. Can you believe it? 1937. Must be the Dionne quintuplets. Wonder how long this place has been abandoned?"

"Too long. Look at all the mouse poop. Disgusting," Victoria says.

My eyes follow the beams across the open attic. "The roof's intact and only one small windowpane is cracked. I see potential — I see our secret sanctuary."

"Come on. Let's go. I'm going to try and hold it until Batoche," Victoria says.

We find our cattle trail and follow it through the bluff and onto a massive field of blue flax. The top of my head hurts. It's probably burnt a bright red part through my blonde hair. War paint. The pain feels perversely good. I suffer as Louis suffered. If I ever have a son I'm naming him Riel.

"God, it's beautiful here," I say and stop to slide the blue neck bandana onto my head like a kerchief. Victoria pushes past me and continues along the trail. I follow her through the ocean of blue, then down along the riverbank, through mud and quicksand until the trail disappears into the river. Beside us, the riverbank has grown in steepness and height. "We gotta go up."

"I'm too tired," Victoria says.

"Well, it's either climb the bank or swim. Batoche has to be up there somewhere."

"I'll climb up first but if I don't see Batoche from here, we're going back. Deal?" Victoria says.

"Deal."

Victoria climbs the eroded bank, first on her feet, then on her hands and knees. I watch until she pulls herself up and over, disappearing with Marx.

"Victoria? Anything up there? Can you see Batoche?" Silence. I scramble up the bank, through the loose dirt, holding onto bunches of grass and roots to pull myself onto the flat field. She's far ahead, walking towards a cluster of old buildings. I run, my lungs burning, passing Victoria, her voice growing fainter behind me. Everything Dad's told me about the North-West Rebellion is underneath my feet. The wagon road, the cattle trails, originally buffalo trails, they lead from our farm straight to Batoche. I am running back through time.

Clapboard buildings line the wooden boardwalk like seniors in an old folk's home, optimistic that young blood might grace them with a visit. My mud caked feet merely skim the surface of the grey boards. Time means little when destiny calls; I have a date with a ghost. The abandoned buildings lead to an invisible Métis neighbourhood. The Métis homes are gone, transformed into a plaque, standing in the grass, marking where they once stood.

The first grave I reach belongs to the greatest warrior, none other than Gabriel Dumont. "Alex would love this."

"Yeah, so — where's this great concession?" Victoria says, then wipes her frayed hair from her shiny forehead. "Oh my God! Alex's hero. Do you think he knows?"

"Probably."

"I thought Alex said that Dumont escaped to Montana and joined Buffalo Bill's Wild West Show," she reads.

"But Dumont is here, under the ground. At least his bones are. So obviously he came back to Canada," I say.

"Or they sent his body back to be buried at home."

"No. He came back. Lived his final days here, unnoticed by the government. That's what it says," I say, pointing to the plaque beside his grave. I sit cross-legged in the grass, between Dumont's grave and Marx. "Why'd he do it? Risk his life to return?"

Victoria crouches down. "I don't know. Maybe he had lost too much to stay away."

Victoria surprises me. Sometimes, completely unexpectedly, she is deep.

She stands up and holds her hair back from her face. "There is no one," she says, stating the obvious. "Doesn't anyone live in Saskatchewan besides us?"

"No. No one actually living lives in Saskatchewan."

"Except us. He's not here, you know," she says to my back.

"I know — they hung him in Winnipeg." I say, knowing she means Riel.

A cloud passes over the sun. "Stood up by a ghost," Victoria says into the stillness.

I retrace my steps along the boardwalk, longing to reach for Victoria's hand and hold onto it, like when we were little, but I can't. She'd think I was an incestuous lesbian or something. Instead I drag my hand along the buildings, poking my fingers into holes that scar the rectory's clapboard siding.

"Are these bullet holes?" Victoria says.

"Yup, battle wounds, to remind of us of the Métis corpses."

"Rotting in that field."

The emptiness of Batoche creeps inside. "No wonder no one lives here anymore. The land's stained with blood."

It is nearly dusk when we finally make it back to our own pasture. I am sweaty, dehydrated, and can barely focus on keeping the truck on the wagon trail. I keep that last bit to myself. For the first time ever, I am happy to see the house.

"Oh-oh. Here comes Dad," Victoria says.

He runs through the corral towards the truck. His legs move fast but his face moves slow. I wish it were Victoria and not me behind the wheel. His hand reaches for the driver's side door before I even brake.

"Where in the hell have you been with my truck? I've been waiting all day for you two," Dad says. He's wearing clean jeans and an ironed, blue checked shirt.

"We parked the truck and walked to Batoche," I say. I want to tell him about Dumont, but he is in no mood.

"No more driving privileges. The truck is officially off limits." He reaches his hand through the window, opening my door from the inside. A whiff of freshly applied, spicy deodorant stings my nostrils.

"But we didn't drive on any roads," I say. He ignores me. "Why? Until when?"

"Until I say so, that's when. Out of the truck. I've got to make it to the university before everyone leaves. The university is screwing me around. I can't feed you two on one course. Out, now! That means all of you." Behind his glasses, his eyes appear magnified with adrenalin. His glasses look comical on top of them. Marx won't budge. The red on Dad's neck crawls up the sides of his face, resembling red mutton chop side burns. "Marx, get the hell out of the truck. Move — bad dog!" A whimper escapes Marx's floppy lips. Alex sighs, a heavy about-to-vomit-his-soul sigh. He jumps in the truck. "Open the gate, Lydia!" he demands through the open window. Victoria and I lift the corral gate. He speeds past with Marx at his side.

"Why is he taking Marx with him to the university?" Victoria says. Her fists clutch the back of my arm as though, somehow, I'll protect her from the craziness that is our father.

"No clue. Maybe he's finally snapped, lost his mind." The truck brakes abruptly at the end of the driveway. Dad jumps out and starts to yell. I can't make out the words. He gets back in the cab but leaves the passenger side door open. Marx emerges from the truck. He's being forcibly pushed out, arse first. He tries to jump back in the truck but the door slams shut and Dad drives off, spitting gravel and leaving Marx behind in a cloud of dust.

Mom sits at the kitchen table. A flypaper plastered with dead flies swings low over her head, threatening to attach itself to her hair. She's been crying. Her eyes turn turquoise when she cries.

"What's wrong?" I say. Mom closes her eyes and shakes her head. "Tell me, Mom, please."

"Nothing. Nothing is wrong. Just leave me alone, okay?"

Victoria opens the fridge, looks inside momentarily, then slams the door.

"What can I drink? I'm dying here!"

"Close the fridge. Have a glass of water," Mom says.

"Are you crazy? The water tastes like shit," Victoria says. Her braids are nearly completely unravelled on top.

"Upstairs, now!" Mom says.

"Get a grip," Victoria says, stomping up the stairs.

"Victoria can be a real bitch sometimes," I say, bending over Mom from behind and wrapping my arms around her shoulders. Her hair smells stale, a little greasy, and kind of like dandruff. It smelled good in Vancouver, like peppermint from the mousse she used. "Mom, when was the last time you washed your hair?" I say. She forcibly breaks free of my embrace. She bolts downstairs and slams her bedroom door. I wait, standing behind her empty chair until I no longer hear her muffled sobs.

There is nothing in the fridge but milk and Dad's light beer. I hate milk. I take a beer and climb the oak staircase to my room, pausing to look out the landing window at the giant orange beach ball rising above the poplars. The dingy staircase wall is painted warm amber in its light. It's too beautiful. A sharp pinch of sadness twists beneath my ribs. I know what it is: the harvest moon. Prairie summers don't last forever.

TWO

The mosquitoes are rampant because there is no wind. I can't go outside. I am trapped in the tower with George and his incessant kneading. His needlelike claws work their way around my bed, slicing pinprick holes in the down duvet as he purrs. Everyone except George is foul. Dad has only one course to teach, Victoria is hormonal, and Mom found six dead woodpeckers in the furnace. The birds have been dead so long they're mummified. I guess that explains the smell of death in the basement. I have to laugh at myself, thinking it was Victoria and her farts. The tower walls have faded to the colour of recently deceased flesh. Trust Dad to bring home shoddy, reduced-to-clear mistint paint.

I flip through last year's yearbook for something to do. I hate my picture. I had my hair chopped off like Rod Stewart to be different. Thank God it's grown out again. Victoria looks like she's about eight with her two tight French braids and that toothy movie star grin. The yearbook is losing its charm. I've not only memorized every face with its name, I can tell you how many zits are on each and every sorry-faced loser too.

The chickenshit has risen once again from beneath the floorboards like the phoenix, reclaiming my room as its territory. The smell is directly proportionate to the temperature: the hotter the day, the stronger the stink. What's ironic is that Mom is seriously considering buying chickens. For the eggs, she says. Chickens would ruin everything. We would officially cross over to the other side, a backwards metamorphosis. The ancient house is our chrysalis, trapping us until our metamorphosis is complete: our chic city wings will be plucked from our backs, and we'll emerge as fat, white larvae, like the ones living in the corral cow-pies. Maybe if I submit, it will release me sooner. Never. In the words of Walt Whitman, "Resist much, obey little." My new mantra.

The only solution is to torch the place, but even that would be impossible. The house is indestructible, determined to outlast the land. Three years ago a grass fire took out everything on our section of land: the barns, corral, old outhouse, and shed. Everything burnt to the ground in one blazing inferno — everything except the house. After the flames died and the smoke cleared, my father's exhausted feet crunched through the crispy charred earth towards a lone vertical protrusion: the house, a tall white streak of silence rising from black ashes.

The wind's come up. Outside is a possibility. I sneak out the front door unnoticed by the folks. I take Dad's old ten-speed that leans against the side of the house. "You'll be my trusty steed today," I say. It's hard to pedal. I concentrate on the sound of the tires on gravel, imagining it's the sound of hooves, galloping towards freedom. Damn this province! If the wind is still, the mosquitoes are deadly. But when the wind blows, it gusts, making it impossible to bike.

I huff and puff my way towards the riverbank. I follow the road that separates the riverbank from our land. The river is wide, nearly a kilometre. It's fast and deep too. There's no way across but by ferry. The crossing is about ten kilometres south of our place. Dad says the river is a liar. The water appears smooth and glistening in the sun, but the current is like a piranha eating away at the sandbars from underneath. He says it'll take you so fast, they won't find your body until it washes up on the shore of Lake Winnipeg, though he's been known to exaggerate danger to make a point.

No cattle in the vicinity, so it's safe to explore our field. I jump off the bike and squeeze myself under the barbed wire fence onto our pasture and walk towards the ancient buffalo pit. I sit inside the shallow circle indentation, close my eyes, and massage the warm, sandy earth through my fingers. I lie back and let my head fall against the pit's warmth. The soil is sweet with cow turd and ancient buffalo dung. Thousands of buffalo roamed our land a hundred years ago. They'd lie down in the pit, like me, and roll to shed their heavy winter coats. I am always on the lookout for proof of their existence, like a sun-bleached buffalo skull with horns intact. So far, the only evidence I have is the pit.

The wind suddenly turns gale force, thrashing the field, forcing the grass to dance. The motion is hypnotizing. Sand cuts into my eyes and grits between my teeth. I squeeze back under the barbed wire, clasp the handlebars, and pull the bike under the fence, onto our land. The barbed wire catches my skirt. I yank it, tearing it free.

The bike won't move. The chain's off and it's too stiff to get it back on. I shake the hair from my face but it is useless. It whips into my eyes, nose, and mouth. There is no escape. I push the bike blindly towards the direction of the farm. The wind is a wicked accomplice; it lifts my skirt, pushes my legs, and steals my breath, forcing me back to the house.

Suddenly, the sound of hooves, too many, pounding the earth. They're coming at me fast: cattle, spooked by the wind. I turn and drop the bike, trying to find them, wanting to escape their path. The pasture is empty for as far as I can see. My scream is silenced in the fury; the ghosts of the buffalo, too many of them for my eyes to see or my brain to hold, but I know they're there. They run with the wind.

Abandoned homesteads dot nearly every field this side of Hicksville. Dad says families left their possessions during the dirty thirties and moved to the city in hopes of finding work. The entire region was a dust bowl. Victoria and I have been raiding as many of the empty houses as we can fit into our schedule, which means we explore every empty building between the river and Hicksville every single day. We take what interests us or is useful. Bandits of the West, Lydie and Vic, unarmed but dangerous (or demented).

"Why are we following the wagon trail?" I ask Victoria.

"Don't know. Let's cut through the field." We head diagonally across the pasture to the farthest corner, in the opposite direction of the river. Gophers rise and stand at attention, like meerkats, guarding their massive underground city. As soon as they spot Marx they vanish from the line, one by one. We create trails, exploring pastures and fields that we've never encountered before, until we spot one, a house, smack in the middle of acres and acres of wheat.

"The field's ready for harvesting. Try not to flatten anything, and stay close to the fence," I say. The wheat stalks reach our hips. We edge close to the shore, along the vast golden ocean of grain. The decrepit farmhouse looks similar to ours with an A-line roof; only it's a story shorter and the white paint more faded. I step cautiously onto the open porch and peer in one of the front windows. A few things are scattered about inside. I push open the front door, my hand not leaving the knob. The wind shakes the thin glass windows. The entire house rattles.

"There might be rats — or bats. Call me when the coast is clear," Victoria says.

"Wimp," I say and walk into the house. Sun shines through the side windows onto peeling plaster walls painted in soothing hues of turquoise and soft yellow. Mouse droppings are everywhere but no vermin in sight. "Come on in, if you're woman enough."

Victoria stumbles inside with a grimace on her face but feet on a mission. She lopes straight for an old phone on the wall. "Look at this — you crank it. Hello, hello, Pizza Palace? This is Victoria Buckingham. I want two large cheese pizzas delivered to the little house on the prairie, pronto, and throw in two ice-cold beers. Thank you. Goodbye."

"How long are they going to be?"

"Twenty minutes or it's free."

I climb the wooden staircase hesitantly, afraid the wood might be rotten. The boards creak beneath each step. The upper hall is a tunnel of open doors. The air is heavy and smells slightly of mildew and Dad's cigar before it's been lit. The first door leads into a narrow, salmon-pink bedroom with an elegantly scrolled iron bed frame. Victoria hovers behind me and walks past me into the room, opening the closet door and disappearing inside. "Oh my God, Lydia — look at these."

The closet is a miniature room with a single bar holding clothing that hangs limply from wooden hangers, waiting for their owner to arrive home and put them on. Victoria lifts out a long dress, black with rust coloured grape bunches. "Try it on," she says.

"Empire waist, nineteen thirties my guess — let me showcase my bosoms," I say dramatically, and smooth the dress over my boobs.

"Put it on."

"No way."

"Come on! Don't be a chicken."

"I can't. It's weird, I know, but it belonged to someone. Someone who thought she'd come back for it but never did."

Victoria's smile fades. "That's morbid."

"A princess bed is just what the sanctuary needs. We'll bring the truck next time, get as close to the field as possible," I say and clutch leather baby booties to my chest.

"I take it those aren't too personal? You've stolen them from a baby, you know," Victoria says.

"Yes, my hands burn with guilt and shame. But I can't just leave them here, waiting for some chubby little baby's feet that will never fill them."

We haul the useful stuff to the secret sanctuary. The place is evolving into a little atelier on the prairie. I made a straw mattress for the princess bed, and the woodstove even works. So far though, our atelier has not entertained any guests. Our only acquaintances in Saskatchewan are the dead — the ghosts of Batoche and the abandoned homesteads.

The door into the house opens and Mom, with her bouncing fresh-washed hair and clean slippers, slides her way across the wooden porch floor. "Here. Keep this out here. I don't want it inside. It's ugly. Don't bring it in again," she says and thrusts an afghan onto the old porch sofa. "You know you're going to have to clean this all up again, right?" she says, eyeing the porch shelf lined with prairie artifacts.

"Yes, we know," I say.

"Good. It's a front porch, not a junkyard," she says, then disappears back into the house. The loud hum of an ancient floor polisher vibrates the porch windows.

"Hey, I like that. I cuddle with it in front of the TV," I say and pull the ratty afghan to my face to sniff its comforting smells. "Mmm . . . Vancouver."

"Marx barfed on that," Victoria says.

"When we first moved here. I washed it."

"No one's touching this museum," Victoria says.

"I know. I only agreed with her to get her off our case," I say and take in the full effect of our natural history museum. "I'm royally insulted."

"I know. Like, how could this possibly resemble a junk shop?"

"She's in one of her cleaning frenzies. Seriously, the university will probably offer us money for this collection some day."

Our collection consists almost entirely of little shew and mice skeletons inside of glass bottles. The bottles are drinking bottles mostly, with long, narrow necks. Dad says grass fires are fast, too quick to melt glass. The terrified creatures ran inside the bottles, trying to escape the raging firestorm, and were cooked alive. The bottles sit on the shelf that runs the length on the porch, directly under the front windows. The sunlight illuminates each skeleton perfectly.

Dad steps into the porch from outside as though he's been hiding in the barn from Mom. He moved a desk and chair out there last week and christened the room nearest to the door his "summer office." I doubt he actually gets any work done out there. He's only uses it to hide from Mom when she's in her "I hate Saskatchewan" mood, which happens to be her main mood lately.

"I'm going to the university. Tell your mother," he says. He steps down the front steps, stops, and pokes his head back inside. "In case you go into the pasture today, I've got an angry cow. She's a rogue, thinks she's a bull. Without warning she'll charge. Be careful." He shuts the porch door softly behind himself, leaving a clean, spicy scent lingering in the porch with us.

I open the porch door. "Wait, Dad, wait!"

"What is it?"

"How do you know she's dangerous? Did she charge you?"

"I've got to go, see you tonight."

Dust clouds roll down the road, following the pickup. "I bet she chased him around the corral."

"Yet another species of woman that he's pissed off," Victoria says.

I laugh because it seems like such an adult thing to say. As I shut the porch door, the door into the house opens simultaneously.

"Where is he?" Mom's eyes follow the dust trail up the road. "Where in the hell is he going now?"

I shrug my shoulders.

"He said the university," Victoria says.

Mom slams the door shut, disappearing back into the house, but not before I hear her say, "Asshole."

The midnight train. Alex still isn't home. Damn him. I'd be asleep right now if he wasn't so bloody inconsiderate. Maybe he's been in an accident. I don't want to know. I tiptoe into the sewing room to gaze down the long drive. Headlights bump their way down the gravel road. The beast is back.

I watch, hidden in the dark sewing room, as he walks towards the house. There's a scramble of feet and the front door opens. Mom locks the front porch before he can get in. He rattles the door loudly and whisper-shouts, "Mary Jane — Mary Jane!" Then he hammers at the window with his fist. He pounds the glass for what feels like forever. Mom suddenly slams the heavy wooden front door. He stops banging and lopes to the side of the house, out of my view. I hear the shuffle of Mom's fast slippered feet on the kitchen floor and the thud of the bolt securing the back porch door. I run to the staircase-landing window. I catch a glimpse of his face in the yard light. He smiles in nervous disbelief before disappearing into the dark. I turn to head up the last few stairs to my bedroom. A ghostly white face in the moonlight meets mine. I gasp. Victoria's been shaken from slumber by the drama of the night. I step into my bedroom and lock the door.

I tiptoe down to the museum first thing in the morning to admire our collection in the early light. Victoria is already there, sitting on the porch chesterfield, her bare feet drawn up under the hem of her cotton nightgown, and George curled up purring on her lap. "A whole lot of door slamming went on last night," she says, as I walk past.

"They better not have broken any of our specimens." I lift a seaweed-green wine bottle to check the shrew skeleton inside. Its little feet are pressed together with its neck down, as though praying. "Alex didn't get home until after the midnight train."

"I know."

"Mom locked him out."

"Obviously," Victoria says and pats the chesterfield. With each pat, a plume of dust fills the porch. "Where is he?" she asks, stretching her legs out from under her nightgown.

"I figure he gave up and slept in the barn," I say. "We should go and check."

"No thanks," she says.

I sit down on the sofa beside her and pull the afghan over my lap. "What the museum needs is a buffalo skull. That's my quest, the holy grail of specimens. What did Mother do with the dead birds?"

"The woodpeckers?" Victoria says.

"Yeah."

"I think they went to the dump," she says.

"Go check to see if there's anymore."

"Why?"

"One would be nice under glass," I say and point to an empty glass milk bottle sitting on the shelf.

"Gross. They still had their feathers on," she says.

"Just check for me, okay? All you have to do is go down and open the furnace door and report what you see inside. I'll do the rest."

"You're weird."

"I know. Please?"

"You'll play a game of Clue with me after lunch?"

"Okay, just be quiet. I don't want Mom freaking out on us," I say and gently detach George's claws from her lap.

Victoria creeps across the painted porch floor and disappears inside, leaving the heavy oak door slightly ajar. I pick up the milk bottle and hold the mouth to my eye. One woodpecker might fit; they're petrified and all shrunken. Victoria's heavy feet thud up the stairs. She's out of breath when she reaches the museum. "Why are you so bloody loud?" I say.

"He's down there," she whispers, her eyes bulging. "He slept with Mom."

"How do you know?" I whisper.

"I saw him. Their door was open."

"So, the sorry asses are all cozy together this morning," I say, no longer whispering. "What about the bird?"

She looks clueless, then shakes her head. "There wasn't any."

"What are you doing?" Dad suddenly steps from the house into the porch in blue boxer shorts.

Crap, Victoria woke him. "Nothing." I don't want him to figure out it's a museum. He'll only make it seem ridiculous.

"I'm leaving for Langham in a few minutes. Does anybody what to come?" he says.

"Why?" Victoria says.

"If you want to come, be in the truck in ten minutes," he says.

Victoria and I sit in the back seat, sweating. As usual, Dad waits until we're all in the truck before he decides he has to go to the can. "He does this every time," Victoria says.

"And it's never a quick pee. It's always an agonizingly long number two."

He emerges from the front porch in cut-offs and leather sandals. His wire-framed glasses turn dark in the sun.

Dust from the gravel road fills the cab. I pull my shirt over my face. "I can't breathe. Can't we close the window?"

"No. It's over forty degrees in here." His navy T-shirt has a wet circle on the front from sweat. He stops the truck as we approach the river, opens his door, and steps onto the road. I open my door and choke in fresh air. "Not yet Lydia. Get back inside," he says.

"Why do you get to stand outside? It's not fair," I say.

"He's selfish. He doesn't care if we're cooked alive," Victoria says.

Victoria and I wait, panting, inside the cab, until the ferry guy unhooks the rope and signals us to drive on. "Oh my God. It only holds six cars. What kind of a ferry is this?" she says.

I glance back at the riverbank. It looks almost exotic from this distance, lush and green. "Now, Dad? Can we at least get out and look?" He nods.

The wind blows the hair off my face and sprinkles it with river spray. I close my eyes and fill my nostrils with the fishy smell; it feels almost like crossing the Georgia Strait.

We dock on the other side of the river and drive down more gravel roads, nearly identical to the ones on our side of the river. We finally reach Langham, a small, unremarkable town. "Even Langham looks more interesting than the hole near us," I say before realizing we drove right through without stopping. Dad pulls off the gravel road onto a dirt road then stops abruptly.

"Why are we stopping?" I say.

Alex sticks his head inside the open driver's side window. "Hurry up. Get out. You won't want to miss this," he says.

Raised wooden boxes stand in rows beside the truck. "Why has he taken us to a bee farm?" Victoria says.

The place looks like a grotty little operation with a bunch of old trailers tossed randomly around. "I hope Alex isn't planning to stock up on honey. I wouldn't trust anything from this dump." I say.

A man approaches Dad. He seems eager, like he's been waiting for us. His gait is fast, bouncing upwards with each step. He shakes Dad's hand and grins at Victoria and then me. He won't stop smiling. It's painful. His teeth haven't seen a toothbrush in about a year. A long streak of misery, Mom would say.

"Go on, girls, go take a look at your horse," Dad says.

Victoria shrieks as she climbs the fence. "Are you serious? You bought us a horse?"

"Go on, take a look at her. She's an Arabian, silver-blue roan," he says, smiling big and unabashedly.

"What's her name?" Victoria yells from the pasture. She's smack in the horse's face, stroking its long nose. The Arabian shakes her head, widening her brown eyes until their white edges appear.

"Silver," Dad shouts.

I watch from the fence as Silver trots from one side of the corral to the other, then stops again, a few feet away from Victoria. "Can we afford a purebred Arabian?" I say. Dad glances down at me beside him, as though he's only just realized I'm there.

"She's not registered," he says.

Silver trots gracefully along the fence, eyes wide, nervously searching for someone. "She knows something's up. Doesn't she?" I say.

Dad laughs. "Go on, get in there, introduce yourself," he says.

I don't tell him that I am a little afraid of her. I climb the fence and step cautiously towards Silver. Victoria's arms are wrapped around her thick neck. I gently touch the end of her black nose with my fingers. Suddenly Silver tosses her head and steps backward, freeing herself from Victoria's grasp. I step back simultaneously towards the safety of the fence. In her dark eyes I see that she is very bright, and I also see recognition; she and I are both slightly wild, with the tendency to spook on occasion.

$$\maltese$$

The morning sky is painted pink and green. My eyes sting with sleep but my mind says go. Victoria pushes open the bathroom door, too tired to act surprised to find me on the toilet. Her hair looks like she just rubbed it with a balloon, and her eyes are puffed with sleep. "Silver?" I croak in a morning frog voice. She nods, putting her finger to her lips and covering my hand with hers to stop me from flushing the toilet.

We step out of the house in our white cotton nightgowns, gently closing the back porch screen door so it doesn't bang. Marx isn't sleeping in the hay stacked beside the house.

"Look, they're all together," Victoria says. Silver is way out in the pasture, grazing beside the cows. The grass is cold and wet. It sticks to my bare legs. Marx raises his head as we approach the herd, then rises from the dewy grass and bounds to greet us.

"What's this, Marx? Are you a horse now? Silver's little colt?" I say and scratch the folds under his chin.

Silver lifts her head from the grass to acknowledge us. She is breathtakingly wild looking, a mustang with a long silver and black mane and a tail that touches the earth, no halter, nothing on her. I kiss the soft spot between her nostrils. She smells like fresh grass and something else — warm blankets. Victoria kisses Silver's nose right after me, as though staking her territory. I retaliate by running my hand down Silver's smooth back, warm from the morning sun, and patting her rump firmly as I saw Dad do last night. Victoria wraps her arms around Silver's neck. "That's my good girl," she says. Silver's ears flatten back, and she exposes the whites of her eyes.

"I wouldn't do that if I were you. She doesn't like it."

"And you know what she likes and doesn't like?"

I step back and scan the pasture. The sky's turned ocean blue. No white caps to be found. "Should we try and ride her?" I say.

"Dad said not until tomorrow."

"Why do we have to wait until tomorrow?"

"He's going to teach us how to ride Western," Victoria says.

"It won't hurt to just walk around a bit out here. It's not like we haven't ridden before."

"Silver only knows Western — Dad'll kill us if we corrupt her."

"Not if he doesn't find out," I say.

"How? We have no saddle or bridle on her," Victoria says.

"Bareback. Hang onto her mane."

Silver stands still as the Queen's Guard. I boost Victoria onto her back. "Vic! You're not wearing any underwear for God's sake! You can't ride a horse bare back with a bare butt. Gross."

"It's not my fault. I never sleep in panties. Mom says a vagina needs to breathe."

"I know, I know. But she doesn't mean all day long. You're disgusting sometimes."

"Like you ever sleep in gotch. I'll wrap my nightie around me like riding breeches. Okay?"

"You better or I'm not getting on behind you." Victoria pulls her nightgown underneath her and sits on it. "Some riding breeches. Okay, guide her to that rock over there and I'll get on too."

There is no guiding Silver. She shuffles along, one hoof at a time, only moving to reach the next blade of grass.

"Come on, Vic. Don't hog her all to yourself!"

"She won't move. I can't."

"At least make her raise her head. She doesn't have to keep eating. Silver isn't some magical unicorn — steer her!"

"How can I steer her without a bridle?" she says.

"Nudge her in the armpits with your heels."

Victoria swings her bare feet outward and brings them swiftly back in, kicking Silver firmly behind her front legs.

To prove the point that she is no unicorn, Silver bolts, streaks past me so fast she almost knocks me down. Someone is on her back with no bridle to instruct her. She is free. She is a mustang. Victoria's white nightie billows behind her as she holds on for her life. "I said nudge, you idiot! Not kick! Victoria, you get back here right this minute. I want to ride too!" Even as I shout the words, I know they're useless. Victoria has no control. Silver steers herself in a straight line across the pasture and into the biggest poplar bluff on our land. I run. By the time I reach the edge of the bluff, there is no sign or sound of either of them. The bluff swallowed them. "Victoria!" I shout. Silence, except for the rustling of poplar leaves in the morning breeze, then a chilling voice from behind me: Alex. He runs through the pasture towards me, stark naked except for white boxers and a pail of oats. He runs past, calling Silver and shaking the oat bucket.

"Where'd they go?" he says.

I point to the trees. Alex walks towards the bluff, slapping the oat bucket and calling Silver's name, then he stops to listen; nothing, then the crunching of branches. Silver appears from the thicket of poplars. She shakes her head and trots to the oats. Her back is bare.

Dad slides a rope around her neck and turns towards me. His authoritative eyes bore into mine. I don't dare look away. "Where is Victoria?" he says.

"I don't know." My stomach feels as though I'm on an elevator, free falling towards the basement. I run, top speed, through the bluff, dodging poplar trunks and willow branches. I will find her in the blur of green and brown. I slow my pace instinctively, as though scripted. She appears to me as a celestial being in a white gown with a crown of branches and leaves. Her nightgown is torn up the front. She has a huge grin on her face. It stretches across her cheeks, separating two trails of blood flowing from her forehead. I want to cry but I laugh instead, a short nervous laugh. I step towards her with the desire to slap her face. I squeeze her upper arms in my hands instead and plead with her wild eyes.

"Wow," she says, "that was incredible."

The elevator hits bottom, a pang of envy. Dad appears beside me.

"Do you girls know how dangerous and stupid that was? You could have been killed. Silver could have broken a leg. What were you thinking? You never get on a horse without a bridle," he shouts, his face all red and blue veins. "I'm disappointed in you two." He thrusts the oat bucket at me. "Take this back to the barn."

Dad lifts our grounding just shy of a week, once he's deemed we're good enough riders to meet great-grandfather's strict rules of horsewomanship. If his grandfather were as bossy as he is, it's no wonder my nana left home at sixteen. On the positive side, he said I get to ride first, seeing as I did not crash Silver into the bluff last week.

"Up ahead, over there, do you see it? It looks like a house. Come on," I call from my majestic perch. Silver and I walk calmly but purposefully down a long, flat dirt driveway. Victoria struggles behind on the gravel road, riding the rusted ten-speed, its wheels spinning dust. She's pissed because the deal is, she rides the bike there and I ride it back. "There" is our undecided future destination, which just might be the intriguing little house we're approaching.

The property is even more treeless than ours. The only splash of colour that dots the bleak, straw-coloured landscape is the fuchsia petunias planted in the front garden and the tall caragana bushes that line the drive. I jump from Silver's back and pull off her bridle, tying her harness to a fence post. Victoria arrives, dragging the bike. The chain is off. "It's fucked," she says, then heaves it into the grass. Her face is red and her legs are streaked black with bike chain grease. She wipes her hands on her cut-offs, then reaches for Silver's rope and begins to untie her.

I grab her arm. "What are you doing?"

"What are *you* doing? Someone obviously lives here," she says.

"We never fulfilled our quest to find real neighbours, the living kind. Maybe you want to spend the rest of your life collecting bones but I don't. By the way, you've got squished bugs in the corner of your eyes."

"I'm not going," she says, dabbing her eyes with the corner of her T-shirt.

"Stay," I pause just long enough so that Victoria thinks I'm referring to her, then I add, "Sit, Marx. Stay with Silver."

The front door to the small house swings open and an old woman steps onto the porch. I am reminded of a story from fourth grade: *The Teeny-Tiny Woman.*

"*Bonjour!*" she says. "*D'où venez-vous?*"

My brain shoots out grade nine French before I even know what I'm saying. "*Nous venons de* . . . Buckingham farm," I say and point in the direction of our land.

"Grand'Mère," she says, pressing her bony finger into her chest. Her white hair is pulled elegantly from her small, lined face into a French chignon at the back of her head. "Come."

"*Napoleon! Des petites filles sont ici,*" Grand'Mère shouts into the front room.

Napoleon half turns from a TV screen, nods and says, "*Salut,*" in a deep voice and returns to his program. He appears to be watching CBC in French. I've tried to watch it myself a few times since we moved here, out of desperation, but my French isn't good enough to enjoy it.

"*Asseyez-vous, asseyez-vous,*" she says, pointing to the tall wooden chairs around her kitchen table.

The smells of roasted coffee beans and cigarettes permeate the house. Grand'Mère pauses in front of a huge black stove trimmed with gleaming chrome. She lifts up one of the burners to stuff a small log into the flames below. She returns to the table with three steaming mugs. The liquid is extremely hot and black. I sip it reluctantly. The coffee makes Mom's dark roast taste like coloured water in comparison. Victoria blows into her cup repeatedly, as though afraid to drink it. Grand'Mère slides a china bowl filled with sugar cubes in front of Victoria. She takes one, then two. I count eight before I am too disgusted and avert my eyes.

"Beautiful Arabian you girls ride," Napoleon says, turning away from the TV. His face is startling. His eyes are large and dark like Grand'Mère's and his skin tanned but less wrinkly than his mom's. His head is big and the bones in his cheeks and jaw are pronounced. For an old guy, he's handsome.

"Thank you. Her name is Silver," I say. "Do you have horses?" I look at Grand'Mère but speak loud enough for Napoleon to hear. Grand'Mère chuckles and shakes her head. Her eyes are nearly black. They shine like still water at night and her face is a mass of glorious, tanned wrinkles. I can't stop starring at her, afraid to turn away, afraid I'll miss something important. It's as though her eyes are speaking, even though her lips are still.

"*Non.* Long time grand, big horse. Many big horse," she says, still smiling, reaching high above her head.

"Once, a long time ago. But not now," Napoleon says without turning from the television set.

"Ah . . . Napoleon, he like the horses. He tame much wild horse, not so long ago." Grand'Mère says, topping up our coffees with more steaming black liquid. I bury my smile into my mug but don't dare take a sip, knowing my lips will instantly blister. My gaze slides just over the rim of my cup, secretly watching Napoleon.

Grand'Mère disappears into what seems to be a storage room on the other end of the kitchen. "The kitchen sink has a metal pump — no faucets," Victoria whispers.

"It's so hot in here. I'm going to pass out," I whisper.

"*Servez-vous,*" Grand'Mère says and places a plate of chocolate-dipped biscuits on the table. The plate is as lovely as the biscuits, trimmed in gold and covered in pretty little flowers.

"Where's your bathroom?" Victoria says, reaching for a biscuit.

"*La toilette,*" Napoleon shouts from his chair. His silver and coal black head doesn't turn around.

"*La toilette?*" Grand'Mère says.

"*Oui, la toilette,*" I say.

She chuckles, stands up and throws the shawl from the back of her chair over her shoulders. "Come," she instructs. The top of her head barely reaches my shoulder, but she walks fast. She leads us outside through a screen door at the back of the kitchen. We follow her slight frame towards a pen filled with big, fat, grey birds with floppy red skin hanging from their beaks. "Turkey," she says, pointing to the birds. "Gobble-gobble," she adds. She stops beside the pen, and gestures towards a little wooden shack about twenty feet away. "*La voila.*"

It's an outhouse. "Merci," I say, over enthusiastically. "There you are, Victoria. In you go," I add. Grand'Mère walks back towards the house, wrapping her shawl more tightly around her small shoulders.

"I don't have to go. I was just wondering if they had one," Victoria whispers.

"Just pretend. We don't want to be rude."

She narrows her eyes. "Why me? Why can't you do it?"

"You're the idiot that asked. Just get in there — I don't want them to see us hesitating. They'll be offended," I say, pushing Victoria's back. She steps inside and closes the thin door.

"You owe me for this one, woman," she says through a crescent shaped window.

The chickens are loose in the yard, Mom's new bantams. I try my best to at least appear to snub them (out of self respect); they are, after all, the same species that are responsible for my room reeking of rotting corpse. I admit though, the hens are cute — six little miniature chickens. Some are pure white and others speckled with brown.

"Something smells good," Victoria says as she approaches the house.

"Mom must be baking again. She seems to make something new everyday."

"Yes. Things that use up a lot of eggs!" Victoria says.

I laugh, suddenly realizing the correlation between the chickens arriving and mom's baking obsession. Mom flips an angel food cake upside down to help loosen it from the pan. I place a jar of saskatoon berries in syrup beside the waiting platter. "Here, Grand'Mère gave us these."

"That was thoughtful," she says.

"Aren't you going to ask us where we got the saskatoons?" Victoria says, rolling her dusty, sweat-soaked T-shirt until it sits on top of her little white bra.

"Angel food again?" I say.

"Saskatoon berry shortcake," she says, examining Grand'Mère's jar. "I can't let all these fresh ingredients go to waste. Who did you say gave them to you?"

"Grand'Mère, an older French woman who lives down the lane," Victoria says.

"Have I even met the woman?" Mom says. She stops, looks first at me, then at Victoria, and places her hands on her flour-marked hips. "No, I guess I haven't," she says.

"Nor her bachelor son," Victoria says.

If I were closer to Victoria I'd either stomp on her bare foot or pinch-twist her skinny arm. "Don't worry, Napoleon's ancient. He's nearly seventy," I say. I don't dare tell anyone about my budding interest in Mr. Ancient, the mysterious cowboy.

I keep quiet during dessert, but in truth, I can't warm up to the saskatoons. My parents think they're delicacies, but to me they taste like gravel dipped in almond extract.

"Next spring the river bank will be loaded with saskatoons. We'll pick buckets full and you can freeze them, Mary Jane," Dad says.

"That would be fun. Though I don't know — I don't need anymore encouragement to eat dessert. I've gained fifteen pounds since we moved here."

"You wear it well," Dad says.

For some stupid reason, I laugh. Everyone stops eating. The silence is awkward so I feel obliged to speak. "I wouldn't notice either, except, you wear those polyester pants, nearly everyday lately." I leave out the word hideous, as to not offend. But, seriously, the pants have got to go. I have fantasies about accidentally throwing them in the furnace. She can look good; she used to in Vancouver. Her hair was longer, and she never left the house without makeup. I miss her petal pink lipsticked lips. "Mom? Why do you wear the same pants everyday?" As soon as I've said it, I regret it. Her fork freezes just below her lips.

"Do you think I like dressing like this? Do you?" She pushes her chair back from the kitchen table. "I'm one hundred and fifty pounds for God's sake. What does it matter? No one sees me anyway," she says and darts downstairs, leaving her saskatoon berry shortcake unfinished.

I leave my bedroom door open just enough to hear the goings-on of the house. The hall light sends a pencil stream along the floor to my bed. The house is unusually quiet. I can't hear a damn thing except Victoria singing off-key. I don't recognize the song. Bare feet flap against the floor into the hall: Victoria, on the way to the can. A nose with a face attached pokes itself through the crack in the door. "You really fucked up royally tonight," it says, far too loudly (as it still has its bloody Walkman on).

"Leave me alone," I say, in knee-jerk reaction time. "And fuck off while you're at it," I add, once my brain has caught up to my mouth.

⚡

The last Saturday of summer arrives. It seems as though we were only just thrust onto the doorstep of this towering relic of a house. Yet Vancouver seems like an ice age ago. I won't let the day go. I will hold it inside my soul and let it simmer through all the unknown months ahead.

School starts in August in Saskatchewan. What kind of a backward province starts school in August? September is the natural month to start, the day after Labour Day. To attend school before Labour Day seems sacrilegious.

Victoria is in the kitchen, making a cheese sandwich with Dad's processed cheese slices. He and Victoria are the only ones who can stomach fake cheese. She leaves the fridge wide open while she works. She has a Prissy Tits pretense about her. It's a cover. She's just as terrified to start school as I am.

"What's up? It's only nine."

"I'm taking a picnic into the pasture," she says, already dressed in jeans, her cowboy boots, and a satin quilted housecoat.

"What's with the housecoat?"

"It's comfortable."

That word, picnic, suddenly makes the thought of a processed cheese sandwich seem almost palatable. "Can I come?"

"I don't care," she says. I pull on dad's old cowboy boots and fill an empty plastic pop bottle with orange juice.

"Dad found a coyote's den inside here last spring," I say, climbing to the top of the biggest rock pile in the pasture.

"Are they still here?" Victoria says, looking between her legs into the cracks between the rocks.

"No way. He said they're noisy. You can hear the puppies cry."

"What's with these piles of rocks? Why are they here?" Victoria says.

"The ice age. A wall of ice literally picked them up and pressed them into the ground. The first homesteaders, which would be our great-grandparents, collected all the boulders into piles so they could cultivate the fields," I say.

"How'd they move them without modern machinery?" Victoria says.

"Probably hooked their workhorses up and dragged them around. There used to be more rock piles. Dad said the University of Saskatchewan is built of stone, our stones. They bought our rocks and built their campus."

Silver and Marx wander over to join us. "Marx never leaves her," Victoria says.

"I know. It's adorable."

"He thinks he's a horse."

Silver tosses her head, wanting to be petted. I hold my apple up to her lips. She flashes a toothy grin and snatches it between her teeth and chomps. It falls from her mouth into the grass. She bends her long neck down to find it again and finish it off.

"Horse teeth are so cool; they're like human teeth only longer and interesting to look at," I say.

Victoria laughs, "I never thought about it before but it's true."

Marx places his front paw on my knee and whines. Silver's teeth nibble at the plastic bread bag on my lap. "Get lost, you two!" I say and push their heads away with my feet.

"Aren't you even the slightest bit curious?"

"About what?" I know she means starting school.

"What do you think they'll be like? Backward or a little bit with it?"

"Backward. For sure backward. What are you going to wear? Mom still hasn't to taken us into Saskatoon. I don't know what she's waiting for. I have nothing decent."

"I guess I'll just wear these jeans," Victoria says.

I can't help but feel pity for her. They used to be her new jeans. The jeans she christened on moving day. Now they look like crap. Too many mornings riding bareback and too many afternoons spent knee deep in sooty soil, looking for skeletons.

"Marx! Get lost. I'm hungry," I say. They're working as a team. He's distracted me long enough for Silver to snatch the sandwich bag and gallop across the field. "You get back here, you greedy girl!" I laugh in disbelief.

"Here, girl! Silver, come get my fresh apple!" Victoria shouts.

"There is no way we're going to catch her. She's too smart."

"I just hope she's smart enough not to eat the bag."

"Um, yeah — let's not tell the folks about this."

The truck is parked in front of the house. "They're back early. Wonder what's up?" Victoria says.

Mom is in the kitchen, standing at the ironing board, pressing one of Alex's good shirts. "Where were you two?" she snaps.

"Just out in the pasture," I say.

Dad slides past me with a beer in his hand. "No-back-to-school shopping. Not this year," he says and parks himself in the big orange chair on the back porch and takes a slow sip of beer.

"It's official. Your father's sessionals have turned into one sessional. Isn't that right, Alex? Anyway, you two will be fine. No one here has seen any of your outfits from last year — besides, you'll be miles ahead of the local trends," she says sarcastically, then puts down the iron.

I spot a few of my winter clothes from last year in the laundry basket, waiting their turn. "There's no way I'm wearing this hideous thing to school. It's totally out of style now," I say and yank last year's white cotton pirate shirt from the basket and throw it across the kitchen. "You can't do this to me. Make me go to that hick town school in old clothes. How cruel are you?"

Dad swoops in for the kill. "Get upstairs, get out of my sight, and start acting your age. Sugar Daddy gives you a roof over your head, food to eat, a dog, a horse — don't you forget who pays your bills."

"Who's the Sugar Daddy in this family? My dad has no sugar — isn't that right, Alex!" I yell. I run up to my room and attempt to slam the door, but last night's pajamas are caught underneath it. I want to hurt someone. Maybe myself. My father can't stand the sight of me and my mother doesn't care. I am nothing to them.

I hear him downstairs, "I need to go back to the university. Do you need anything for supper tonight?"

"Why now? It's Saturday, for God's sake," Mom says.

"I'll take that as a no," he says and leaves, taking the truck into Saskatoon.

Sugar Daddy doesn't make it home until dark — long after his supper has found its way into Marx's dish.

THREE

"We have a new student this year. She's from Vancouver, BC," Mr. L. Polinski says as he hands out the class outline for English. I am exposed sitting in the desk, everyone staring. Open wide, earth, and swallow me quick. Don't say my name, don't say my name. To remain anonymous forever is my only wish. "Welcome Lydia — Lydia Buckingham." He said it.

Mr. Polinski turns to finish the paragraph he started to write on the chalkboard, a mess of crap sentences that I assume he wants us to correct. A low voice sounds behind me, "Fucking pig." I hear it again. "Fucking pig." I turn around. The culprit is a pimply-faced, miniature boy with long greasy hair hanging over his eyes. I can't believe the low voice came from someone as puny as him.

"Excuse me?" I say.

"Bucking-ham . . . fucking-ham . . . fucking-pig." he says in his slimy way.

"Fuck you, creep," I retort. I move to an empty desk one over and two up. *I'm watching you, you ugly psychotic toad.*

Victoria and I meet at lunch and walk to the post office to pick up the mail for the folks. It's not even a real post office. It's a rectangular cubicle of a building with walls covered in rows of small, square metal boxes. No one works there, so you can't buy stamps or post anything.

Once inside the empty post office, we lean against the wall of mailboxes and scoff down our sandwiches. Mine tastes like sawdust. I can barely swallow. My throat is too tight. I hold the sandwich tenderly. It's tuna salad. Mom's loving hands made it. A tear rolls down my cheek. I want to go home, far away from this cold, alien nation. Victoria and I don't talk. We're both too miserable to speak.

"I hate school. I swear, all of the kids in my class are weird," I say, walking like a zombie past Mom, who stands on the front porch.

"Didn't you meet anyone interesting?" she says.

There are only twenty-four grade tens in the entire school and they are all related.

"Oh, come on. It can't be all bad."

It is Hicksville High.

"Did you like your teacher at least?"

Polinski. Puke. Polinski is my homeroom and English teacher. He wears a short mustache over too-thin lips. I used to like English but that could change.

"Come on. Say something, anything about your first day!" She turns to Victoria for information. But Victoria pushes past her, slamming her tote bag then herself down on the old chesterfield. An apple rolls from her bag and onto the dirty porch floor. Her mean eyes stare beyond the skeleton bottles and out the front window.

I pause on the first stair before climbing up to the tower. "The day was a living nightmare. Sorry, Mother, but I won't rehash it for anyone."

Two weeks pass, then three, and I still don't notice an improvement. Three seems to be the magic number. Things finally start to change, not so much for me but for Victoria. She marches by me during morning break with Mr. Forney, the principal, right beside her. I mouth, what's up? as she passes. She slices across her neck abruptly with her finger.

I hear all the gory details next period from Nathan Dyck.

"Hey, Fuckingham, I heard your sister's in trouble for busting up some guy's nuts — with her foot," he whispers gruffly.

"Bugger off, pervert. You're just wishing it was you."

If the guy is anything like Nathan Dyck, he had it coming to him. I'd like to have done the honours myself. I'm proud of her.

I meet up with Victoria at lunch. "The school called home," she says.

"Shit."

We walk to the post office as usual. It's no longer about picking up the mail. It's all about escape. Some guy calls out to us as we leave the schoolyard, "Hey, it's Spiff and Spiff junior!"

"Who is that loser?" I say. I want to neuter him.

"I think he's in grade eleven. How does he even know who we are?" Victoria asks.

"He's a total dipshit, his parents are first cousins, you can just tell."

We sit together on the bus ride home, closer to the front than the middle. It's safer up front with all the little kids. I have avoided staring, but from what I can tell there's a whole lot of pimples, perms, and ball caps going on back there.

Victoria struts off the bus like a regal feline, her tail in the air. She doesn't seem the least bit worried, so I'm worried for her. She may be naive but I know our parents. They're lurking, like a couple of hyenas, in the front hall — effectively blocking my route to the tower.

The news about Victoria seems to set my parents off. The day spirals from bad to worse. "This is your fault. Why didn't you teach your daughters about boys and their sensitive private parts?" Mom says.

"You're their mother. Sex Ed is their mother's job," Alex says.

"My job? Why is everything left up to me? You're their father! Start acting like one!"

"My income is feeding those two. If you'd get off your ass and do something with yourself — get a job and help support this family!" Alex shouts.

"How? With what vehicle? You leave me stranded on this fucking farm day after day. How can I look for a job from here? You're a rotten, selfish son of a bitch! I hate you!" Mom screams.

"Jesus, look what you've unleashed," I say to Victoria.

We hide out in the basement building Barbie houses. Mine is going to be a posh sixties-style bungalow. I set up in the darkest corner, behind the furnace, well out of the view from Mom and Alex's bedroom. The pungent odor of old cat spray lingers, but it will be a cozy spot once Alex fires up the beast of a furnace.

Victoria's building a modern condo on top of the little bar fridge that sits pathetically in the opposite corner of the dark basement, waiting for someone, at the very least, to plug it in.

"Quiet," she says.

I listen. Nothing. Things seem to have quieted down. "Shall we brave the battlefield?" I whisper.

"You first."

I lead up the wooden stairs, holding my breath, motioning Victoria back with my arm. I hear a loud *crack*! We've come up too soon. Mom's frantically whipping Alex with a wooden spoon. He tries to shield his head with his hands. She smacks his wrists. She's noticed us standing at the top of the stairs. She throws down the spoon and comes towards us. We split up and run. She catches up with me in my bedroom. Her eyes are wild and angry. But at the same time I see recognition; she's not out of her mind. She snatches a wooden school ruler from my dresser and proceeds towards my bed. What is she doing? Is she totally insane? I roll onto my back and flail my legs in my classic protection move. I use it on Victoria every time we fight. I don't want to do it — I'm wearing a jean mini skirt and my fuchsia panties are on full embarrassing display — but she's left me no choice. If I keep my legs moving fast enough she can't reach my torso or face. She lifts the ruler and smacks it down hard on my leg. The steel ruler's edge cuts through the skin on my thigh. It stings.

"What are you doing? I haven't done anything!" I say.

"You're brats, all of you. Spoiled rotten, selfish brats," she says.

"I hate you. You're a horrible mother. You're insane and cruel," I cry.

She stops hitting me, drops the ruler, runs down the stairs, and out the front door. I stand, my legs shaking, and look out my bedroom window. Her silhouette runs through the dark field towards the river.

Victoria cowers at the top of the staircase, listening. I push past her. Alex stands at the base of the staircase, his hand on the banister knob. His gaze fixates on my bloody leg but he says nothing.

"Where'd she go?" he asks and turns to follow her. "Girls, help me find your mother."

My father is afraid so I am afraid. She might be heading for the river to throw herself in.

"Victoria, are you coming?" I say.

"No," she says without emotion, then rises and disappears up the stairs.

I find the flashlight in the kitchen junk drawer and call Marx as I walk into the prairie night.

The sound of a chainsaw cuts through my sleep, gnawing away at my brain. I hate that sound. Alex is on a mission: to prepare us for the winter. I think he's lost one hundred years somewhere out in the pasture. We're living in the eighteen eighties.

Alex treats poplar wood like it's rare milk. Milk to feed his precious baby, the huge, gas-filled baby that squats in the middle of the basement belching out thick black smoke. Although the furnace burns both oil and wood, Alex insists on wood exclusively. It's cheaper and the labour's free.

I drag my socked feet downstairs in a stupor. Mary Jane waits, sitting all bundled up in the kitchen, in her polyester pants and parka — check, double check.

"Hurry up and get dressed. Your father needs us out in the bluff. There's a lot of wood to haul," she says as though last night never happened. Apparently she is not a child-beating, suicidal maniac after all. She's a farmer's wife extraordinaire.

"Whoopee-yee-haw-cow-paddy," I say and open the fridge.

"What did you say?" Mary Jane's voice is sharp. It stabs my post-sleep brain. I focus my attention on the inside of the fridge. "Hurry up, Lydia. There's no time for breakfast. You slept in. Victoria's already out there. Dress warm. There's no snow but it's cold — and shut the fridge," she adds, banging the back door behind her.

I wait, staring at the jug of orange juice before slamming the fridge door shut. I gaze out the kitchen window at the bluff closest to the house. There's Victoria all right, sifting through the dead wood . . . goody two-shoes. She's dressed in a toque and parka with her pink robe and pajama pants sticking out the bottom — too good to help rescue her suicidal mother but not too good to be little Miss Wood-Hauling Prissy Tits.

"There. That's it. I'm done," I release my last load into the woodpile beside the house. My shoulders ache. Mary Jane begins to organize the pile. Forget that, I am dying to have a shower and eat something. I look back at the bluff. There's my slave driving father, dressed in his cow-poo jeans and ripped parka, still out there wandering, hopeful that he'll stumble upon one more rotten log to chop up.

I talk to as few people as possible at school and fantasize my days away. I'm probably doing serious damage to my psyche that I'll pay for when I'm older. I live in one long daydream. But the alternative, the reality of Hicksville High, is too painful. I'm doing squat in Saskatchewan, unless of course you count the Post Office Club at noon, the Zombie and Zits Bus Riding Team after school, and my personal favourite: The Prissy Tits Wood Hauling Club. We meet on all Saturday and Sunday mornings at various poplar bluffs.

Victoria is still my post office buddy, so her weeks aren't much better. We don't talk much at school. It's an uncomfortable place to be. Communication only draws attention to our awkwardness.

"You know what Polinski said to me this morning, after you traded lunches with me?" I say once we're huddled inside the warm post office.

"What?"

"Why is it that the only time you smile is when your sister walks into the room?"

"What a perv. Like he'd ever say that to a guy."

"It was a rhetorical question, anyway. Look around the classroom, buddy! Isn't it self-evident?"

"Who's your least favourite classmate?" Victoria asks.

"I don't know. They all suck."

We shut up and suffer in silence.

The temperature plummeted in the night. Out my bedroom window there is nothing but white. It is shocking against the clear blue sky. I know I prayed for the chickenshit smell to go away but the cold, it's unbelievable, nothing like Vancouver. Even though the truck's block heater was plugged in all night, it still won't start. Mary Jane and Alex can't go into Saskatoon for their Saturday morning constitutional of coffee and errands. Instead, Mary Jane calls Granny to complain about our finances. Our house in Vancouver still hasn't sold. I am secretly pleased. I love that house. However, Alex and Mary Jane are in shitty moods because of it. After a lunch of Alex's homemade soup concoction of Asian noodles, frozen peas, and bouillon, they retire to the living room to drink and listen to Mary Jane's Kris Krisofferson album, even though it's not even four o'clock in the afternoon. Just listening to the guy singing about beers for breakfast makes me want to cash it all in myself. Too close to home, Kris. Way too close to home.

Victoria sits beside me at the kitchen table sipping hot chocolate. "What are they drinking? It looks disgusting," she says.

"Coal tar shakes."

"Is that what they're called?"

"No, I made it up."

"What's in the coal tar shakes that makes them black?" she says.

"Water."

"Seriously?"

"Correction, our water, Vodka, and orange juice, that's all they are. Some strange chemical reaction takes place when you mix the well water with alcohol. It turns black — like a magic potion."

"Alex said it comes from the bowels of the earth — an underground river, three hundred feet under the house."

"He had it analyzed by the government — I read the report. It contains every element known to human kind: huge amounts of iron and sulfur, all rocks and minerals — more of a solid than a liquid, really. No one under the age of three is supposed to drink it."

Victoria stops sipping her cocoa. "What? Are they trying to poison us?"

"Only toddlers can't drink it. Lethal diarrhea."

"Death by diarrhea."

"Relax. Alex says each glass is like a multivitamin — the worst of it is the taste."

"Like dirty diapers."

Mary Jane must be getting tipsy. She's rehashing how horrible Alex treated her when they were first married. I hear her voice above the lyrics, "You used to go out every night . . . your communist friends . . . leave me alone in that tiny apartment . . . two crying babies . . . come home two, three o'clock in the morning . . . stoned," her voice is getting shrill.

"It'll be a simple Christmas this year," Alex says.

That's code for skimpy.

"We'll manage. The girls are getting older now. Christmas doesn't mean as much to them anymore," Mary Jane says.

Speak for yourself, Mary Jane. I still love Christmas. I haven't decided what's worse, selling our house or getting squat for Christmas. I guess I choose missing Christmas if it means we get to move back to Vancouver. At least in Vancouver I can go outside every single day without the danger of my flesh freezing in less than a minute. Their conversation is getting painfully dull: talk about the septic tank and truck transmission. I am bored, dead bored.

After an afternoon spent in a serious coal tar shake stupor, Mary Jane and Alex decide to tuck themselves into bed early. The master suite is anything but impressive. It's like a cell, boxed into the front right corner of the basement, encased in two-by-fours and Gyproc, an Alex special. I don't know why he insisted on building it. They could fit into the sewing room if they really wanted to.

They've donned matching toques and lay buried under layers of duvets to keep warm, as Alex still refuses to feed his big creepy baby (the bird crematorium) oil. He hasn't deemed the weather cold enough to require back up. They do nothing but read down there. Alex reads and rereads a box of old *New Yorker* magazines beside his bed. Mary Jane reads one of at least a dozen novels she borrowed from the Saskatoon library. She'll go through the entire collection in three weeks. I predict that the two of them will spend all winter tucked into their dungeon bed.

The first yip of a coyote sounds from outside. That means it's almost eleven. I pull a thin black case from my closet shelf. Inside, on blue velvet lining, my flute glistens like polished silver, untouched since the final grade nine concert. Hicksville High doesn't have a band. I carefully take her out, slide the pieces together, then press my lips gently to her rim. I blow as though blowing into a glass bottle. The sound is low and mournful. It's exactly what this house needs on such a night as this. The wind has turned wicked and the entire house quivers with the chills. I play the melody of "Life On Mars" from memory. I taught it to myself last year. Our band played a lot of crappy jazz and some old movie theme songs but nothing like Bowie. Bowie is a god. I play Bowie along with the coyotes as they howl to Marx.

My fifteenth birthday arrives with little fanfare. Victoria and I build a Barbie town in the basement — Paris, France. It's too cold to do anything else except homework, and homework isn't as exciting as Paris. Our Barbies are Canadians in Paris — expats. Victoria's Barbie is a famous painter. Mine is a fashion designer who works at Chanel. The basement is still dark, dank, and depressing, but warm because the bird crematorium is fired up and belching out her black smoke.

I hear the sound of the truck motor, and then the truck doors slam shut. The parents are home from Saskatoon with the groceries. "What time is it, Vic?"

"Four fifty."

"Whoa, time flies. I can't believe I'm still in my pajamas."

"I'm going up," Victoria says.

I stay, determined to stuff my Barbie into her velvet evening gown. I sewed the sleeves too narrow. But this baby is going on if I have to cut off her hands to do it.

Victoria trots back downstairs. "Mary Jane's making pizza for your supper — and they bought pop."

"All right!" I say before she runs back up the stairs.

Alex creeps down the stairs. I don't look up. He sits on the wooden box Victoria's using as the Louvre. It can't be good. Alex never wants to talk to me. My stomach twists into a knot.

"Your mother and I are worried about you," he says.

That's new. I sense a snakebite coming on. "Be careful. You're sitting on Victoria's art gallery," I say.

"You're too old to play with dolls. Why don't you do things like other teenagers? It's not normal to chum around with your sister all weekend at your age," he says and slithers his way up the stairs.

I don't want pizza anymore. My stomach hurts. My flannel pajamas are babyish with puffed sleeves. Why did Mary Jane even make these hideous pajamas for me? I'd stay down in the pit forever but I have to go pee. I climb the two long staircases lethargically, like a pathetic waste-of-a-life would. I don't dare look at myself in the bathroom mirror. I know just what I'd see: a big, ugly disappointment, a crying, freckled baby face with stringy hair.

As I sit on the cold toilet, tracing the pattern of the ancient linoleum with my big toe, it occurs to me that I don't do other things because I'm a prisoner. I take the bus to and from that freaking hick school and that is all. They never take us into Saskatoon, the nearest neighbours are six kilometres away and they're seniors for crap sake. I do very well for myself, thank you, entertaining myself all weekend long in this hellhole. And what about Victoria? She's only a year younger than me. Why isn't she a freak for playing with Barbies?

Mary Jane globs cream cheese icing onto my peanut butter cake as I plunge my finger in the bowl surreptitiously for tastes. Alex clomps into the back porch from outside, the scent of fresh chicken feathers on him. "Take a look at this," he says, lying long leather straps across the kitchen table. I hate him for the Barbie ambush but my fingers can't help themselves; they slide across the table and gently touch two large glass buttons with red roses painted inside.

"These are cool," I say, unable to stop myself.

"Your great-grandfather's harness. I found it in the old shed a couple of summers ago along with sleigh runners. I had the presence of mind to move it to the house. The runners survived the blaze but not the sleigh. I'm going to build a new box." He pauses to wipe his cold nose on the back of his red hand. "I want to hitch Silver to it. She can pull you girls around the pasture."

"I've never seen any sleigh," I say.

"We have the steel runners, the most important part of the sleigh. Your great-grandparents used to ride to town on that sleigh all winter long. I'll build a new box for it, then she'll be ready to go." He unzips his parka and sits down at the kitchen table. "What kind of cake is that?"

"Peanut butter," I say.

"Peanut butter?" he says, and squeezes his frosted eyebrows together as though I said dog shit.

"Lydia's favourite," Mary Jane says, placing a mug of coffee in front of him.

"Thank you," he says, then uses his palms to rub the frost from his eyebrows.

Alex's office appears to be abandoned: a stack of university exam books frozen to a rickety old chair, a dusting of chicken feathers settled on the desk. Before the minus forty hit, he used to work in his office on weekends, dressed in his parka and toque. Now it looks like some ominous scene from *Doctor Zhivago*. The barn door bangs open. Victoria stands at the entrance, dressed in snow boots and her long pink housecoat. Her braids are unraveled, framing her face in a crown of fuzz.

"Where is it?" she says, striding past me to the last stall. Lying in the corner of the stall are long, elegant steel sleigh runners. "You call that a sleigh?"

"You'd never guess it's over a hundred years old," I say.

"What's this?" Victoria says and kicks the plywood on top.

"Alex is making a new box for it."

"Yeah, well, Alex doesn't know what he's doing. It already looks crappy," she says, then turns, swinging her pink cloak as she marches out of the barn.

Her words cut through me. Alex is using his own hands to build something, something my great-grandparents treasured, for us. I hate Victoria for putting down Alex, and I hate Alex for putting down me. I hate them both.

Alex pushes his chair back from the table. "That was very nice. If you'll excuse me, the Oilers are playing the Islanders tonight. Mary Jane, bring my dessert, no cake, just ice cream, into the living room when it's ready, please and thank you," he says overenthusiastically, to camouflage his abrupt demands. He saunters into the family room and lowers himself into the La-Z-Boy, puts it in recline position, and reaches for a cigar. There is something comforting about the exotic scent of a Cuban cigar. A single obnoxiously-exhaled smoke ring floats from his lips and hovers, like a noose, over his head.

Victoria sniffs the air and coughs. "Second-hand smoke is twice as bad for us. You're slowly killing your children. We're dying here, breathing your toxic waste."

"Promise?" Alex says, without turning from the TV.

"Take this in to your father for me," Mary Jane says, handing Victoria a heaping bowl of vanilla ice cream.

Victoria shakes her head. "No, I need to breathe." The pink-robed goddess leaves the room, carrying a substantial piece of my cake upstairs with her.

Happy birthday to me.

The school bus spits Victoria and me out into minus forty-seven. We run for the house. I throw off my parka, sprint up to the bathroom to pee, then head for the tower. I've been taking a break from the Barbies. Not because of what Alex said, but because it's depressing sitting down there in the dark smokiness. I put Bowie into my tape recorder, lie down on my bed, and dance my feet up the wall over the black and white fashion photographs. I ripped the most striking images from the school's stash of *Seventeen*, *Flare*, and *Vogue* magazines. It's not like anyone will even know they're missing; fashion and style are lost on the culturally vacant minds of Hicksville High.

The tower door abruptly opens and reveals my pale-faced mother. "It's your sister."

"What?"

"She ripped up all of your father's cigars and flushed them down the toilet," she says.

Suddenly, it seems, my day is about to improve and the bright spot, once again, is Victoria and her stupidity.

"Somebody had to do it," she shouts from her bedroom.

"Yeah, somebody with a death wish," I shout back.

"I wish she hadn't done it. He's going to explode," Mary Jane says.

"You never know, Mom, she is his favourite."

As a precautionary measure, I insist that Victoria hide under her captain's bed. The impending excitement inspires Victoria and me into a harmonious period of heightened sister bonding. "Come on, Vic! How old are you? I swear women have two holes and not just one," I say as I recline on top of her bed.

"How do you know?" she says from under the bed.

"Okay, how do you explain being able to pee with a tampon in?" Victoria's silent. "I don't know what happened to you, kid. I educated myself reading *Cosmo* and *The Joy of Sex* when I babysat in Vancouver. Where were you?"

"I don't believe you," she says.

The truck pulls up to the house. I lie still on Victoria's bed and stare at the ceiling, listening.

"What's for supper, Mary Jane? I'm famished," Dad says.

"Hamburger soup and homemade buns," she says.

I am dead sick of hamburger soup. She makes it every Friday. Her buns are delicious though. I take my place at the kitchen table. We eat in total silence except for Alex's slurping. The basement door rattles. George's furry black and white paw grasps underneath it, trying to open it. The door is directly behind Alex's chair. No one makes a move to let him up.

"Where's Victoria? Why isn't she eating?" Alex glances at Mary Jane and then at me.

"She's hiding from something," I say, focused on the tomato broth left in my bowl.

Alex rips off a big bite of bun with his teeth. He chews it for what feels like five minutes. Finally, he swallows. "Someone better tell me what's going on," he says.

I'm surprised by the anger in his voice. He leaves the rest of the bun drowning in his soup and places his elbows on the table. "Tell me what's going on, Lydia, or you can leave this table immediately," he says.

There are three buns left on the tray and the butter dish is nearly empty. I don't want to look up. His eyes will burn holes through my brain. I glance at Mary Jane for support. She avoids my gaze. "She wants you to quit smoking," I say.

"So. So what?" he says.

"Your daughter has disposed of your cigars. She's worried about your health," Mary Jane says calmly.

Alex's face flashes from white to red in an instant, and my face turns from white to red. I stop chewing. "Where is she?" he says, wrenching his chair back from the table.

He lunges upstairs in an attempt to find her, then runs back down the stairs, passes us, a blurred angry streak, and opens the basement door. George bolts through, like a cat out of hell, and disappears onto the back porch. Alex thunders downstairs and remerges in less than a minute holding an empty cigar box.

"That's it. I'm outta here," he says, knocking the basement door open so hard that the doorknob knocks a chunk of plaster from the wall. He storms down to his bedroom.

Mary Jane follows him. "Alexander, calm yourself down. This isn't a big deal. You can buy more cigars tomorrow."

His voice is loud and deep. "I am sick and tired of this bullshit! I have no home. No one respects my private property. All I do is work for this family and I'm done — done with all of it!"

I spit out the bun that suddenly feels and tastes like a chunk of Styrofoam. He can't leave. We'll be stranded, totally alone; no car, Mary Jane has no job. I jump up from the table, run into the hall, and take the truck keys from the ledge under the hall window. I fly up to the bathroom and drop them into the rust-stained toilet bowl, covering them with toilet paper. He'll never see them in there. I wait on the staircase landing.

He's clutching a big leather bag and has a smaller bag tucked under his armpit, his toilet kit. "Where are the keys, Mary Jane?" he demands.

"I don't know," Mary Jane says.

"Lydia?" he shouts up the stairs. "Very good, very good. It doesn't matter, I have another set in the glove box." He lunges for the hall closet and snatches his parka.

My plan has failed. The elevator hits the bottom of my stomach. We will die alone. I leap down the staircase and out the front door. I beat him to the truck and lock every door. I've done it. We're safe. There is no way out of here now. My adrenalin is high. I don't realize the temperature until I start to shake. I'm wearing only a short-sleeved T-shirt and jeans.

Alex strides from the house with his parka unzipped. His face is set, determined and angry. He won't look at me. He pounds on the windshield, "Lydia, get the hell out of my truck, now!" He turns, walking away, disappearing behind the side of the house.

Breathe . . . it will be all right. Things seem to have climaxed and everything's calming down. He'll sit out in his office until he's frozen solid then slink back into the house when we're all asleep.

I debate with myself when a good time to exit the truck might be. My trembling legs say any time soon. Suddenly, Alex appears from behind the other side of the house. His stare is terrifyingly unrecognizable and he is carrying something in his hand. The silver blade shines in the yard light. He's brought the axe. He strides towards the truck without flinching. I slide out of the driver's side and into the passenger's seat. Alex raises his hands over his head. It happens instantly, but at the same time, it's as though I exist in a slower version of reality. Glass shatters all over my lap. A scream escapes from my throat but it doesn't sound like me. My brain scrambles to put it all together: my father's smashed out the passenger side window with an axe. It is in a million little pieces all over me.

Mary Jane screams from the porch, "Alex, what in God's name are you doing?"

I slide back to the driver's seat, unlock the door, and run. I run up to Victoria's room and roll back her bed. "Get out of there, you fucking coward! Look what you've done!" My entire body vibrates. There are glass pieces in my hair and little cuts on my right arm. Victoria crouches under her bed, her eyes wild with both fear and excitement. I hear the truck speeding out of our driveway. "Good riddance!" I shout. I shake so badly that my teeth knock together during the "riddance" part.

Alexander spent the night in Saskatoon at the King George Hotel. He actually spent two nights before showing his sorry face on our porch again, all serious and quiet. Victoria spots the truck first, parked in front of the house. I race to the front door and lock it, then to the back door and lock that too. He's already standing inside the porch and knocking on the front door. "Come on, let's see what he wants," Victoria says. I hesitate. He's an asshole. But my curiosity gets the better of me. Victoria opens the door.

"I'd like to talk to your mother. Can you please tell her I'm here," he says, with no acknowledgement of either Victoria or me.

"Mother! It's your long lost husband," I yell.

Mary Jane surfaces from the basement. "Yes? What do you want?" she says, cold as Saskatchewan.

Victoria follows me deeper into the living room and we sit side by side on the chesterfield. Alex speaks in a low, quiet voice. I can't make out any of his bullshit.

Mary Jane walks into the living room, "I'm going into Saskatoon. Your father wants to take me for a drink — to talk," she says, avoiding eye contact.

"She's so easy, a doormat," I say as the truck pulls out of our ice-packed driveway.

They had their drink. Suddenly everything is peachy, and Alex moves himself back into our shabby, tall house along with a brand new wooden box of Cuban cigars.

Somehow, Victoria has managed to make a friend. I'm not that big on Twyla. She's a born-again Christian. She struggles with "the whole evolution thing." Though I can't blame Victoria for falling for her — beggars can't be choosers. I need to find a girl to chum around with at lunchtime. I don't even have to like her. I just have to tolerate her.

The daily walk to the post office is lonely and depressing without Victoria. My sandwich tastes like cardboard slices with sawdust sprinkles. It's hard to swallow. I force myself though. I hate the going-to-barf-and-then-black-out feeling I get when I don't eat. I manage half the sandwich, and wonder how to kill thirty more minutes.

It takes all I have to eject myself from the warm room into the frigid air and walk back to school. My thighs feel like frozen chicken legs by the time I glide, unnoticed, through the front doors. I am alone in a sea of pimply-faced geeks. My eyes sting and water. The hallway is blurry. I can't identify individuals. It's an improvement.

FOUR

The septic tank backed up. I don't know the details. I suspect the house has grown tired of us and all of our shit. Alex is down in the poop filled pit with a blow dryer and a flashlight. I feel a little bit sorry for him but mostly for my mother. She's always his first mate on all these type of chores.

"It would happen, of course, during another cold snap," Mary Jane says.

"Minus fifty-five with the wind chill," I say.

"Thank you for that, Lydia," Mary Jane says sarcastically.

"Is this tight enough to fit now?" I say and hold up the mini skirt I've been sewing. "They're going to die when I show up at school in the new year: death by culture shock. Everyone is beyond out of style in Hicksville."

"Maybe they just have a different kind of style," Mary Jane says.

"It's different, all right. I call it Hutterite chic," I say.

Mary Jane puts down Victoria's balaclava and picks up the waistband. "Another inch — see, it has to fit perfectly, no overlapping," she says, then pulls the balaclava over her stale hair. She joins Alex outside in the shit pit as I slink into the bathroom and lock the door. If I disappear, Alex might forget all about me. I'd rather be across the hall, finishing the skirt, but it's too risky. Victoria's an idiot. She's out in the open, sitting on the chesterfield reading, just asking to be involved in the shit fiasco. The front door opens and slams shut. An icy blast slides its way up the stairs and under the bathroom door.

Alex thumps the snow off his boots. "Girls come down here, family meeting. It's extremely important."

I unlock the bathroom and pause at the top of the landing. "What is it?" I say.

"Down here, now!" he says. His face is scarlet and his hair white with frost. Victoria leans against the wall in her housecoat, her gaze is set beyond the front hall, beyond our family. Mary Jane steps in from the porch. In her frosted balaclava, her head appears frozen, mid scream. She resembles that Edvard Munch painting, *The Scream*.

Alex has prepared a speech. "I've just sucked raw sewage — frozen shit — through a pipe the size of a straw. I am not, I repeat, not stepping a toe down into that septic tank again this winter. And this next part is crucial. Are you all listening? Mary Jane, girls — you cannot flush tampons down the toilet. You got that? Never. Do I make myself clear?"

How does he know I use tampons? I eyeball Victoria. She's stunned into silence too. I don't think she uses anything yet. Alex's speech is not over: "There's the toilet paper issue. Someone has been using too much of it. It's plugging the system. Only four squares each — maximum. Do I make myself clear?"

"Crystal — four squares," I say.

The speech fucked up Victoria. "He can hear me unroll the toilet paper. He counts the sheets based on how many times he hears it spin around," she says.

"I've never seen him, " I say, but even as I say it I get a strong mental picture of him hovering outside the bathroom door, listening. Victoria hasn't pooped since the speech. It's Christmas holidays so she can't even try going at school. She is truly stuck. We've decided to sleep together, in the tower, over the break. It's amazing how I can cuddle right up to that warm, annoying body of hers when it's life or death. Alex sets the thermostat to fifty degrees Fahrenheit and no one's allowed to touch it. The irony is that there is a huge hot air vent right outside my bedroom that he's sealed shut by jamming a piece of wood in it. He says hot air naturally rises, if we open the vent they'll have no heat in the dungeon.

I have on a toque, socks, and flannel nightgown, yet my feet are ice blocks. I try warming them on Victoria but she kicks like a wild horse. I wait until after the coyotes have left the pasture and the midnight train has gone. I slide out of bed and tiptoe down, holding my breath on each step. In slow motion, my finger guides the thermostat dial up one degree at a time until it hits fifty-nine. I inch up the stairs and crawl into bed. It creaks. I wait — nothing. Alex is still asleep. Mission successful.

The heavenly purr of the furnace blows hot air up to the big sealed vent. The tricky part: I tiptoe to the grate and delicately remove the wood jam. Careful, one millimetre at a time, sliding the hinge back, opening the grate, and releasing the heavenly hot, smoky air that fills my nightie. I sit, puffed up like a blowfish, for one glorious moment. My toe hits the hinge and it snaps loudly into full open position. I'm paralyzed. Alex heard that. He's coming up the stairs. I jump into bed and lay still, pretending to be in a deep sleep. I hear him pause on the main floor and readjust the thermostat. He makes his way up towards my room and stops to jam the grate shut. Victoria and I lay deadly still, softly snoring, tucked under my duvet.

Maybe it's the pathetic sight of us in our toques, one of us faking a snore that touches some empathetic core inside him. Or maybe he's just too tired to try and figure out which one of us did it. But he leaves us as we are and slithers back down to the dungeon.

⚡

The truck wheels are frozen solid. It takes Alex a while, rocking back and forth, to release them. We bump along icy ruts on square wheels. Japanese trucks aren't designed for Saskatchewan. The seats are solid blocks of frozen foam, no give whatsoever. The cold seeps through and chills my bum. The trip is long even though it takes only about half an hour to reach Saskatoon. The landscape surrounding the car is white and flat, like a giant skating rink. There are no trees to protect the highway; snow continually sifts across, blown by the steady wind. I doubt we're even driving on the road. We seem to hover above it, driving through a white moving blanket.

"Where are we going, anyway?" Victoria says.

"Downtown," Mary Jane says without turning around. She's all cozy and warm up front with Alex, running her hand through the back of his hair. Alex moves his big head around like he's Marx, looking for the next scratch. He glances into the rear-view mirror and catches my eyes.

"What's with all the makeup? I said we're going to Saskatoon, not Paris," he says.

"Black liner prevents snow blindness," I say.

"What is this?" I say, bewildered by the parents' destination choice.

"This is where we go for our constitutional coffee," Mary Jane says.

"What? The bleeping Army and Navy for God's sake? Who shops here?" I say.

"Disappear," Alex says to us.

"Do your Christmas shopping and meet us back here in an hour," Mary Jane says and hands a ten-dollar bill first to Victoria and then one to me.

We stand, in shock, watching the parents climb the staircase into a café designed to resemble a ship. "Cool restaurant. Mom said the building used to be an Eaton's."

"Wish it still was," I say.

We ride to the floor above on a narrow, ancient wooden escalator then, on discovering the second floor is full of giant bras and armpit-high panties, we take an elevator back down again. "Let's go check out the Salvation Army Thrift Store. I saw it on the way here. It's down the street," I say.

"Why?" Victoria says.

"The amount Mary Jane gives us to spend on clothes gets us nothing. If I want to look good, I have to make it myself. I want to find some old fifties dresses to rework."

"We're supposed to be Christmas shopping. Mary Jane won't want you taking off on me." The thought of abandoning her hadn't occurred to me until she mentioned it. In her braids, puffy parka, toque, and snow boots, Victoria looks like she belongs in Hicksville. At least I refused the toque Alex kept throwing at me, and the Sasquatch boots too.

"Come with me then," I say, hoping she'll decline.

She furrows her eyebrows and shoots me the death stare. As soon as the elevator doors open she bolts down an aisle of Christmas ornaments without looking back.

Sorting through depressing polyester and armpit sweat-stained dresses makes me rethink the logic behind my mission. I may just abort the seedy operation early. The dresses are horrible seventies scraps. An item in the men's department catches my eye. The royal purple satin and velvet are too stunning to resist; I purchase the vintage smoking jacket for the full ten dollars.

Warm air hits my frozen feet as I spin through the Army and Navy's revolving doors. Victoria's hard to miss in the toque. She's on the first floor, in the makeup department, sniffing lip gloss. "Where are the folks?"

"Don't know," she says.

"What'd you get them?"

She pulls grey work socks out of a plastic bag, then a bottle of pink nail polish. "It's all I could afford," she says. There is something about the gifts, simplicity verging on pathetic, that triggers an unexpected urge to cry.

"She doesn't even wear nail polish," I say.

"I know — what'd you get?"

I open the top of the plastic bag and pull out a portion of the jacket.

"What the hell is that?"

"A smoking jacket. Vintage. 1920s."

"That's not even museum worthy," she says, disgusted by the musty odor, I presume.

On Christmas Eve morning the prairie delivers her first gifts: a bright topaz sky and pristine snow so bright, it hurts to look at it. Mary Jane is the first to spot them from the sewing room window, two dark objects making their way through the field towards our house. "Two masked riders. How dangerously alluring," I say to Victoria. The riders park their snowmobiles beside the truck and dismount.

"Who are the masked men?" she whispers to me.

"We'll assume they're men, hope. When those helmets come off, I better not see grey hair and wrinkles," I say.

One of them knocks on the front door. No one has ever knocked on that door. It's as though we've forgotten what comes next, after a knock on the door. "Is someone going to open that?" Mary Jane says, pushing past the statues that were once Victoria and me. I'm not disappointed. They're both male and they're not old. I recognize them. They're in grade eleven at our school. They must be lost. Victoria and I shuffle our statue legs towards the front entrance. Why did I decide to wait to wash my hair?

"We're just riding around," says the dark-haired guy. He rides our bus, always sits way in the back.

"Come in, I guess," I say, looking for approval from Mary Jane as she stands in the hallway.

"Brady," the dark-haired guy says and holds out his hand.

"Mary Jane — the mother," Mary Jane says as she politely sakes his hand.

The redhead smiles shyly. "Mark," he says.

Brady bends over to take off his boots before stepping onto our front hall carpet. Red hair dude follows suit.

They seem tall; I feel short. No one says anything.

"They ride our bus," I say to Mary Jane.

"You're classmates?"

"No," I say at the sametime as Brady.

"Perhaps our guests would like to sit in the living room — I'll be upstairs finishing my Christmas sewing," Mary Jane says and raises her eyebrows in an "I'll be listening" warning. She acts like her sewing project is top secret but it's the same every year: Victoria and I receive matching flannel nightgowns with ruffled collars that turn us into Mary and Laura from *Little House on the Prairie*.

I walk casually into the living room and sit in the winged chair. Victoria follows. She stands beside my chair with her hands stuffed into the pockets of the pink housecoat. "You can come in here," I say.

"Sure," says Brady and puts his helmet on the hall carpet and unzips his jacket, laying it over the banister.

The boys sit, side by side, on the chesterfield, leaving the rest of the long sofa empty. They look ridiculous, all cozied up like that. Victoria takes a seat on the arm of my chair. My gaze floats from one sorry face to the other, wearing a perky yet inviting smile, I assume. Victoria won't quit staring at me, afraid to even look towards the sofa. With her freckled nose and oversized round front teeth, she looks a little like the dorky *Mad Magazine* guy. It's all I can do not to elbow her off the arm of the chair and send her crashing to the floor.

"Do you want to listen to some music?" I say. Victoria makes a move towards the stereo. I pull her sleeve. There is no way I'm letting her choose the tunes. She'll put on something mortifying, like Air Supply. "Ditch the housecoat!" I whisper.

"I was going to put on Roman Holliday," Victoria says and slaps my hand.

"Have you guys heard of Roman Holliday?" I say.

"Don't think so," says Red. Brady shrugs.

"They're a British band — virtually unknown in Canada," Victoria says with a British accent. *Ditch the housecoat and ditto for the accent.*

Victoria returns to her perch on the arm of my chair as the Roman Holliday album starts to play. The room is still for what feels like too long. "Do you even know our names?" she says, still staring at me instead of the guys. I want to smack her but I control myself and slap her leg gently. "Well, excuse me, but I was just trying to be polite!" she says.

"You're Victoria, right?" Mark says.

"What about her? Do you know her name?" Victoria says, placing her hand on my head as though I'm her pet. I forcefully remove it.

"Lydia," Brady says and beams as though he's on a game show. I blush the instant he says my name.

"Do you guys have any tattoos?" Victoria says.

"Victoria!" I say, mortified.

"Maybe," Brady says. "Push over a bit, would ya?" he adds to Mark, then stands up to pull at his jeans before sitting back down again. Mark shuffles a full cushion to the other end of the sofa.

"Well? Tattoo — anyone?" I say, trying to sound bored.

Brady rolls up the long sleeve of his baseball style T-shirt.

"Mark?" Victoria says, looking at him.

Mark hesitates. "It's obvious isn't it?" he says as he holds out his freckled arms that protrude from short sleeves.

"Tattoo virgins," I say, feeling a sudden rush of confidence. We are Lydie and Vic, unarmed but dangerous.

"There might be one hiding one somewhere . . . else," Vic says.

"You wouldn't be hiding any hideous tattoo from us, would you?" I say, looking directly at Mark because looking at Brady might make me blush again.

"All right, you win. Let's take it off, Mark," Brady says.

For a moment I panic, unsure what he means by "take it off". Their shirts come off in unison; no Pillsbury Doughboys, they're strong farm boys. The muscles in my face start to twitch. I cannot return to Lydia. I'll blush like an awkward idiot. Lydie I must remain.

"Tattoo virgins — you guys need tattoos," Lydie says.

"Macho ones," says Vic.

"Victoria can fix that," Lydie says.

"I can?" Victoria says.

"She's an amazing artist, " I say and walk into the kitchen and open the junk drawer. The only felts are dead felts, so dry they squeak. I take two ballpoint pens.

Victoria holds the ballpoint pen as though I've just handed her a knife and told her to stab someone with it. I nod in the direction of Mark.

I take Brady's wrist in my hand and press the pen tip into his flesh. His wrist is boxy and oversized compared to my own. I lose myself in the creation, drawing up his entire arm, across his chest, then down his other arm. He smells clean, like fabric softener. Good thing he's not hairy. His chest is a garden in full bloom, his arms twisted vines and hearts. "Turn around," are the only words I say to him. He mutely obliges. His back is my masterpiece, an ode to Bowie.

"Does that say Bowie?" Brady says, struggling to read the image on his back in the credenza's mirror.

"Yeah," I say.

"As in David Bowie?" he says, then slides on his T-shirt.

"Lydia's obsessed with him," Victoria says.

"I am not. It's just that I get him — and his art. It's an artistic connection," I say.

Brady smiles at me through the mirror. I try to smile back but my lips are frozen. Suddenly, I am no longer dangerous.

"What's back there?" Mark says and flaps his hand all over as though somehow his hand will be able to feel the tattoo and report back.

"Not to worry. It's only Silver and she's gorgeous," Victoria says.

"What the . . . " Mark says, with his back facing the credenza's mirror.

"Seriously. It's okay. It's just one huge horse head," I say. I don't tell him that with all his giant freckles, it looks like an Appaloosa.

Victoria and I stand at the window on the landing as the two black dots disappear into the white field.

"I can't believe they let us tattoo them," Victoria says and uses her fingernail to scrape a heart on the frosted windowpane.

"We branded those boys — their blue torsos are screaming to the world now." I scratch an arrow through her heart.

"What are they saying?"

"Touch me: I'm a hormonally challenged farm boy," I say in a low, dorky voice. "That was great though, wasn't it?"

"Yes — yes, it was," Victoria says.

Our Christmas guest list, in its entirety, includes Alex in his cow-poo jeans, Mary Jane in plaid polyester, Victoria in her pink housecoat, and me in my new smoking jacket. I used some of the dark purple velvet from Mary Jane's fabric trunk to reline the jacket. "The velvet is dry clean only," I say to George. George hisses into the mike. He's overstimulated himself on catnip, a present from me. He sounds demonic. I record his evil sounding growls onto a tape with my new ghetto blaster.

Mary Jane and Victoria make Christmas Morning Wife Saver in the kitchen. I won't be touching it. I hate eggs.

"We need wood," Alex says as he marches through the kitchen.

"It's Christmas morning, for God's sake," Mary Jane says. "Wait until breakfast is ready at least."

"No thanks. I'm not hungry." He pulls on his boots and leaves out the back door.

"He's always been weird about Christmas. He says it's a capitalist creation," Victoria says.

"He drinks too much on Christmas Eve and then he's miserable Christmas morning," Mary Jane says.

Alex barges into the kitchen, snow plastered up to his knees and his eyebrows white with frost. "I need help. Everyone get dressed and meet me at the far poplar bluff."

Nothing feels more uncomfortable than pulling cold snow pants and a parka over my Christmas outfit. We sink into the snow and wade across the pasture towards the bluff. Cold seeps inside my boots.

Alex cuts the chainsaw's engine. "The truck's stuck. I need you to load up all the wood I've cut into the back. Then I need everyone to help push me out," he shouts. His face is grey, like the cold has drained it of blood. I cannot believe all the work ahead of us. He's managed to cut up every single dead tree in the bluff.

"He's done this on purpose," Victoria says.

I'm too miserable to acknowledge her comment. The work involves wading through thigh-high snow, lifting cut logs, and hauling them to the back of the truck. Marx sits comfortably inside the cab. Lucky Marx. I cannot feel my hands and feet. My shoulders are pinched tight, my head aches, and I might barf into the snow. I am nobody, nothing. I take us in, my family. We are the most pathetic bunch alive. "This is not the Christmas I'll make for my family when I'm an adult, no way," I yell over the sound of the chainsaw. Everyone ignores me. Victoria's eyes are turquoise and her nose is red. I have to pee. I work fast. The sooner the truck is full, the sooner we'll be out of here.

Finally, the box can hold no more wood.

"Lydia, get in and drive. Don't turn the wheels. Just focus on taking her straight out of here. The rest of you push," Alex says. I take the driver's seat and crank the heater fan to max. It blows frigid air. I hit the gas. The wheels spin, creating deeper and deeper ruts; Mary Jane's turn. We give it all we have left, with Alex on one side of the rear bumper, Victoria in the middle, and me on the other side. Exhaust and snow spit into my face. It's impossible to breathe. There is movement, the truck swerves dangerously and then, somehow, we manage to get it back on the road. "Keep going, Mary Jane!" Alex yells. "Take it back to the house."

Alex hangs back.

"What's he waiting for," Victoria says.

"Who knows? Maybe his imaginary son, so he can walk back with him." I say. Victoria and I walk together in silence. My feet are frozen flippers. I cry tears, no sound.

It's dark in the barn. It takes a minute for my eyes to adjust. "Where is it, Dad?" My mind envisions a bright red sleigh with bells and a fur throw but I can't find it.

"Right here," he says, patting a piece of wood. It's still just a wooden box made of plywood. He's not even painted it.

"Where do we sit?" Victoria says through the woolen scarf wrapped around her head.

"Up front. The box is for wood. Won't have to worry about the truck getting stuck in the pasture again. Silver can haul wood all winter," he says.

It is the box of Frankenstein. I refuse to look at Victoria. I don't want her to see my disappointment. She'll think she's won. "Poor Silver," I say.

⚡

"I love her fuzzy winter coat and her icy high heels," I say, mesmerized by the perfectly round ice balls formed under Silver's hooves.

"Here, give me that. We better chip it out or she won't be able to pull us," Victoria says and snatches the hoof pick from my hand.

Alex arrives in the corral, his arms loaded with porch sofa pillows and the old afghan.

I stare nervously at Alex. "Go ahead, tap her with the reins. She's ready," he says. I lift the long reins and gently let them snap on her round butt. The sleigh lurches forward. My mouth gapes open as we slide past Alex. He stands tall in the snow, a misplaced Viking with bushy blond hair and a pink face. He brings one hand out of his jeans and waves. I can't wave back — the reins.

Silver steps lightly and smoothly. The motion is hypnotic — *swish, swish*. The world is quiet. The pale grey sky turns into a warm flannel blanket, the snow into fluffy white pillows. Big, beautiful, plump snowflakes fall occasionally onto my lap. Prairie snowflakes are usually small, precise, and crisp. Vancouver's are big, sloppy, and fat. These are something in between — perfection.

"This reminds me of that poem by Robert Frost," Victoria says. "The woods are lovely, dark, and deep. But I have promises to keep."

"And miles to go before I sleep, and miles to go before I sleep."

We stop speaking and listen to the music of sleigh runners cutting through the snow with a steady beat, the occasional jingle of the harness bell, and Silver's steady breath. She's working hard, pulling our load through the snow. "Tap her reins. Let's get going faster. Make her trot," Victoria says. I ignore her. "Come on, this is going to take all day. I don't want to come home in the dark." I tap the reins gently. Silver doesn't react. I snap them firmly. The sleigh jerks, snow flies. Marx stands up and attempts to jump out.

"Sit! Bad dog! Stay!" My toque slides over my eyes. "Sit Marx! Victoria, make him sit down."

"No, not the trees, Lydia!" Victoria shouts. I pull Silver and the entire operation to a stop. "Out of my way, woman," Victoria says, snatching the reins and sitting down on top of me.

"Get the hell off me, Victoria!" I shout and pinch her arm as hard as I can through her down parka.

"It's my turn! Alex said. It's halfway. Move it," Victoria says, not moving from my lap.

I push her off and slide over. What a bitch. I almost feel like jumping from Frankenstein's box and walking home. I close my eyes. A gnarly willow branch pierces my cheek. "Ouch! Shit." I touch my face. There's blood on my mitten.

"Victoria! Stay on the open field for fuck's sake." Marx lays his big, heavy head on my lap, whining occasionally in protest. Never again; if I'm going to die by sleigh, I want to be the one driving it.

It's a Christmas miracle that we arrive uninjured and even though it has been months since our last surprise visit, Grand'Mère has scalding hot coffee waiting.

"*Les petite filles sont ici!*" she says and kisses our cheeks. Napoleon turns from the TV, smiles and nods in our direction.

They've obviously had a quiet Christmas. Aside from a three-foot artificial Christmas tree beside the TV (smothered in heavy garland), the place looks exactly the same as the last time we visited. I sip my coffee and nibble a chunk of dark chocolate. I take another sip of coffee and alternate it with a bite of chocolate. "Try it, Vic. Take a sip of coffee and then a bite of chocolate. It's a transcendental taste experience."

Victoria takes a cautious sip with a large chunk of chocolate bobbing inside her mouth. "Whoa . . . this is orgasmic," she says. I kick her under the table. "What?" she says with a mouth full of chocolate. I can tell she has no idea what orgasmic means, and Grand'Mère gives no indication that she does either.

I refocus my attention from the orgasmic idiot to the wall behind her. On it is an old framed photograph of a family standing in front of a wooden house. The women are dressed in dark long dresses. I point to the picture. "Who are those people?"

Napoleon stands slowly, still watching the TV, then he turns and walks to the photograph. "Family." He smoothes down his black hair with his hand. He's wearing a crimson cotton shirt, unbuttoned to reveal a white undershirt under-neath. The deep red looks stunning against his skin. "This young man here, he's my grandfather, Napoleon Bouvier. I was named for him. This little one, that's my Uncle Leon. All these are my aunts, and this woman is my grandmother. Grand'Mère wasn't born yet."

Grand'Mère points her long bony finger at her father's image. "Cousin to Louis Riel," she says.

"Really?" I say.

"*Oui*, Louis Riel cousin my father, Napoleon Bouvier."

"Napoleon, what do you know about the North-West Rebellion?" I say. I surprise even myself with the bold move. I am a little shy of Napoleon, mainly because he is a little shy of me and so . . . manly.

"My grandfather fought in the battle alongside Dumont and Riel. Let Grand'Mère tell you about it. She likes to talk about that," he says, then he says something in French, too fast to understand.

Grand'Mère begins to speak in fluent French, her voice sounding younger than her eighty-eight years. I glance at Victoria in a panic, understanding nothing but my hero's name, Louis Riel. When she says it, in her rapid French, a shiver runs down my legs, like I have to pee. Grand'Mère pauses to drop six cubes of sugar into her coffee, then slides the bowl down the table towards Victoria.

Napoleon's low voice translates all she has said into English. They have done this before. Grand'Mère's lips are thin and creased; Napoleon's a slightly plumper, softer version of his mother's. I can't be sure whether it is French or English that I understand. The translations are almost undetectable, both of their voices smooth and hypnotizing. "Your farm was once many farms, narrow strips of land, each one on the riverfront, all belonging to the Métis. Everyone had access to the river. One hundred years ago, the government stole the land. They took it and divided it into sections, huge farms belonging to only one person. This was the beginning of the battle between the government and us, the Métis. The Indians joined our fight. They were starving peoples. The government killed all of the buffalo, forced them off their land, onto reservations. They were Big Bear and Poundmaker's Cree. We were the dispossessed — united, fighting for our land. Batoche was our home and site of the last battle." Grand'Mère's lips are still. Victoria stares, as though frozen, with her mouth hanging open, chocolate oozing from the corners of her lips.

Grand'Mère leans forward, her eyes intense. "Most tragically, it is the site where the true west was lost — no buffalo, no land for the Cree and the Sioux, and no more Métis farms."

I'm guilty by genetics. My great-grandparents profited from the government's victory. They were foreigners, Europeans, looking for cheap land and lots of it. We live on stolen land. Grand'Mère and Napoleon don't seem to hold a grudge. Grand'Mère hands me a jar of fresh cream and Victoria a jar of saskatoons to take home to Mom. She kisses both of my cheeks and Napoleon does too, his scratchy cheek brushing against my skin.

FIVE

New year. Old bus. The sunrise reveals a landscape of doom: grey snow, grey sky, grey sticks they call trees, grey buildings, black and white magpies — crazy birds. Why do they stay? If I had wings, I'd fly all the way to California. Victoria sits, staring out the bus window in a mute stupor. Perhaps Twyla the Twat will perk her up.

As soon as I step from the bus, I feel it: hostility. The sky is too low. The school is a prison encased in barbed wire. I can't do it. I can't go in. I stand frozen, watching. Everyone from the bus wanders inside the school except me. It's a spontaneous decision, but I make it. I walk. I walk home. It's seventeen kilometres to our farm and minus seventeen degrees Celsius outside. I follow the train tracks across the prairie, listening for trains. The snow in the ditch is level with the tracks. I step off the tracks, thinking it might be safer to walk in the ditch. My boots are heavy anchors and the ditch an ocean. I sink up to my crotch — back to the tracks. The landscape is serene, no humans, no traffic, only the occasional magpie. The sky has turned from prison grey to a warm, creamy café au lait.

If I concentrate, I believe I can detect the scent of sage, rising from beneath the snow.

It takes me four hours. By the time I reach our road, reality hits. If I go home, they'll kill me. I walk past our drive to the spot were the buffalo pit lies buried underneath the snow. I only have a few hours until sunset. I have no choice but to sneak unnoticed through the corral and hide in the barn.

It's cold inside the barn but not freezing. The chickens flap their wings and cluck out to me in greeting. "Shh! Quiet, birdies!" Marx cries and scratches at the barn door. Marx — I hadn't planned on him finding me so soon. He must have spotted me walking through the pasture. "Go away, Marx. Off! Off!" I whisper harshly.

The barn is sparsely decorated but at least it's fairly clean, aside from the dusting of chicken fluff. Man, do I need to pee, and I'm starving. It's going to be a long day, and then what? I haven't thought it through. I need Victoria. I dig into my bag lunch. Wait, I must ration. Who knows how long I'll be out here? I eat only half of my sandwich and stash the rest back into my knapsack.

I doze off for a while, huddled in the hay pile. The bus — yes, it is the bus. I scramble up from the hay and out of the barn, keeping low as I sneak along the side of the house.

"Victoria!"

I've startled her. "Lydia? Why weren't you on the bus? What are you doing out here?"

"I need some money," I say.

"What are you talking about?" she says, her confusion turning into irritation.

"Just enough for a one-way bus ticket to Vancouver. Please — can you help me?"

"Why?" she says.

"I can't go back to that hellhole ever again."

"What happened?" Her irritation turns to curiosity.

"It doesn't matter. I need to pee. Could you distract Mom so I can go upstairs and then sneak me some money and maybe a little snack?"

"I don't know — what do I tell her?"

"Don't tell her anything. You haven't seen me since this morning on the bus, got it?"

"All right, I'll try and sneak you something. But maybe you'd better just pee outside. It's too risky."

She walks inside and I run to the barn. She never said anything about the money. That's the most important part. Without the money, I'm trapped. If I can get to Vancouver, I can stay with Granny and Granddad, go back to my old school. I'll wait until morning to pack up my things. Mom's going to Saskatoon for a doctor's appointment and the house will be empty.

I eat until I've polished off my entire school lunch. Mom's cupcakes have never tasted so good. Minutes drag on like days. Where is that little asshole with my snack? It's black outside when Alex finally arrives home. *Stay calm, things are working out, stay calm . . .*

Alex has been home for about fifteen minutes. I hear the back door swing open and the rush of snow boots. I lay still, listening. It's an ambush. They burst into the barn. I'm going to pee my pants. Mary Jane's the first one into my stall, her flashlight is blinding. "She's in here," she says triumphantly. It takes a few seconds for Alex to catch hold of me. He forces me violently out of the stall.

I am led straight into the back seat of the truck. Mary Jane opens the front passenger door and slides in beside Alex. He starts the truck and heads out the driveway onto our road.

Victoria's a no good, stinking rat. She was conspicuously absent during the surprise attack, the traitor. I hope she's ashamed of her yellow-bellied self. "Where are we going?" I say.

"You're going to see the principal and then the RCMP," Alex spits out.

"Why?" No answer. He's driving too fast and there's no way out.

"Why? How can you do this to me?" I say.

"How can you do this to us?" Mary Jane spits back, cold as the air in the truck.

"Please don't do this to me!" I say. My throat is so tight it hurts to speak.

"It's against the law for you to stay home from school. The police and Mr. Forney can explain it to you," Alex says. He says it with that weird voice of his, the one he used to tell me all the horrific things wrong with the farmhouse. It's tinged with sadistic pleasure.

"Please, don't take me back there. I hate it! It's a living hell."

Mary Jane looks out her window into the dark night as though she has night vision.

"Hey, I have an idea, what about private school? Or home schooling? Or why can't I go to school in Saskatoon — catch a ride with Alex each day?" They refuse to acknowledge me; ice.

I cannot let the principal find out. It will be beyond mortifying. I am not the teenaged delinquent that my parents think I am. I watch out the window as we pass yard light after yard light, getting closer to town. "Please — please, I'll never do it again. I'll go to school everyday and never complain, ever again. Please don't do this!" I cry. They are cold, fixed. Alex keeps driving towards Hicksville. I want the road to go on forever. The gas station on the outskirts of town appears far too soon. The tears stop. I am too stunned to cry anymore. My parents despise me.

The sun has set by the time Alex stops in the school parking lot. The lights are still on inside the school. The teachers must still be there. My father leaves the engine running and walks in the front entrance to find Mr. Forney. I want to bolt but I remain seated behind Mary Jane, paralyzed with fear. My bladder aches with the pressure of a day's worth of pee.

Alex emerges from the school and jumps in the cab. "He's gone home," he says to Mary Jane.

There is a God.

"Please, I promise I'll never skip school again. I'll go to school every single day for the rest of high school if you please just take me home."

Alex looks at Mary Jane. They are silent. Please, someone say something, anything.

"You'll go to school tomorrow and everyday after that?" he says, finally acknowledging me.

"Yes," I say solemnly. "I promise."

That seems to do it. They've run out of steam. Alex backs out of the school parking lot. He drives past the RCMP detachment and doesn't stop. I begin to shake, first my legs, then my arms, and finally my teeth start to chatter. No one speaks. A monumental place in time: my parents might be my worst enemies. They are no safe haven to run to. Even Victoria seems safer than them and I hate her. Though, despite the hate, I feel a strong urge to cry in her cowardly arms.

I am a zombie, the living dead. I get on the bus, get off the bus, and walk into the school, void of emotion. Nothing can touch me. *Fuck you*, I mouth to everyone I pass, just under my breath. Mr. Pervert Pants Polinski, my English teacher, is the first sorry ass to pry.

"Where were you yesterday, Lydia?"

"I had an appointment," I say, flat as the prairie. That frightens him for some reason and he leaves me alone.

In my absence, I've been partnered with Michelle Dyck to edit our *To Kill a Mockingbird* essays. I pity her, being distantly related to the psychotic toad Nathan, though I give her credit for being quiet and aloof.

"Were you at the chiropractor's or something?" Michelle asks.

"No." I know I should probably say something else, to be cordial, but I don't.

"Only asking because I have to go after school today."

"To a chiropractor?" Old people go to chiropractors.

"Yeah," she says, and retreats back to her quiet aloofness.

"Why?"

"Toothache. I hope he doesn't pull it this time."

"Shouldn't you see a dentist?"

"My mom doesn't drive in the city."

"Your chiropractor is your dentist?"

"I guess."

"Where to you go to the doctor?"

"Same place."

"To the chiropractor?" I cannot camouflage my incredulousness.

"Yeah."

This time I let her sink back into her detachment.

It's too cold to go the post office so I hide out in the sewing room at lunch, working on the jacket that matches my mini. It's a difficult pattern, my first fitted jacket. I like having the place to myself. I can relax a little without all the inbreds and their snide comments: Sexy Legs, every time I wear a mini, followed by Fuckingham, Spiff, and Ice Princess. Fashion is what separates me from other school loners. I am not a disillusioned, lost youth; I am Ice Queen by design — fashion is my armour, my coolness untouchable.

Noon announcements blast into the room, announcing the Snow Queen finalists. How tacky. No one has beauty contests anymore. This place is backward. The intercom spits out my name: Lydia Buckingham.

Victoria arrives within minutes. Her freckled face is a surprising relief amongst a sea of motley locals. "Did you hear the announcements?" she says.

"It has to be a prank. What nitwit would nominate me? Don't they get it? I hate everyone and everyone hates me."

"I bet it was that pervert, Nathan Dyck," she says.

"Puke! Don't make it any worse than it already is. Though, it is sort of flattering, I guess — like winning best pig at the country fair."

"You haven't won yet, Wilbur. I gotta go. We'll talk on the bus." Victoria says.

"Don't worry, I won't let my name stand. I don't believe in sexist beauty contests," I say to the back of her long blonde hair.

Footsteps sound behind me. *Get lost. If you're not Victoria, I'm not interested.*

"Hi," a male voice says.

I'm afraid to turn around. I never thought I'd talk to him again. We've effectively ignored each other on the bus for five months. I search under the machine for the bobbin that tumbles from my stunned fingers.

"So, how was your Christmas?" Brady says.

I raise my pink face from beneath the machine cabinet. "Good — how was yours?"

"It was all right," he says.

I scan his arms, for any remnants of the tattoo. "You washed off Bowie," I say.

"Yeah," he says and laughs as though embarrassed. He gazes out the window for a moment, at the snow-covered field filled with puffy, fighting children, then down at the turquoise fabric in my hands. "What are you working on?"

"A jacket."

"Did you design it?"

"Sort of. I'm altering a pattern — so, what are you into besides fashion?" I say.

"Fashion?" he says.

I hold up the sleeve of my jacket. "You're in the sewing room," I say.

"Oh, right. I'm into fashion," he says, pinching his hockey jersey.

"My guess is you're into hockey."

"Good guess," he says.

"Not really — you're Canadian and you're male."

"Isn't that a little sexist?" he says, and hoists himself onto the kitchenette counter.

"No — Mrs. Leach would cringe," I say, referring to his butt on the Home Ec teacher's clean counter.

"Let her," he shrugs.

"You're going to be in the NHL when you grow up?" I say. It comes out more condescending than I intended, but I am the anti-Canadian. I don't care about hockey.

"I'll play hockey for as long as I can and then go to university," he says defensively. "You're not a fan?"

"Wayne Gretzky's not bad," I say. *Not bad looking, that is.* "But I'm not going to pretend to enjoy watching a bunch of losers fight and make millions doing it." He's speechless. "So, what do you want to study?" I say to change the subject.

"Computer engineering, then I'm going to move someplace hot and get rich."

"Interesting," I say, though it sounds godawful boring, except the rich part and the someplace hot.

"People talk about your clothes. They say you're New Wave," he says and jumps off the counter. His scent wafts towards me and triggers a Christmas Eve memory of fabric softener and a hint of spice.

"People?" I say, and try not to breathe him in.

He laughs. "Okay, some people, that go to this school — so, are you? New Wave, I mean?"

"No. I'm just me."

The bell rings.

"See ya," he says.

That was weird — and a little wonderful. I guess he can't let go of the sensuous tattoo session. If only he were a stranger to these parts — but his last name is Melenchuk, like fifty percent of the kids at Hicksville High. He's one of them. There is no way I can date the enemy. Like Romeo and Juliet, it will never work.

Mary Jane is napping in bed when we get off the bus. I return to my duty of calling George. We haven't seen him for three days. No one seems to care but me. I hike into the pasture shaking the bag of cat food. Marx bounds towards me, hopeful I have treats for him. "Find George — go find George." The paw prints in the snow that lead away from the house are too big to be a cat's. Coyotes. My gut says they got him. "George! Georgie-Porgie! Here kitty, kitty, kitty!" I call across the barren landscape.

Mary Jane yells from the back porch. "Lydia! You're in your slippers for God's sake. Get inside, now!"

They're not even my slippers, they're hers, but at least she's up. She stands in the kitchen looking dazed. Her eyes are at half-mast and her hair is sticking straight up in the back. "He's probably found a female in heat. He'll come home when he's ready," she says and yawns. She opens the oven drawer and unearths the big frying pan and heaves it onto the stovetop.

"What are you making?" I say.

"Supper," Mary Jane says and pauses to scratch her head.

"It's only four o'clock."

"What's your point?" she says, ready to fight.

"Nothing. No point whatsoever."

"How about burgers and fries tonight, girls?" She says in a fake perky voice, the opposite voice of her previous comment.

I collapse on the loveseat beside Victoria and stare at the TV. I turn up the volume as Mary Jane starts banging around in the kitchen.

"I haven't been sleeping well lately. For no reason, I'm up in the middle of the night," Mary Jane says over the sizzle of frying hamburger.

"What do you do?" Victoria says.

"Not much. I look out the porch window until I start to feel sleepy," she says.

I don't know how she can stand it; the porch is freezing at night. Mary Jane is saying something about nursing. I turn the volume down and listen.

"When, Mom? I need you here," Victoria says.

"Don't worry. Not until next fall," she says.

"What are you talking about?" I yell.

"I'm thinking of finishing my nursing degree. That's all," Mary Jane says.

I get up and walk to the kitchen doorway. "I think you should. I don't know how you can take being on this farm all day," I say.

Mom looks behind me, at the TV in the living room, still holding the spatula. "Look at that woman. I can't believe she has her own show," she says, referring to a local Saskatoon talk show host. "She looks like shit on wheels."

Well said, my beautiful mother in polyester pants with bed-head and a greasy spatula in hand.

Polinski looks me up and down, as usual, as I make my way to my desk. Everyone notices and laughs. He's oblivious. I feel like a piece of meat. I hate that man and everyone else for laughing at his googly eyes. I bury my face in *Fahrenheit 451*. Suddenly, rank coffee-cigarette breath alerts me that the pervert is standing beside my desk. I slap through a few pages of the paperback, a pathetic attempt on my part to warn him to retreat or I'll attack.

"Miss Buckingham, Mr. Binstead wants to see you in his office, immediately, " he says.

Retreat it is.

What's left of the vice principal's hair is dark brown but his beard is grey. Never trust a man with a beard.

"Mr. Binstead," I say after I read the nameplate on his door.

"Miss Buckingham, have a seat," he says. He uses the old silent stare routine to try and freak me. Like I give a whoopee-ding-dang what he thinks of me.

"There's been a suggestion that perhaps you need to rethink your wardrobe choices," he says.

"Oh," I say. I know where this is going. Playing stupid is the only way to deal with stupid. More silent staring on his part. I reciprocate. He shifts in his chair. I've flustered him and being flustered appears to make him irritable. He looks at me as though he wants to grab me and shake me.

"We like to keep our wardrobe choices somewhat conservative at the school," he says.

I study the dirty green indoor/outdoor carpet for a long while until, I swear, I see an insect crawl across it. "You know, Mr. Binstead, my wardrobe showcases the latest fashions. If you taught anywhere else on the planet you'd know that."

"I think everyone needs to be reminded of what's appropriate from time to time," he says.

I bet he has no chin underneath that beard. He might be part Neanderthal.

"No place is more out of style than this school," I say. An accident, I wanted to say something more eloquent.

"Style is not the issue, Miss Buckingham — try to keep your skirts no more than an inch above the knee," he says through clenched, yellowing teeth. Bet he's a smoker.

"Well, it should be. Short skirts are in. Long skirts are out," I say and jump up from the fake leather office chair. "Anyway, I always wear opaque tights so no one ever sees any skin," I add, then vacate his office before he has a chance to say more.

What a loser. No surprise that Polinski has enlisted the vice principal to do his dirty work. At least I've identified my main foe and it gives me strength: Polinski. Binstead is nothing but a patsy.

I sit down in English class and stare at Polinski. I send him my most vile *back off, pervert* thoughts. He's an obsessed psycho. I saw him looking through the door at me during chemistry class yesterday, outright staring. Mrs. Proctor, the Chem teacher, thought he wanted something and opened the door. That sent old Pervert Pants scurrying down the hall like the vermin he is. I wish I hadn't made that pact with my demon parents. Two and a half more years in this school with freakin' Mr. Pervert Pants may just be my ticket to hell.

However, my return to English class is not a complete tragedy. Suffering stimulates the creative mind. I shut out Polinski's incessant nattering about comma splices and I write. I write my favourite poem to date.

Pervert Pants Polinski

Your skirts are too short
The word from the boss
The boss is a man
A man who looks me up and down
His eyes bulging from his pants
His students are there,
Snickering, laughing, nudging
Me, their peer, suddenly a sex thing
Play by the rules
Be conservative
Be a misogynist
Conform to a life of mediocrity and grey slime
Where She is sinful
Where She sits behind her father
Where She must
Quit whining like a woman and get to work.

As soon as I swing open the heavy post office door, I realize that it has lost any appeal it once had. The place stinks of wet socks and the flyers on the floor scream annoying capitalist propaganda. My sandwich is as appetizing as the snow-soaked flyers. The only thing pleasurable is squatting within the narrow borders of the sunbeam that shines through the glass door.

Brady calls me in the hallway after school. "Lydia!"

I pull myself from the long line of bus traffic and step to the side, where Brady waits against the cinderblock wall. Stopping feels awkward. I don't talk to anyone in public at Hicksville High, though I've never seen so many interested eyes. You'd think we were celebrities.

"Where were you at lunch?" he asks.

"I had to pick up the mail for my parents," I say.

"You walked into town?"

"Yeah."

His school jacket hangs open, revealing an Ozzy Osbourne T-shirt underneath. I imagine my ballpoint flower garden blooming under the shirt. His bare chest flashes in my mind. His nipples are dark, way darker than mine, verging on chocolate milk colour. Focus Lydia, forget his nipples, try to remember what he just said — nope, can't remember a thing. Instead, I shuffle through my binder as though I've something important to show him — the poem. It will have to do.

"I just wrote this. It's for the literature annual," I say and hand him "Pervert Pants Polinski."

"You didn't really enter this?"

"Yes. Why? You don't like it? You don't think it's good enough to grace the pages of the school's literature annual?"

"Come on, there's no way; you'll be expelled." He laughs.

At least I don't have to relate to Brady on the bus ride home; he sits at the back with all of the big boys. He dresses better than other Hicksville High guys, less dorky, more classic all-American: faded jeans, T-shirts, and leather runners. Nothing special, but it's amazing how ditching a ball cap can civilize a look. I smile vacantly at him as he passes my seat.

I jump off the bus and head directly to the barn to feed the chickens and help Victoria haul hay into the corral for the cattle and Silver. On the way inside, I stop to fill Marx's bowl with kibble. We work fast because our reward is to sit on the family room loveseat and stuff our faces with soda crackers, orange juice, and cheese, cheddar for me and processed slices for Victoria. We don't talk. Neither one of us mentions Mary Jane's conspicuous absence until the news comes on. The sun gradually fades beneath the pasture, leaving the house in darkness except for the light from the television.

"It's six o'clock. Do you think we should check on her?" I say.

"I'll go," Victoria says. She's back up in about thirty seconds. "Well?"

"She's okay. She's just folding laundry and crying about the rust patches on the sheets."

"In the dark?"

"No, the stair light's on. Oh, but I turned that on when I ran down — yeah, you're right. It was dark down there."

"She is down there doing laundry in the dark? God."

"I don't think the pills are working," Victoria says.

"What pills?"

"Alex said the doctor put her on Halcion."

"Halcion? What the hell is that?"

"Some little pills for depression."

"Well, those little pills are putting strange ideas into her head. She is seriously freaking me out."

I greet Alex at the door. "Alex, you better go check on Mom. She's been in the basement crying all day."

He hangs up his "university" coat and heads downstairs.

I sit on the toilet and count out four squares. What kind of an idiot thinks four squares is enough for anything? I believe the right number is four squared. Sixteen sheets ought to do a fine job. I hear clanging and banging coming from the kitchen. Good, Mary Jane must have finally come up.

I hurry down to the kitchen. It's only Alex. "Where's Mary Jane?"

"She's tired. Just leave her. You're in for a treat tonight, Lydia. I'm cooking," he says, rubbing his palms together over-enthusiastically. "I'm making my special, shipwreck."

"Oh joy," I say. I know his shipwreck. He throws whatever he finds in the fridge and/or floor (I speculate) onto rice and mixes it together.

⚡

It's obvious Polinski has read the poem. "Late again, Lydia. Bring me a pink slip," he says. I'm not even late. I only took Victoria's lunch down the hall to her classroom to switch it for mine. We make our own lunches since Mary Jane's been on Halcion, and there is no way I'm eating one of Victoria's processed cheese sandwiches.

I hand him the pink paper and put my English essay in the pile on his desk. I get out my binder to look for the *Fahrenheit 451* questions we're supposed to be working on:

Discuss the meaning behind Beatty's words: *Forget them. Burn all, burn everything. Fire is bright and fire is clean.*

It's another trick question. Polinski doesn't really want my take on those words. My essay on *To Kill a Mockingbird* plops on my desk in front of me.

"I just handed that in," I say.

He slides his hands into the front pockets of his pants and taps his foot. "I won't accept it. It's not ready," he says.

"But I proofed it and Michelle proofed it — I edited it three times."

"I want you to proof it again," he says.

My mouth drops open. There is no way he could have looked at it that fast. I scan the room. No one else has their paper handed back. Michelle Dyck catches my gaze and rolls hers in solidarity with me. I snatch the paper and stand up. Once I'm up, I feel stupid. I have an audience; now both of the Dycks are watching. Nathan's too curious to even smirk. I have no choice but to walk out of the room, clutching my paper. I head for the bathroom; there's nowhere else to go.

The loser who calls me Spiff is sitting on the floor of the hallway holding a metre stick. "What's the hurry, Sexy Legs?" he says as I pass him, then he lifts the back of my skirt with the stick. "Forget to shave?"

I smack my skirt down with my hand and keep walking, no time for inbreds. Once I'm safely in the girls' shower room I stop to sit on the bench. The essay's exactly the same as when I handed it in. He's made no corrections or comments. Someway, somehow I'm going to have to go back to the classroom. No doubt I'm in trouble for my stage exit to the right. I pray there isn't another visit with Binstead for this one.

I'll tell him I have diarrhea. I'd love to have the guts to do it, but once a diarrhea girl, always a diarrhea girl. No one ever forgets that word.

The hall is empty. I feel rank breath on me, just as I take my seat. "Lydia, stay after class for a moment. I want a word with you," he says. Only a word? I have two for him.

Surprise, he doesn't like the poem. He's involved VP Binstead in everything. Bad move, bad for me. Mary Jane and Alex have received separate phone calls about my rude, unacceptable behavior and my inappropriate poetry.

For the first time ever, I actually have a real reason to take my lunch to the post office. I have a damaging letter to intercept. I open the heavy glass door and step inside. There's a letter in our box, one letter amongst several flyers. It's from the school, addressed to Dr. and Mrs. Buckingham. It's the same crap: disrespectful . . . inappropriate . . . poor choices . . . don't care attitude.

Our stop. I've said nothing to Victoria; I can't trust her, not since the barn ambush. "Drive on, James!" I want to shout to Jim, our driver. "Take me anywhere but home." Last time the school phoned home the folks went ballistic. I still have the scar on my leg from Mary Jane and her ruler. I drag my Sasquatch boots across the yard. I could hang out in the barn for a while but I'm starving. I risk the house, like a fool. I keep the Sasquatch boots on and head out to retrieve two logs from the pile beside the house. Down the stairs I go, like a good little helper, topping off the furnace for my family. I throw the letter in the furnace along with the logs and watch it burn. No one is the wiser.

Victoria has already parked herself on the family room loveseat with a column of soda crackers. She munches them like a hamster, showering the loveseat in crumbs. Then she stands, shakes the crumbs from her pink housecoat, turns on the TV, and sits back down with her kibble. I understand the hamster mess; Victoria's setting a trap. The old Mary Jane would never tolerate this kind of disorder. I doubt the new Mary Jane will even notice.

Mary Jane finally comes upstairs at four forty-five. It appears as though she's had one long crying jag. The whites of her eyes are blood red and her irises are a brilliant cerulean blue. She clamours about, putting together a supper of fish sticks, rice, and peas. Not a typical Mary Jane meal. She usually makes something from scratch. Alex comes home and heads outside to chop wood. His routine is to keep chopping through supper and right into dessert.

Mary Jane picks at her supper, rearranging the rice on her plate. "Did I tell you my new plans?" she says.

"What new plans?"

"I'm going to buy a motorcycle, a decent one. I'm going to drive down the coast to California."

I stare straight ahead, unsure if I should laugh or cry.

"Sorry, but I'm only taking Victoria. She's my baby. She still needs me," she says and reaches beside her to clasp Victoria's hand and squeeze it.

"Very nice, Mother. Very nice," I say. I glance up and meet her vacant eyes. All I can think is, *poor Victoria*.

Alex stomps into the back porch. He's made it in early, before dessert, lucky him. He unzips his ski jacket and sits down at the table with his toque still on. We are about to enjoy one of several frozen cream pies, purchased by him on sale because they were past the expiry date.

"What flavour is this?" Victoria says.

"I'm guessing the mystery flavour is whipped dust," I say.

"Did you feed Silver?" Alex asks Victoria.

"Yes. I just did, before supper."

"Very good."

They don't say a thing about Polinski or my poetry. The school had to have been bluffing. I bet they couldn't get ahold of either one of them or the Halcion's erased Mary Jane's short-term memory.

Six

Mary Jane sits at the kitchen table in her polyester pants. Her eyes are glassy and red, but at least she's up and dressed.

"Why didn't you go into Saskatoon with Alex?" Victoria says.

"Yeah. What happened to the Saturday morning constitutional?" I say.

"I could not stomach another Saturday morning spent sitting in the Army and Navy cafeteria, watching your father drink his coffee in slow motion. It is so godawful boring. I'd rather kill myself," Mary Jane says.

"I kinda like the boat. It's so retro, it's cool," I say.

"You go with him next time if you like it so much," she says.

I want to tell her off, tell her that she's being a selfish cow, that coffee at the Army and Navy sounds like paradise to me because I haven't been farther than Hicksville in months. What makes my blood boil is that she knows Alex would rather take Marx into Saskatoon for a coffee date than me. But I bite my tongue. She's in no mind to tangle with.

"Well, It's officially the first day of spring and, despite any sabotage attempts, I am going to enjoy my day sliding through cow shit. Thank you very much!" I say.

"I almost forgot. It's tournament day," Victoria says.

"What tournament?" Mary Jane asks.

"Curling, Mother. We made a rink in the corral," Victoria says.

"Did I mention the trip I'm planning?" Mary Jane says.

"Come on, Vic, meet you out back. It's time for the Tournament of Turds," I say, not waiting for Mary Jane to rehash her bizarre plans.

The corral rink is made of cow pee-stained ice from the spring freeze-thaw. Ice cream buckets filled with frozen water are our rocks. Victoria slides past me, her pink housecoat billowing behind her as she frantically sweeps in front of the ice cream pail with our old kitchen broom. I bite my bottom lip to stifle a laugh. She couldn't look more imbecilic.

"Time! The rock's stuck in a big cow-pie. Hold it — I'm wrong, it's a huge pile of horse buns," she says.

I throw the rock again. She runs beside the bucket, pink frills flowing, sweeping the ice. My rock stops short of the red food colouring circle Victoria drizzled on the yellow ice. She takes off her mitt and begins to chew at a nail. Distracted once again, she stares beyond the yellow and brown rink, beyond the corral fence. I doubt she even sees the pasture through those eyes. "Your shot!" I yell in an attempt to bring her back from wherever it is she goes.

I pry a large pile of horse buns loose from the frozen pee with my mitted hand and carry it carefully. "And now, may I present you with the well deserved Turd Trophy."

"Gross! You're disgusting, Lydia. Get that thing away from me."

"Hey, get back here, you Champion of Turd!" I say and chase her.

⚡

The first day of spring ended along with spring. We're being pummeled with more winter. I keep hoping that they'll close the school but it has to dip lower than minus forty with the wind chill. It must be hovering at thirty-nine point nine degrees everyday. The drifts have blown in the driveway again so Victoria and I have to walk to the road. I take off my mittens and hold the tips of my eyelashes between numb fingers. They give off enough heat to melt the frost and release my eyes. The bus can't come soon enough.

As soon as I sit down for English class, I sense something's up. Polinski is late. He's never late. Nathan Dyck has become my personal Hicksville crier, whether I want it or not. "Hey, Fuckingham, your boyfriend isn't going to make it today. He's got crap to deal with," he says.

I narrow my eyes. "Turn around," I say.

"No shit. Someone crapped in Polinski's desk," he says.

We wait for the substitute teacher. It's the first and only time I feel camaraderie amongst my fellow grade tens. The classroom is vibrating with energy. It's the most exciting thing that has happened all year. For a second, I lock smiles with Michelle Dyck. Rumours are swirling, whispers that it was one of the boys in grade eleven, Lyndon, the inbred creep who calls me Spiff. "Any word on when he's going to be back?" I say to the slimy toad still staring at me. Nathan tosses his greasy mane to the side.

"No. Looks like someone's taking a stress leave," he says in mock surprise.

I'm in love. Who would have thought a Tuesday could be so beautiful? Who would have thought that English is my new favourite subject? The new English teacher is young and hip: Mr. Kent, a.k.a. Super-Stud. He just graduated from university. He is so *GQ*. Smells good too. In those jeans of his, with that rugged turtleneck sweater, I want to throw myself into his arms, smell his neck, and melt.

"Lydia, isn't it?"

Is he talking to me? He said Lydia. He is talking to me. Be cool, for God's sake, don't blow your first chance to impress him. I nod.

"Would you start Act II Scene I, reading the role of Brutus. I'll read for Lucius," he says.

It's just the two of us, as though we're having a private conversation in front of the entire class. I bet he's only like twenty-two or something. That makes us only seven years apart, nothing. Mr. Kent, you make Julius Caesar fascinating. I'm actually enjoying Shakespeare.

Brady's not on the bus. He's been missing all week. His little sister, Katie, still takes the bus so I know his family hasn't relocated. I watch Katie from behind on the ride home, working up the nerve to ask her about her brother without appearing too obviously concerned. It's their stop. I look around his yard for any sign of him; nothing. "Katie!" I shout, not too subtly. She turns around, surprised. "Why isn't Brady in school?" She looks a little shaken by the question. She doesn't know me. I guess I qualify as a stranger.

"He's in Edmonton," she says, turning to walk off the bus. "Hockey school," she adds.

Well, at least he's alive and not purposely avoiding me.

"Do you think anyone's going to make supper tonight?" Victoria says. "What time is it?"

"Seven ten."

"Holy shit! Where's Alex?"

Victoria shrugs. "Probably at the faculty club boozing it up with one of his communist girlfriends."

"Doubt it. Who'd be stupid enough to date that cheap-skate?" I open the fridge. "There's nothing to make. Mom, I'm starving. What can I make us for supper?" I yell into the basement. Silence. "Is she even down there?" I say. Victoria shrugs. "I'll go check."

I barely touch the knob and the flimsy, nearly weightless door opens, faster than I anticipated. She's lying in bed, in the dark, with the covers pulled up tight under her chin, staring at the ceiling. My mother the corpse.

"Mary Jane? Should I make something for supper?"

She closes her eyes. I wait, watching the sheet rise and fall with her breathing for a few minutes, then go back upstairs, leaving her bedroom door ajar.

"Looks like it's gonna be a cracker and cheese kind of night," I say, to Victoria.

"Shh . . . I hear movement down there." Victoria says. Mary Jane thunders upstairs with unusual speed, rushes past us, and up to the bathroom.

"What was that about?" Victoria says.

"No idea, but at least she's up."

"It's too quiet. What can she be doing up there?" I whisper to Victoria in between bites of cracker.

"It's been like half an hour," Victoria says.

She gets up from the loveseat and places her milk glass in the kitchen sink. "At least the basement's free. I'm going to organize the Barbies — you coming?"

I want to go down and join her but something inside me tells me not to. "In a minute," I say.

As Victoria descends the basement stairs, I ascend the oak staircase, sliding my hand along the glistening golden wood. I press my ear to the bathroom door and listen. Nothing. I knock. "Mary Jane, are you okay in there?" Nothing. I speak louder, "Mom? Are you in there?" Nothing. "Mother, please answer me. I need to go to the bathroom — let me in." I rattle the crystal doorknob. I hear a shuffling sound. "Mom! Victoria's fallen downstairs; I think her arm is broken." She turns on the bath water and drowns out my rattling.

I walk downstairs and rummage around in the kitchen junk drawer. Ouch, a paper cut. I suck on my finger and continue to forage . . . found it, the skeleton key. I knock one more time then use the key. As the door swings open, lavender fills my senses. I expect her to be in the bath but she's not. She sits, fully clothed on the toilet, methodically slicing her wrist back and forth with a dull razor blade. There is no blood. I lunge forward, snatch the blade, and toss it behind the tub.

"Jesus, Mother, what are you doing? You're so bloody dramatic! What do you want? Your children to clean up the blood?" I stand in front of her, forcefully holding her wrists. She looks like a guilty child. I lead her by the hand, out of the bathroom and into my bedroom and onto my bed. I'm the mother; she's the fucked-up kid. "You sit here and stay still. I'll be right back." I say in my new grown-up voice.

Victoria's in the middle of a wedding. "Victoria, you have to go up to my room and sit with Mary Jane. She tried to slice her wrists. She's totally out of it. Just keep her calm and keep her there until I get Alex."

"Where is he?"

"The truck just pulled up. I've got to go talk to him."

"I'm busy," she says, irritably, pulling the veil over the bride's face.

"You get up those stairs right now! This is a fucking emergency situation!" I say.

She looks up and slams down the bride. "You've got one minute," she says. The pink frills of her housecoat flutter regally as she ascends the staircase. I want to rip those pink frills right off her back and stuff them up her royal ass but I have no time.

I open the porch door before Alex has a chance to. He looks startled. "Mary Jane tried to kill herself. She tried to slice her wrists with a razor blade. I found her in the bathroom. You have to come. She's in my room."

"What do you mean, sliced her wrists?" he says in a pissed off tone, as though I'm at fault because I bear bad news. As Alex climbs the oak staircase, I hear the back porch door bang shut.

Victoria sits at the top of the stairs. "She took off," she says.

"Fuck, Victoria! Why didn't you stop her?" I yell. "Alex. You've got to help me find her. She's suicidal."

"She's not suicidal. She's gone for a walk," he says.

No one gets it. I can't let that crazed woman wander the prairie alone. The river still freezes at night. I circle the house. Where could she disappear to so fast? I hold my hands in front of my mouth, not knowing what to do next, then run to the poplar bluff nearest the house, where the coyotes gather at night. Wolf willow fills the damp spring air. It's usually a comforting smell but tonight it smells like terror. "Mom, where are you? Please, Mommy, I need you."

A giggle; it's coming from somewhere near. I walk aimlessly through the bluff. I'll never find her in the dark, amongst so many branches. Suddenly, I catch a glimpse of her in the moonlight, pressed back into the willow bushes, barely visible, except for her face. Her eyes are wild, her mouth turned up in a thrilled smile. She's trying to suppress laughter and remain hidden. She giggles.

I wrap my arms around her shoulders and lead her back into the house. I've become the professional, the calm psychiatrist, gently leading my patient to her shock therapy session. "Everything is going to be okay. I'll get you some tea. You can lie down and relax." I guide her down to her room. Victoria follows. I mouth, get Alex. She nods and is gone.

Mary Jane reclines on her bed as I stand over her. The patient is getting restless. I don't know how much longer I can keep her occupied. No sign of Victoria and Alex. I wonder if she can even find him. Maybe he's not even in the house anymore. Footsteps on the stairs — thank God, backup has arrived.

Alex stands at the entrance to the bedroom. "What happened, Mary Jane?" He sounds like a concerned husband now. Her face becomes animated, thrilled to have his attention.

"Why does it matter? You don't care about me. You don't care what I do."

"That's not true," Alex says in a fatherly tone.

Victoria slides into the room past Alex. We surround the old iron bed, watching the patient who suddenly seems quite perky. She likes being the star.

"We've got to take her to the hospital. They said she's still at risk. It's common for them to try again." Victoria is serious. Suddenly, it seems, she's the professional head shrinker.

"Who? Who said?" Panic rises in my brain.

"The professionals," Victoria says.

"What professionals?" Alex says. He's on to her too.

"I called the suicide crisis line — someone had to," she says.

"Great, now the whole world knows — we're on a party line, you idiot!" I say, then add, "Maybe she's right. Mom, you should go to the doctor," I say.

"No!" she screams. "I'm not going!"

"Alex? Please, talk to her."

"You're never going to get me out of here. I'll never leave this house!" Mary Jane shrieks. She is frighteningly serious. She holds onto the iron bars of the headboard and wraps her feet around the bars of the footboard.

"She doesn't want to go," Alex says, as a matter of fact.

"I'm calling the police then," Victoria says. "They'll make her go."

"You're not calling the police," Alex says.

"You can't stop me," Victoria says.

His face flashes red. "I won't let them in. I'll barricade the door. No one is forcing your mother to go anywhere," he says. He's turning into Mary Jane. I am the only one left with rational thought patterns. I turn to Victoria, my only hope. I grasp her arm and lead her outside the bedroom.

"Alex will do it. He'll lock us in here and the police will surround the house. They'll shoot someone. They'll kill us all before Alex will back down." She meets my eyes but says nothing. "Promise me — promise me, you won't call the police." She's thinking about it.

"All right. But if she kills herself tonight it's on your hands."

Alex walks out of the bedroom with his pillow under his arm. "I'm tired. I'm going up to bed."

"No! Alex — Dad, please, you have to stay with her. Watch her. Sleep on the floor if you have to but don't leave her," I say.

"She's fine. I'm tired." He walks up the stairs.

"See. He doesn't care about me. He never has. Look how selfish he is!" Mary Jane shouts from the bedroom.

I've had it. I wash my hands of the lot of them. I drag my anguished self up from the dungeon and into the tower. I shake for a good five minutes, then I walk down to the kitchen. Alex isn't sleeping, he's watching TV in the living room. I place a kitchen chair in front of the fridge and stand on it while opening the liquor cupboard. I take out the vodka and fill a glass one-third full. I put it back carefully and then the chair. I open the fridge, take out the orange juice and fill the rest of my glass. I take the murky black potion up to my room and lock the door.

I drink the vodka quickly. I'm clumsy, banging my head into the doorframe as I get up to go to the bathroom. "Fuck the world!" I shout.

I can't sleep. I'm terrified of violence. I don't know what exactly, but anything might happen. God only knows. I'm relieved I have a lock on my bedroom door. I put Bowie in my new ghetto blaster and wait for the midnight train. David Bowie is a god. His voice is so distinctive and sexy . . . a gentleman rebel. *I, I will be Queen* . . . too tired to wait for the train — shut off Bowie — close eyes.

The sun is high. My head hurts. It feels heavy and abnormally large. Its weight causes my neck to sway in an odd way to balance the load. I feel like checking my head in at a hatcheck and getting rid of it for a few hours. I don't want to get out of bed. I'm afraid to leave this safe nest, but I can't stay locked the chickenshit tower forever. I unlock the door and step back into the weird world that is my family.

The house is quiet. The truck is gone. "Victoria?" No answer. I wander down to my parent's room. The bed's made, but no suitcases on the floor. Nothing looks as though a crisis took place. The back door shuts. I leap up the stairs. Victoria walks into the kitchen with a basket of little blue, green, and blush coloured eggs.

"Those little bantams lay the most exquisite eggs. Where are the children?" I say.

"I like the green ones. They've gone to Saskatoon for their constitutional." She sticks her finger down her throat.

"It's like nothing happened. They put us through hell then treat themselves to coffee in Saskatoon." My voice is tired, no fight left. I wrap the velvet smoking jacket tightly around my body and carry my heavy head into the pasture for a little peace. My feet tread on slushy patches of snow and last year's flattened grass, optimistically dotted with fresh lilac crocuses. Alex is useless. Whenever Mary Jane's down and out, I see the real him, clinging protectively to what's left of her like a frightened child. I am alone, a woman trapped in the wilderness with three unruly children, far from all I know, and all I know is black.

I have the urge to see the cow cemetery. To date, I've only seen fire ravaged skeletons on our land. I avoided the pit all summer, afraid of swarming horse flies and the possible stench of rotting carcasses. But on the safe edge of winter, with spring just around the corner, I fear the dead no longer. Maybe it's the question from English class stirring in my brain, the one about burning and fire being clean.

The pit contains the skeletons that came after the fire, the blackleg bodies. Marx and I came back with Dad the summer after the fire. We drove out from Vancouver together, eating his processed cheese sandwiches on whole wheat, no butter, for two days straight. When we arrived, Dad let me choose a cow and calf as my own. I chose a Black Angus pair, Magic and Midnight. They were coal black and beautiful. Whenever they laid down to rest, I could never find them against the black, burnt-out field. I said goodbye to them that summer, for the first and last time. They died that winter of blackleg.

The cemetery is hard to miss, bones at awkward angles against the sunless sky. The cattle carcasses are almost totally gone, only bare bones remain between tuffs of hair and cartilage . . . coyotes. They're piled in what used to be an old homestead's cellar. Now, it's a deep pit filled with stained bones. I remember Beatty's words from *Fahrenheit 451*: "Fire is clean." Fire is kinder to the living. Death by fire leaves nothing remaining but white bone. The living can forget the agony that preceded the bone. I don't like the stained bones. I cannot forget, and I don't want to know who they were. I've got to get out of here, away from the stain of death and suffering.

SEVEN

Friday night is officially a girl's night in, whoopee-yee-haw-cow-paddy. The girls include Victoria, the chick with the Halcion eyes, and me. Mary Jane sits in a toque at the kitchen table while I unload my bag of goodies — makeup and hair accessories. She's started to emulate her husband's indoor attire lately. "Hello, McKenzie brothers? Bob? Doug? I think I just found your long lost sister." I pull off her toque and toss it into the back porch. It lands on the orange chair.

"Where's Victoria?" she says.

"Your fashion stylist is braving the rickety ladder up to the attic — she's searching through the trunk for some snazzy outfits."

"The attic? I think there might be bats living up there," she says.

"What Victoria doesn't know won't kill her," I say.

Mary Jane's face is my canvas: thick coats of sparkling blue eyeshadow with bright blue mascara and a ghostly-white powdered face. Her lips are crimson. I slide the lipstick past her lips, draw a lightning bolt directed towards her left eye, then trim it with sparkling violet eyeliner. "Ziggy Stardust has arrived on the prairie," I say.

"I don't think so," she says.

I brush her hair into a flat, spiked wave on one the side of her head. Victoria stumbles down the stairs in Mom's ancient go-go boots and unloads her arms, dropping an assortment of Mom's outfits from the sixties and early seventies onto the chesterfield.

"I don't know," Mary Jane says, glancing into the living room. Her words could mean a whole lot of things so I don't pry.

"We're going for Devo here," I say and blast Mary Jane's head with a full aerosol assault.

I hear a car door slam. Alex is home from one of his meetings. He walks through the kitchen in his boots and stops at the living room entrance, rubbing his hands together as though he's nervous, excited, or cold. I can't tell which. The smell of civilization clings to him: tobacco, beer, and other people's cologne. I wait for his reaction to his wife.

"Are you going out, Mary Jane?" he says, then disappears downstairs, not bothering to wait for an answer.

His enthusiastic energy reeks of society, of fun — a painful contrast to our night of quiet, isolated boredom. The two opposing energies hang in the air, causing our camp to feel the bitter, sharp assault of the unobtainable; he's not one of us anymore.

"Was he serious?" I say.

"The hell if I know," Victoria says.

Mary Jane walks clumsily towards the credenza in the dining room, her spike sandals barely keep her upright. She studies herself in the mirror. I'm not feeling totally confident about the silence. Her Ziggy Stardust smile crinkles and droops in slow motion. "I look like a freak!" she shouts, then cries a low mournful sob. The first emotion I've seen from her in days.

Victoria bends down to unstrap Mary Jane's spike-heeled sandals, "Forget it, Mom, we'll help you change back."

"I blame you for this," Mary Jane says.

Our eyes meet in the mirror; I know where Victoria gets her cold dagger glare.

"I should have never let you talk me into this. I should have known you'd do something like this," she says to my reflection.

"All I did was the makeup," I say.

Alex resurfaces from the basement. "Mary Jane? What's wrong?" His concern seems forced.

Mean Mary Jane becomes an expressionless zombie again, then she darts from the living room, up the staircase into the bathroom, and locks the door. Victoria shrieks in pain and collapses on the chesterfield, cradling one of her hands with the other. Mary Jane must have pierced it with a spike heel mid flight. Alex glares at me. I give him stunned innocence and shrug my shoulders. Though I know, as Mary Jane has made it clear, that somehow, some way, this is my fault.

She's filling the tub. I dare to knock. "I'm having a bath — can't you kids leave me alone for one bloody minute!" she yells. More bath water and then, "I'll be out in a minute." The voice is fake perky. Victoria and I sit on the wood floor outside the bathroom and stare at the dark, complicated, antique wallpaper pattern as though it were a puzzle. We wait, in silence, for at least twenty minutes.

"What's going on?" Alex shouts upstairs.

"Mother," I say.

"Leave her alone," he says, then climbs the staircase. Once he reaches the landing he says, "Let her have a bath. Disappear."

"It's too quiet," I say.

Alex's jaw tenses and his brow tightens as he steps over our legs towards the bathroom. "What's going on in there? Are you all right, Mary Jane?" he says, then raps once on the door.

Banging starts on the other side of the door, like she's kicking it, or worse, hitting her head against it.

"Maybe it's Morse code," Victoria says.

Alex doesn't look away from the door. He stares at it, waiting for it to open, I guess. "Mary Jane?" he says finally.

"Get me out of this fucking nightmare," Mary Jane says. She starts to cry, I think, then the crying turns into laughter, manic laughter, then back to crying again.

"What is it, Mary Jane?" Alex says.

"I said, take me to fucking Saskatoon, asshole, Sask-a-fucking-toon, Saskatchewan," Mary Jane yells.

"All right, Mary Jane. I'll take you. Open the door," Alex says. I don't wait for him to ask. I run for the junk drawer, salvage the skeleton key, race up the stairs, and hand it to him. Then I dart back down, terrified of what I might see if I stay.

Silver spike heels descend the staircase, followed by Alex in his black dress socks. She's still in the funky outfit but her makeup's smudged and she clutches a prescription bottle. I can't tell if there is anything in it. She stops at the base of the stairs.

"You girls behave yourselves," she says, in a surreal, calm manner. Mascara circles frame her hollow eyes.

Alex laces up his teaching oxfords.

"What are you doing? Where are you going?" I say.

"We're just going for a drink. We'll be back in a couple of hours."

"Are you insane? A drink? Mother's in no shape for a drink!"

In the spike heels, Mary Jane teeters through the porch and down the front steps towards the truck.

"Look at her, for God's sake!" I say.

Alex pushes past me and opens the passenger door for Ziggy Stardust-gone-wrong.

"Mother! Do up your sandals!" I shout. She ignores me.

I sit in the cold porch, watching the tail lights until they melt into the black. I imagine this is how Mary Jane must feel in the night, when she sits alone, waiting for morning. I stare through skeleton shadows until the warm, magical smell of popcorn slides under the porch door.

Victoria stands, inside a bubble of normal, at the stove popping popcorn. "What? So I'm hungry," she says.

"I'll melt some butter," I say, then join her in front of the old stove.

"Watch that burner," Victoria says, prying the spoon out of my fist. "Don't stir with a metal spoon. Use a wooden one or you'll get a shock."

We clang around the warm kitchen, inhaling the comforting smells of hot oil and butter. The wind's howls are shrill, almost screams. Victoria bangs the heavy pot on the burner, trying to silence the screaming.

"Needs more salt," she says.

I stand in front of the TV and slow dance with tinfoil-covered rabbit ears, trying to figure out what movie is on.

"Stop there — it's *The Shining*," Victoria says.

I run into the porch and grab the afghan.

"I want Marx," I say and turn off the lights and sit next to Victoria in the loveseat.

"Me too." Neither one of us moves. Getting Marx would involve walking through the kitchen, then the back porch, opening the door, calling into the wind, and waiting for Marx to run in from the pasture.

The movie's over. Still no Alex and Mary Jane. A bad British comedy, starring a dirty old man, is on the TV. Victoria snores beside me, her limp hand hanging inside the popcorn bowl. I am terrified to step from the loveseat. The energy of madness that lingers in the house is eerily similar to that in the Overlook Hotel.

"Come on, Vic, wake up. Let's go up to bed."

She awakens suddenly, her eyes full of terror.

"Where's Mom?" she says. In her silky, pink housecoat she appears fragile and young tonight.

"They're not home yet. Come on to bed. You can sleep with me. I'm freaked by that movie."

I wake with a sick feeling inside my gut, dread — Mary Jane. I walk down the stairs, still half asleep. Alex stands at the stove, making coffee.

"Where's Mom?"

"She's staying in town for a few days," he says.

"Town? What? You mean Hicksville?" I shout, unaware of my voice strength.

"Shh . . . Saskatoon," he says.

"That's the city," I say, not that it even matters. "Why? She seemed fine last night when you went for drinks." I know it's a lie. "Where's she staying? We don't have friends there — she better not be staying at that dump, The King George. We can't afford it," I say.

"Settle down, Lydia. Your mother's depressed. She needs to be on new medication. She'll be home soon — and most importantly, she needs you to support her through this. She needs you to look after the house and Victoria for awhile, until she gets home."

"What are you talking about? Depressed? I'm depressed, for God's sake!"

"Your mother's having a nervous breakdown, all right?"

The words are a punch in my stomach. "What in the hell is that, really? It's that bloody Halcion she's been popping for months. It's totally fucked with her brain. Just take her off that fucking drug and bring her home!" I yell.

"Settle down and watch your language. The doctors know what she's been taking. It's just going to be a few days," he says.

Her fly swatter hangs from a hook beside the fridge. It's spring. The flies are waking up. She'll need it soon.

"I can't believe this. All that talk about California and taking Victoria with her and now she just dumps Victoria on me?" I run up to the tower, stopping on the landing to shout, "You never did tell me where she is!"

I lock the tower door. In my dresser mirror an ugly, blotchy, freckled baby face cries silent tears. Chickenshit. The flies aren't the only thing coming to life with the spring thaw. The phoenix rises again.

I hate her.

Ziggy Stardust! That's why they were so quick to lock her up. She looked totally insane in the makeover outfit and smudged face. Her hair! I sprayed it until it was plastic. They must think that she looks that bad all the time. We made her look like a freak. Victoria was right, we should have turned her back into herself.

$$\lightning$$

The few days turn into a few weeks. Mary Jane's no longer even in the province. She's too fragile to face us, her daughters, but not too fragile to go home to Mommy and Daddy in Vancouver. Alex can't look after everything on his own. This place is falling apart. The house is filthy and the cupboards are empty. I heard Alex on the phone asking about her therapist. She's seeing one of the best in Canada and she's expensive, I know that much. I think he might be hiding something from us. I'm beginning to wonder if she will ever be coming home again.

Victoria sits on her unmade bed. Her room is a mess, clothes and blankets everywhere. "It's not fair. Twyla's mom takes her shopping in Saskatoon every Saturday. They go out to buffets together. Where's my mom? Oh, she's on vacation somewhere I can't talk about," she says, throwing a stuffed horse at the window. She starts to cry.

"I don't get what's so great about buffets," I say.

Victoria doesn't respond; she keeps on crying. She seems unable to stop. Maybe I've pushed her too far, told her too much about Mary Jane. "Of course Mary Jane's coming home. She'll be here in a few weeks. She'll be so much better, like the old Mary Jane." She continues to sob. I hug her and kiss her cheek. She abruptly quits crying. She stares into space for a long while. "Victoria, snap out of it!" No response. She sits there like a zombie. "It's me, Lydia. Remember, Lydie and Vic, unarmed but dangerous?" I read in one of Mary Jane's old psychology texts about catatonic states that the mind can retreat to when under severe stress; this must be one. Mental illness is genetic. She must have inherited it from Mary Jane. I slap her across the face. She doesn't react although I've left a bright red hand mark across her cheek.

Alex is in his La-Z-Boy watching hockey. "Something's wrong with Victoria." I wait, counting three smoke rings. "She's upset about Mom, and now she's gone into this trance and she won't respond to anything."

Alex doesn't look up. "Leave her for awhile. She's probably tired," he says. He doesn't get it.

I make a call to Granny and Granddad's number in Vancouver and ask for Mary Jane. "Hi. It's Lydia . . . Mom . . . I need your help. I'm worried about Victoria. We were talking about some family problems, and she just freaked out and went catatonic on me. I can't get her to respond to anything. She's been like a zombie for about fifteen minutes. Could you please, lie to her if you have to, just tell her that you're all better and coming home soon and everything is going to be all right again."

"Put her on. Let me talk to her," Mary Jane says.

I lead Victoria downstairs in her zombie-like trance, stand her in the front hall, and hold the phone up to her ear. "It's Mary Jane, she's coming home soon. Here's Victoria!" I shout into the phone.

A fake and cheerful voice says, "How's my baby girl?" and I can't make out the rest but whatever she's saying, it works. Victoria slumps into a heaving pile of sobbing pink frills. She drops the phone.

"Thanks, Mom, I think she's going to be okay. Talk to you later, bye," I say and hang up the phone. I bend down to embrace the sobbing pink blob. I hug her, huddling on the hall floor until she stops crying. "I'll make us tea. We can have it on the front porch," I say and take her hand. She wipes her face with her housecoat sleeve.

The cupboard beside the stove holds the sacred stash of white tea that Granny brought back with her the last time she was in Hong Kong. Undetected, Alex swoops in beside me, like Dracula. "Did you phone your mother and burden her with your problems?"

"No, I just phoned her to see how she was doing."

"You'd better be telling me the truth because if I find out you disturbed your mother, I won't be happy." He saunters back to his seat, reclines the La-Z-Boy, and resumes his hockey-watching position.

I am alone. He's not my father. He's a cruel, selfish pig. I place the silver tea ball into the porcelain teapot and carry the tray onto the front porch.

It's a lie-on-the-bed-and-climb-my-feet-up-the-wall kind of a Friday in the tower tonight. My toes gently touch each black and white magazine picture that I've taped up.

Alex shouts up the staircase, "Supper!"

I'm starving but I can't stand the thought of Alex's shipwreck again. He has only three suppers that he can cook: shipwreck, fish sticks with hash browns, and grilled cheese sandwiches with Asian noodle soup.

"Get down here now or you won't be eating anything tonight," he shouts.

I survey the pan on the stove as I walk to the table: rice, obviously soy sauce already added to make it brown, corn, peas, chopped celery, and something disgusting . . . looks like bits of fried egg.

"I don't eat eggs," I say and sit down at the table beside Victoria.

"Elbows, Lydia!" Alex says.

"I just sat down. They haven't even touched the table. Could you please pass me the pepper, Victoria," I say, and continue to stir the rice concoction in circles around my plate. I chase a pea with my fork and attempt to stab the little bugger.

"Knife, Lydia. Use your knife, not your fork," Alex says.

"I can't even swallow, you're bugging me so much," I say.

"Would you two shut up!" Victoria says.

Alex stands up with his empty plate and walks into the family room to watch hockey playoffs.

"One shouldn't inhale their food. Bad for the digestion," I shout. "Come on, let's ditch the old fart," I say to Victoria.

The wind is up. An owl calls from the bluff. Marx leaps from his hay bed, bouncing with each step. He thinks we're going somewhere. I open the truck door. Marx jumps in. "Yes! The keys are in the glove box — let's take an evening drive through the pasture."

"Alex will kill us. He never lets you drive at night."

"Come on. Don't be a wuss. Get in."

"Hurry up and get out of here. Alex will chase the truck," Victoria says, then slams her door shut.

I start up the engine and speed towards the corral. "Quick, Victoria, jump out and get the gate, run!" I speed through the open gate, right through the corral, pausing on the other side. Victoria jumps in.

"Go! Get out of here. He's coming!"

I floor it, speeding off into the black pasture.

"We better make this one long drive. He'll need time to cool down," Victoria says.

The headlights illuminate the flattened spring grass and a muddy wagon trail. I try to keep the truck as close to the trail as possible. "I hope I don't hit a badger hole and roll us," I say.

"Or worse, a cow," Victoria adds.

"Don't say that — don't ever say that," I say, thinking of Silver.

We drive along the wagon road until we nearly reach the end of our pasture, then I veer us off the trail. We skid through wet grass and slide through mud. The ride is terrifying yet exhilarating. I hit something big. The truck lurches towards the stars and then bangs back to earth.

"What was that?" Victoria says.

"Rock?"

"Jesus, Lydia! Learn how to drive. Are you trying to kill us?" she shouts, sounding like our father.

"Shut the fuck up — you should be thankful that you're not cruising around California on the back of some Harley," I say. Victoria is mute. I shouldn't have brought up Mary Jane. I don't want her to go catatonic on me again. I turn the pickup around and drive back towards the yard light.

The game is over. The vodka bottle sits on the kitchen counter. Alex has retreated to the back porch with a coal tar shake. He says nothing as we climb the stairs to bed and neither do we. A red, glowing cigar tip is the only proof of his existence.

I'm half asleep when the train whistle blows. It's the Paris Metro, and I'm late for dinner at Maxim's with Mr. Kent. He's teaching in Paris, and I'm studying fashion design. Alex's desperate voice breaks into my fantasy. "Lydia, I need you to get up and take me to emergency. I'm not feeling well," he whispers harshly. I open my eyes to his terrified face in the moonlight. "Don't wake Victoria. Let's go."

"You go and wait in the truck. I'll be right out," I say. I get to drive on the highway, with Alex. I pull off my nightie and pull on a grey tracksuit. I want to tell Victoria where I'm going, but I leave her asleep. With each step down the stairs, I lower myself into a thicker and thicker stench of sickeningly sweet pot smoke. It's coming from the back porch.

Alex sits hunched in the passenger seat waiting for me. As I turn onto the road, I spot Victoria in the rear-view mirror, under the porch light. She stands on the front steps, waving her arms wildly. I want to stop but Alex starts to tremble all over, so I make the decision to keep going.

His eyes are closed. It must be serious because he hasn't criticized my driving once. I drive on gravel roads until I hit the asphalt highway, retracing the route Alex always takes. My mind might be coasting in and out of reality. Am I driving down an abandoned dark highway? Is Alex really here beside me, hunched over and mute? I head towards the giant orange glow that is Saskatoon. I don't stop until we enter the city, pulling the truck to a halt at my first red light ever. There are no other cars on the road. I could just drive on through — this is an emergency situation. The light turns green. I continue in a straight line through the ghost city. "Where is everyone at 2:00 AM on a Saturday night?" I whisper, so as not to disturb the patient.

"Turn right here," Alex says, lifting his head. I drop him off at the hospital emergency entrance, then follow the signs to the parking lot.

Alex is not easy to find. Everyone avoids my open mouth before I even have a chance to ask a question. "Alex Buckingham," I croak, like a toad that has just been sat on.

"Are you family?" the woman in the white polyester suit asks.

"Yes, his daughter," I say.

He's already in a room; actually it's more of a locker with sheets than a room. At first I don't recognize the skinny, pink man in the bed hooked up to an EKG monitor. Alex is tall, Alex is loud, Alex is bushy-haired and arrogant, the Viking of the prairie. Suddenly, the reality of the situation hits me: Alex might die.

"You look pale. Maybe you should sit down," a nurse in a yellow uniform says as she closes the sheet curtain that I had left open. "We don't want two patients in here."

I sit on a hard plastic chair beside pink Alex.

A doctor pulls open the curtain. "All his vital signs look good," she says to me. "He's had a panic attack. I've given him a sedative." I nod. The doctor leans over and talks to Alex in a low voice but I can still hear everything. "I strongly recommend that you avoid any further marijuana use. In all likelihood, it's responsible for triggering the panic attack."

I call Victoria from the hospital pay phone with quarters from Alex's jeans. She's hysterical. She must have cried for two hours straight. I think being left alone out there may traumatize her for life. But at least she's crying. The fact that she's not catatonic is reassuring.

With the news that he'll live, Alex finds the energy to criticize my driving on the trip back. "I don't want you going over sixty on the gravel. Watch the speedometer," he says.

"Good news, Alex. The sedative's had a positive affect on you; you're only half as irritating," I say.

"Drive — and don't tell your mother about tonight," he says.

All the lights in the house are on. Victoria and Marx are asleep together on the chesterfield. Alex doesn't even stop to complain about Marx. He heads straight down to bed. The back porch still reeks. My dad the pothead. He'd better stick to cigars from now on.

EigHt

Victoria pulls gently on Silver's reins, stopping her at the gravel crossroad. Her hair is freshly washed. It smells like the no-name conditioner Alex bought, fake fruit. No bike today, we double bareback, and no pink housecoat today either. There are still a few small miracles to be thankful for. Vic's frilly mess of a houseboat has yet to leave the confines of our land. No one outside the family knows the true extent of her weirdness.

"Let's surprise Brady," Victoria says.

"Brady?"

"Yeah. Why not? He surprised us last time. It's our turn," she says.

"Once. It was a one-off, not like we have to reciprocate or anything."

"So what's the story on Brady?" Victoria says and presses the left rein into Silver's neck and nudges her heels into Silver's front pits. She's decided we're going to Brady's.

"What do you mean?" I say.

"You know what I mean. Do you like him or not? You know he's crazy for you."

"He is not! I never even see him anymore. We're just friends. More like acquaintances, really."

"Whatever you say," Victoria says.

Just shut up and ride.

A big, nasty looking German Shepherd cross barks as it comes towards us once we turn down Brady's long drive. Marx is the first to meet it with a few good butt sniffs. Neither dog growls.

"It must be a female," Victoria says.

"Duchess, I think her name is Duchess," I say. Silver doesn't seem bothered by the beast as it follows us down the caragana-lined drive towards Brady's house.

A woman answers, a surprisingly young and pretty woman who must be his mom. She can't be over thirty. She looks slightly irritated, like we might be selling overpriced chocolate almonds. "Brady's in the Quonset with his dad, working on his bike," she says. A TV sounds inside the dark house, a cartoon, American TV. They must have a satellite dish. I am drawn to the familiar cartoon noises; they sound like civilization.

"Lydia," I say and extend my hand.

"Brenda — Brady's mother," she says without extending hers. Brady's little sister appears beside her mom. She is dressed for bed in a pale blue nightgown.

"Hi," Katie says. She looks us over with critical eyes. "How old are you?" she says in an abrupt manner that would be considered rude in anyone over twelve.

"Fourteen — you?" Victoria says.

"Eleven — well, ten and three quarters. Want to see my room?" Katie says. She extends her hand. Victoria agrees to be led down the hall, turning to shrug her shoulders before disappearing from view. Brenda waits impatiently, half hiding behind the door, as though she wants to close it and get me off her porch. I would leave quickly and eagerly if my traitor sister and that rude little girl hadn't abandoned me.

"Well, I guess I'll go check out the Quonset then," I say.

She smiles pleasantly and says, "Sounds good," as she closes the door in my face. That leaves me to walk alone towards the swimming-pool green, fibreglass Quonset. I wish his dad wasn't in there with him. Parents make everything awkward. The big metal door is open. They are in there together all right, hunched over a motorbike. His dad is about the same height as Brady and they're both wearing ball caps. His dad looks over his shoulder, gives me a bored glance, and mumbles something to Brady. Brady turns around. The look on his face is pure shock followed by an embarrassed smile. He says nothing, only stares as me. I've never seen him in a ball cap before. His hair looks longer; dark curls fluff out from under the cap. His dad turns to smile at me apologetically, as though sorry for Brady's lack of manners. "Who's your friend?" he says.

"Oh, yeah, um ... this is Lydia ... this is my dad, Bill." He is not the cool Brady from school.

"Hello," I say, then nod in the direction of the patient on the operating mat. "Is that your bike?"

"Yeah, just fixing the brakes," Brady says, taking off his cap and holding it in his hand.

"It's fixed. You can take it. I'm going to check on the calves. Nice meeting you," his dad nods, with a polite closed-lip smile.

We are alone. Brady's body relaxes. He puts his cap on but twists it backwards. "Why ... how ... I mean," he says.

I guess he's not as relaxed as he looks. "Victoria and I are out riding around. We just stopped by to say hi."

"Do you have time to go for a ride?" he says, glancing at his bike.

"On that little thing, with you? I don't think so."

"We can take my dad's over there. It's bigger. I've got helmets." He points across the room to a much bigger bike. It's no dirt bike. It's a motorcycle.

"That looks fast. Your dad won't mind?"

"I ride it all the time. It belongs to both of us. You wanna take a ride on my crotch rocket — baby?" he says in a French accent.

I can't hold back a smile. "Crotch rocket?"

"That's what they're called — in Europe," he says.

I hold on tight as he speeds across the grass-covered field, directly behind the Quonset. The back of Brady's neck smells . . . sexy. If he wasn't from Hicksville, I might think this was a perfect date. He drives fast but smoothly. I relax enough, just enough, to see the amazing sky, all peach and blue streaks. We hit a bump and get air, probably an inch but it feels like a foot. "Sorry about that," he says. We stop. Across the open field a raging dust ball gathers speed towards us.

"What is that? Are there Tasmanian devils in Saskatchewan?"

"It's a badger and he's mad as hell," he says.

"Man, look at those short legs go," I say.

"You okay?" he says.

"Ride on."

We leave the badger in the dust and ride on towards the setting sun. Brady cuts the engine beside an abandoned brick schoolhouse. He sits on the bike, not moving, not talking. "Are we going in?" I say.

"Sure," he says, slightly surprised, as though the idea hadn't occurred to him. He takes off his helmet. His hair is stuck to his sweaty forehead. He's hot. What is wrong with me? This is Brady, the guy I tolerate at lunchtime.

The schoolhouse floor is covered in shattered glass and pigeon poop. Amazingly, the old slate blackboard is still intact. "Rats, no chalk. I feel like writing something," I say, crunching glass beneath my cowboy boots with each step. Brady draws on the board with his finger: *B.M. + L.B.* "Brady," I say in slow exasperation. He raises one of his eyebrows. I raise both of mine. "What?" I say.

"Nothing — I like your boots," he says and nudges my cowboy boot with his foot.

"Thanks — they were my dad's — when he was young," I say, then stare at my boots for a while. Brady touches my hand. We haven't actually had physical contact, not since the tattoo session. I let him lead me through the door and onto the school steps. The sun rests on the horizon line, turning the sky tangerine. "I admit it. Nothing is as beautiful as a prairie sunset — I better get back. Victoria will be freaking." I say. He pulls at my hand, leans down fast, and kisses me on my lips. I watch him kiss me as though in slow motion. He tastes good. He smells good. The ice queen is melting into a mess that is someone else. We stumble down the steps and lay, hidden in the high grass, kissing with wet mouths, swollen lips, and aggressive tongues. His hands are up under my bra. My hands slide up under his shirt, feeling his hard chest and puny nipples. "I remember these nipples," I say as though listening to someone else say it. He lifts my shirt over my head. I lift his shirt off. His chest looks smooth and familiar. He was once my canvas. He put his hands around my back, going for the bra. I look down at my own bare boobs. I can't breathe. "I gotta go. Victoria and Silver are waiting."

"Stay, just for a little while," he says in my ear.

"No. I've got to get back. Let's go." I stand up and search through the grass for my bra and T-shirt. I walk to his bike and stand impatiently beside it.

"Hang on. I can't find my shirt," Brady says.

"It's on the steps," I say, deadpan.

My helmet's on. I hand him his. He looks at me, perplexed. "Come on. Let's get going," I say.

Silver, Marx, and Victoria are gone by the time we reach Brady's yard. The sky has turned into a narrow tangerine streak along the horizon and the rest is indigo fading into black. He drives me home in his mom's little car. I continue to avoid eye contact and it keeps him effectively mute.

"Stop! This is fine. I'll get out here," I say as he turns in to our driveway. I don't dare let Alex catch a glimpse of him.

"See you tomorrow?" he says.

"Sure — thanks for the ride," I say.

If I stand up on my bed and look in the dresser mirror, I can check out my entire naked body. My boobs definitely do not look like ones I've seen in *Playboy*. The kids I used to babysit in Vancouver had a pervert for a dad. He kept a giant stash of *Playboy* in the master bedroom ensuite. All the naked models had tennis ball boobs. Mine are more cone-shaped. No one talks about vaginas. It's hard even to find decent literature on the subject. I read in *Cosmo* once that the bigger the labia the better the lover. That is it, the extent of my sexual knowledge aside from the basic functions. As clueless as Victoria is, I'm dying to talk to her about sex stuff. But she's a wall — beyond miffed that I abandoned her at the Melenchuk homestead.

I pull the T-shirt back on, the same one I wore at the old school house. It still smells like him, my dark secret. I dread school, my mind has been swirling its evil brew, poisoning my rational self. I can't have a Hicksville boyfriend. It's tacky, weak. I wish I were still in Vancouver.

⚡

Only a month of school left, then it is goodbye forever, tenth grade.

Brady finds me at lunch. I knew he would. We walk around the track. "What's wrong? You seem different," he says.

I turn into the ice queen of the century. I can't stop the words that jump from my mouth. "Nothing's wrong. It's just that I'm too busy for a relationship, with anyone. I'm still sort of involved with someone in Vancouver." He looks at me with hurt eyes, places his hand on his forehead, slides it through his hair, then his tall body lopes, with heavy feet, towards the school's side entrance.

⚡

I heard a terrifying rumour that Polinski might be coming back next year. They can't get rid of Mr. Kent; I'll die. He's the only reason I'm still here. Otherwise, I'd pull a Mary Jane and find my way back to Vancouver. I spend lunch chatting with Michelle Dyck. Well, she talks and I listen, mostly. The more she talks, the more fucked up she seems. We have almost nothing in common aside from us both being fifteen and females with generally aloof attitudes at school.

Michelle stops in the teachers' parking lot, rummages through her big black purse, and pulls out a package of cigarettes. She hops on the trunk of an old green car, crosses her legs, and takes a drag. At least she has the manners to attempt to blow the smoke away from me. "Last Friday there was a bush party, down by the river near Nathan's place. It was wicked. This weekend the party's in town," she says.

"I didn't even know the parties existed," I say. No one invites the ice princess, I guess.

"You're not missing anything unless you like to party hard — I mean really hard," she says.

"Whose car is this?" I say, slapping the faded green paint next to Michelle, not waiting for any pathetic Hicksville hard-partying details.

"Kent's," she says.

"Thought so. The U of S parking pass on the back window gives it away." I peer inside the car windows, examining the chaos that is Mr. Kent. Fast food wrappers litter the back seat and floor. There's a gym bag stuffed full of clothes heaped on the front seat. "What a mess," I say.

Michelle hops off the car. "Weird. Do you think he lives in there?"

"Doubt it. The extra outfit is probably a change of clothes in case he pee-pees his pants at school," I say.

"Gross!" Michelle laughs.

"Why is there music coming from the gym?" I say.

"Hang on, just let me finish this," she says and takes a desperately long drag on the vanishing cigarette.

We pass Mr. Kent heading for the staff room. "Going to check out the sock hop?" he says.

"Maybe," I say to him. "Didn't even know there was one," I say to Michelle.

Joan Jett's "Crimson and Clover" is playing. The loud music is hypnotizing; it summons me towards the open gym doors. The bass vibrates my bones. I used to go to dances back in Vancouver, but not here, never here. People here still think it's weird when girls dance together.

The gym is dark except for a disco ball and ultraviolet lighting that makes everyone's faces look black and their teeth neon. For a moment, I might not even be in Hicksville, I might be anywhere else. Someone tall, dark, across the gym . . . it might be Brady. It is him. He looks sexy standing there in the dark. He doesn't see me. He's talking to that big-haired girl in his class. She won't stop touching his arm. She's hot for him. There's no oxygen in the gym. I feel weak and sweaty. I have to get out. I want to walk home again but I'm not up for a chat with the RCMP. I walk into the girls' change room. It's empty. I sit in a toilet stall and cry silently. I don't know what I'm doing, but I'll never be able to face anyone now. Even the muted tears make my face blotchy red and my freckles appear 3D.

I can't take that song anymore, "Crimson and Clover" — it has Brady moving through it in slow motion, and I feel like I'm going to pass out.

NINE

The insects are back: grasshoppers, mosquitoes, black flies, moths, and crickets. The chickenshit aroma is my personal reminder that the days are warming their way into summer. But this morning, it's the comforting smell of coffee that awakens me. Mary Jane has come home.

"Good morning," she says as she sits at the kitchen table, coffee in hand, gazing out at the poplar bluff. Her hair has grown. It's a little longer, softer, and prettier. Her eyes match the colour of a new blue sweater that Granny knitted for her.

"Why did Alex fly back to Vancouver? You just got home," I say, though it is a relief to have him gone. The atmosphere's peaceful without his mania.

"Our house still hasn't sold. He's going to lease it for a year to a new professor and his family. Thank God, the rent will pay the mortgage," she says.

Relief, the longer we can hang on to that house, the longer I can hold on to the hope of returning to my old life. "Did you see our house, when you were in Vancouver?"

"Yes, I did."

"What did it look like?"

"The same. When I walked in I expected to find all of you there, waiting for me."

I like that image of home. "Weird — I never want it to sell. I'm not a Saskatchewan girl."

"No? Not yet anyway."

"Not yet and never," I say too loudly.

"Do you want tea? Granny gave me a new stash."

"Coffee."

She raises her eyebrows. "Things have changed around here. Twyla's parents just picked up Victoria. She's off to church with them," she says before I have a chance to ask.

"They're trying to convert her, you know."

"Oh well, she could be into worse things," she says.

I study her. She seems relaxed, so at peace with herself. It's completely unlike her. I'm dying to get to know this new woman.

"What was it like being in the hospital?"

She stares into her coffee. "I don't remember much about the beginning. It's a haze of hell and sleep. By the end of my stay I got used to it. It was quite comfortable. I had my routine and was afraid to leave."

"Didn't you get bored?"

"A little, towards the end. That's when I knew I was ready to move on."

I take a sip of the poisonous coffee, suddenly realizing the science behind Grand'Mère's ultra strong coffee: it kills the undertaste of well water. "Do you think you're stronger now — having survived it?"

"I used to hope that I was. Having lived in such low places where most mortals never tread. But now, having been there, it will always exist for me. There's the possibility that I could go back."

"But knowledge is strength, Mom."

She stands up and drifts towards the fly swatter. *Don't touch it. Don't pick it up.* The fly swatter might be the key to the house. Touch it and you're a goner, trapped inside a chrysalis of insanity. She stops before taking it from the hook and looks out the kitchen window at the chickens in the yard. "Does knowing of places so dark give one strength? I think ignorance is better, never knowing that such a place exists. Hell being a concept that only the dead and the horrible have to deal with was reassuring."

"Hell isn't just for the evil?"

"No. The living and the good can go there too."

The last day of tenth grade. I deserve an endurance award for surviving ten agonizing months of Hicksville High. But the only award I get is a mention in the yearbook — the most likely to become a world famous fashion designer. Some twelfth grader I don't even know nominated me.

It's my last chance to try to connect with Mr. Kent. I want to give him the card that I found in Saskatoon, the one with a black and white photograph of the Eiffel Tower on it. Alex refused to lend me the money to buy it so I made one, a collage of black and white magazine photographs. I admit, it's a little on the sexy side. I chose pictures with couples embracing, a few bare-chested guys and one bare-backed woman. I want to write: *Here's to our future together in Paris! Lydie xoxo,* but I control myself and write: *We'll always have Shakespeare! Yours, Lydia.*

I hand him the card. He scans it silently. "Thank you, Lydia. Have a good summer," he finally says, sounding a little rattled. I'm too afraid to ask if he's coming back next fall.

⚡

Victoria reclines on her bed reading the July issue of *Cosmo* magazine.

"Where'd you get that?"

"Never mind," she says.

"So you stole it?" I say.

"Okay, I got it in town last week. Twyla and I walked to the store."

I give her the evil eye, just to bug her.

"What? You're the one who told me I needed to educate myself about sex."

"I'm just kidding. Can I read it after you?" She doesn't have time to answer. Alex's booming voice reverberates throughout the house.

"Girls! Family meeting! Everyone in the living room — this is important."

Victoria slams down her magazine and hops off the bed. "Aren't you coming?"

"If it's about tampons and toilet paper again, I'm going to sit this one out," I say and heave myself onto her bed and pick up the *Cosmo*.

"Lydia, down here now!" Alex shouts up the stairs. I bump down each stair in my sock feet.

"Now that you're all here — I have an interview in Edmonton. I have to be there on Monday morning," he says.

"Edmonton? Can we go to West Edmonton Mall?" Victoria says.

"Yes! It's supposed to be the biggest indoor mall in the world. It has an amusement park and everything," I say.

"Sorry, girls. It's just going to be your mother and me. We are only staying one night. We won't be going to the mall."

"What are we going to do while you're gone?" Victoria says.

"You'll stay here. Lydia, you're in charge. You girls can handle one night on your own," Alex says.

"You'll be too busy to get into trouble. You'll have to look after the animals," Mary Jane says.

"Typical. Alex and Mary Jane against the world again. Unfortunately, their world is very small, and you and I are the only other two people in it," I say to Victoria. She ignores me.

"Can we at least get some groceries so we can make ourselves decent meals while you're gone?" she says.

"We do need a few groceries," Mary Jane says to Alex.

"Get in the truck," he says. Victoria and I jump up and down together as though we're much younger and much happier girls, too stupid to realize we're celebrating yet another night of going nowhere.

"Did you get it?" Victoria leans over and whispers to me.

"No."

"Why not?"

"She refused."

"Wimp."

"Do you think it was easy trying to shove a bottle of tequila through the checkout with their vodka? It was a bloody nightmare! She was on to me from the start."

"How in the hell can we make margaritas without the tequila?" Victoria pushes her chair back from the table and scoots herself, still sitting on the chair, towards the fridge, then stands on the chair and opens the liquor cabinet. "I need a flashlight. I can't even see what's all in here," she says, picking up a bottle that looks like wine. Alex makes a sudden appearance, behind us. Victoria slams the liquor cupboard shut and jumps from the chair. That man is way too quiet when he removes his workboots. He pushes aside the chair Victoria was standing on, opens the fridge, and takes out a beer. "It's a hot one," he says and pushes his hand through his thick hair, inadvertently causing it stick up like a hedgehog.

"It's so dark. Can't we at least open the kitchen curtains while we're in here?" I say.

"No. The curtains remain closed. That's an order. It's going to be near forty degrees tomorrow," he says.

"Isn't it better to get a breeze going through this place?" I say.

"No," is all Alex says, then he walks into the living room with his beer.

"Wonderful. We live in a sealed coffin — and this is the hideous satin lining," I say and flick the hem of Victoria's housecoat with my foot.

Alex appears unusually clean, wearing a crisp, grass-green short-sleeved shirt, his thick, sun-streaked hair smoothed flat. Mary Jane looks pretty in a new, sleeveless dress. She waves but her smile is brittle, as though it might suddenly shatter like the window. For some odd reason, Alex signals to turn left onto our gravel road. Perhaps he has always done it, even though, to date, not one vehicle other than our truck and the school bus has driven down the road since we moved in.

Victoria and I stand, watching the dust clouds disappear. "They are going to cook in that truck," Victoria says. She has a bathing suit on under her housecoat. Her skinny limbs are pasty white in comparison to her sunburnt face.

"It will be good for those two to sweat a little — why the bikini?" I say.

"I'm going swimming," she says.

"The river?" I say. A grisly picture flashes in my mind: paramedics pulling her blue body from Lake Winnipeg.

"No, I'm gonna try the pond," Victoria says.

"What pond?"

"The one in Somerset's field."

"You mean the slough?"

"It looks deep enough to swim in," Victoria says, insulted that I called her precious pond a slough.

"Alone?"

"You could come," she says.

I fill a giant plastic pop bottle with orange juice then call Marx in from the field. He arrives with his tongue hanging on the ground. We trudge across the yard towards the neighbour's field in cowboy boots, bikinis, and Victoria's housecoat, a sad event: her ratty pink goddess robe finally crosses over our property line and beyond. My boots slide along the dry grass, grasshoppers darting in all directions with each step. Marx is panting hard. The backpack, heavy with juice, cuts into my shoulders. In the distance the slough comes into focus, surrounded by heat waves and a white salty ring. "It looks like a mirage. Do you think it's still there or all dried up?" I say. Victoria doesn't answer; she runs ahead of Marx and me, towards the mirage.

The water's stagnant and brown, the shore stained white with alkali. "You were right. It is a slough," Victoria says. "We shouldn't have come." We stare into the disappointing pool of sludge for a while. "I dare you to go in," she says.

"You first. I dare you — first one in up to their waist doesn't have to carry any supplies home." I toss the backpack and run, full speed, not even feeling the coolness on my skin until the water's turned thick, like pudding. The density of the mud stops my legs suddenly, and I trip into the water face-first, my feet cemented in mud, arms flailing. My legs won't hit bottom. I sink deeper and deeper. "Shit, Victoria, quick — help me!"

"I'm stuck," Victoria says. "It's quicksand."

I don't know whether to laugh or cry. Victoria chooses to cry. I laugh. Marx joins in, crying from the shore. He tries to step in but sinks fast, pulling his paws back just in time. "Stay, Marx! Stay! Good boy, stay." The brown, sludgy water is just below my belly button. But with every attempt to move I sink farther down. I can't stop laughing. I want to but I feel giddy, almost drunk.

"Shut up! What is wrong with you?" Victoria screams.

"Calm down, Victoria. Like getting hysterical is going to help." In the back of my mind the truth shouts at me: no one knows where we are. Mary Jane and Alex won't be home for the next thirty-six hours, at least. The sun will cook us alive.

"Once it's dark the coyotes will come and they'll eat us," Victoria says.

"Calm down — and by the way, coyotes would only get stuck too." But after I've say it, I have a mental picture of our skeletons, sticking out of the ice this coming winter, chewed bare by coyotes, like the cow carcasses. "I can't see anything from down here except all that tall fucking grass — some fucking pond this is!"

"You're the one who wanted to race in, you asshole," Victoria says, then starts to cry again. I let her sob for a long time.

"Great, the mosquitoes have found us," I say and smack one on my shoulder.

"I'm being eaten alive," Victoria says and continues on with her incessant sobbing.

Marx licks his paws noisily. The sound makes me thirstier than ever. I can actually hear Marx. That means Victoria must have finally shut up. Her head hangs down, the ends of her hair resting in the mud.

"My legs are numb," I say.

"I can't feel mine either," Victoria says.

"It's probably what's keeping us alive. The mud cools our body while the sun bakes our heads."

"Don't talk to me," Victoria says.

A huge insect buzzes in my ears; just my luck, it's probably a wasp. The buzzing becomes louder, more annoying. It could be a motor. I recognize the sound. "Shut the fuck up, Victoria — hear that? It's a motorbike." Victoria stops crying.

Voices sound behind us. They sound like boys. "Lydia? What are you doing in there?" Brady says.

"Don't!" I say. "Don't come in here. It's like quicksand. You'll get stuck."

"Relax. I'll ride back home and get some rope," he says.

"No!" Victoria shouts.

"Don't go. Don't leave us here," I say.

"We need rope," Brady says.

"I'll go back. You stay with the girls," Mark says, then hops back on his bike, starts it up, and leaves a dust trail that drifts towards the slough. Brady sits on the bank. Marx won't stop licking his face. I want to cry but Victoria is finally quiet so I control myself.

"Where is that fucking Mark? I'm going to pass out if he doesn't get here soon," I say hoarsely. "Pass me my backpack, could you please, Brady?"

"Sure, what can I get you?"

"Juice. I've got juice in there," I say, holding out my arms to receive it. I chug down six huge gulps. "Nectar of the gods," I say, and hand it to Victoria. "Leave some more for me," I say. After I'm sure she's taken at least ten swigs, she hands it back to me. "I might have to puke," I say.

"Just don't," Victoria says.

An insect buzzes inside my ear. "Mark's coming," I say.

"You're in good hands. Mark does this all the time," Brady says.

"Not all the time — though a few calves have gotten stuck in the dugout," Mark says.

The rope cuts into my armpits as it drags my body to shore. I heave my mud-caked limbs onto the grass. Marx licks my face. I can't breathe. I laugh, uncontrolled, delirious laughter. "Off, Marx, off! Call him, Victoria," I say.

Brady kneels down beside me. "We should get you home," he says, then clutches Marx's collar and pulls him off. "Seriously, we've got to get going. Come on, get on the bike." Brady reaches for my hand and pulls me to standing.

"I'll meet you back at their place," Mark says and then speeds off.

"Victoria's on there with him?" I ask, stating the obvious.

"Yeah." Brady's nervous eyes dart from my mud crusted navel back to his bike, then settle back on my navel.

"I'll walk," I say.

"No — get on the bike," he says. "Come on."

"I'll get your bike filthy."

"Who gives a fuck about the bike. Get on," he says.

"I'll walk back with Marx," I say.

"Get on. We'll ride slow so he can keep up."

Home — our tall, gloomy sanctuary, sealed coffin tight.

I fill the teak salad bowl with orange well water and place it on the floor for Marx. "There's some beer in the fridge," I say, knowing that it's Alex's and that he'll kill me if any goes missing. Brady stares at my navel again. I push past him, open the fridge, and grab a beer. "What? Just take the beer," I say and thrust it into his hand.

"I hate to admit it, but Alex was right. The house stayed cool with the drapes closed," Victoria says, dropping her forehead onto the cool kitchen tabletop. She sits, ungracefully, at the table in a clean dress, borrowed from my closet. She raises her head. Her eyes focus on the beer in my hand. Her mouth opens but no words come out.

"It's okay. We'll replace them. Have one," I say.

"Replace — how?" she says, opening the beer I place in her hand.

"We'll talk — later."

I drink the beer as though it's water.

I lean over the table in my fresh cotton dress, and pull open the yellow checkered curtains. I stumble over Brady's long legs. His sweaty smell sends a rush of recognition though me . . . the schoolhouse. The muscles deep inside my abdomen contract simultaneously, as though touched by his scent. My heart thumps fast and I gulp in air.

Victoria's goofy laugh rings out from the family room. "Shut up! That can't be true. Bloodsuckers can't crawl into your orifices, can they?" she shouts.

"No comment. That conversation is all yours," I say into the family room, then lean against the doorway, determined to keep an eye on her and Mark.

Brady's hair has gone curly around his face from sweat — and he's staring again.

"Stop it," I say. At least he's not focused on my boobs. Mark can't keep his eyes off Victoria's and she hardly has any.

"What were you doing in that slough anyway?" he says from across the kitchen.

"Swimming," I say.

"Swimming?"

"What were you doing out there riding around so close to us?"

"Looking for you."

"Well, you found me, a damsel in distress — no, make that a heifer in mud."

"In a bikini," he says.

"Yeah," I laugh and choke on a mouthful of beer. I can't look at his face or I'll blush. His eyes are too intense.

"They're staying for supper," Victoria says, suddenly standing beside me and wrapping her arm around my waist in an affectionate manner. The beer's gone straight to her brain. "We're making Mexican, and there's brownies for dessert. You love Mexican, right?" she says to Mark.

"Never tried it," Mark says. His bulky white biceps stick out awkwardly from his basketball tank. The rest of his arms are burnt red.

"Do you like Mexican?" I ask Brady. It comes out sounding like a challenge but he doesn't bite.

"Sure. I like it all right."

I carry a kitchen chair outside to the barbecue pit beside the house. Brady follows with two more chairs.

"Is all this wood for the fire pit?" Brady asks and nods towards the monster woodpile stacked against the house.

"No — for the furnace. We have a wood burning unit in the basement." I say.

"Cool," he says.

"You wouldn't say that if you had one," Victoria says as she struggles down the back porch steps with another kitchen chair.

"It's a beast. Takes up a quarter of the basement," I say.

The smoke from the bonfire blows directly into my face. I move. It follows. "I'm going in to start the chimichangas," I say with closed eyes.

The pan spits as I drop the first wrapped tortilla into hot canola oil and wait for it to brown. I can't hear what's going on out there without me. It's risky as Loose Lips is on beer number two. I pluck a browned parcel from the burning oil with a spoon and place it onto a paper towel to cool.

Brady's voice drifts in through the screen door, "The ghosts of the buffalo? Interesting. I've never heard that before."

I kick open the door. "What? You told them about that?" I say.

Victoria's face flushes purple, as though I've caught her in a lie. "I only told them one of your theories," she says.

"You mean she has more? I'd like to hear them," Brady says.

"Wouldn't everyone? It's true, though, I know they're out there," I say and turn towards the pasture, the slotted spoon still in my hand.

"How about this place? Ever heard or seen anything strange?" Mark says.

"Why? Do you know something we don't?" I ask and sit down in an empty kitchen chair. My half-full beer can waits on the ground beside the chair, just as I left it.

"That's it! You know something, spill it!" Victoria says, sounding drunk.

"Everyone around here knows about your house. It's supposed to be haunted," Mark says.

"What the hell?" Victoria shouts, then turns towards me with red eyes. Yup, she's drunk all right.

"I've never heard that," I say, feeling suddenly protective of our godforsaken property.

"Drop it, Mark," Brady says.

"Spill it," I say.

"You know your place is on the Carleton Trail, right?" Mark says.

"Yeah, the fur traders and explorers used it to cross the prairies — and the army, to get to Batoche," I say.

"They say your section is haunted. That they used this house on their way back from Batoche," Mark says.

"Who, who used our house?" I say.

"I heard soldiers, bloodied from battle," Mark says.

"Someone died in our house?" Victoria shouts.

"The ghosts haunted the owners," Brady says. "Drove the old man crazy. He walked into a blizzard one winter and was never seen again."

"Careful, you're talking about our great-grandfather, you know — anyway, they built this place after the rebellion. My dad said they tore down the original house — it was really small, more like a shack," I say.

"Sorry — mmm, what smells so good?" Brady says.

"Oh, shit! I forgot — the chimichangas! Victoria, I need you!" I shout.

"How many beer have you had?" I say, once she joins me in the kitchen.

"Only two — and shut it. Look whose talking. How many have you had? You spit beer all over me," she says.

Brady walks through the kitchen. "Bathroom's upstairs?" he says.

"Yes. First door to your right," I say.

"Lydia! Get up here. You have to see this," Brady calls from upstairs.

My eyes lock with Victoria's. I hope he hasn't gone into my bedroom. There's a new box of tampons on my dresser and dirty underwear all over the place.

My bedroom door is closed but the bathroom door is wide open and he's in it. He stands at the window, his back turned away from me. His tall, muscular frame and almost black hair is unfamiliar. Yet, he is there, standing in my bathroom, my dark secret. He turns from the window at my arrival.

"Look. Funnel clouds. Two of them," he says. The sky has lost definition. Clouds have become murky, lost in a shadowy brew.

Brady and Mark inhale the chimichangas, even the burnt ones. I can't decide which is more entertaining, watching the sky or the guys eat. "I guess you like Mexican," Victoria says to Mark. His mouth is too full to answer.

"I have a strong suspicion that he'd eat a sock if it were deep-fried," I say.

Victoria jumps up suddenly, pointing out the kitchen window. "Look, that one's touching down!" The candelabra flames are dangerously close to her flowing hair.

"Watch — your hair," Brady says and shields the candle flame with his palm.

"Turn on the radio. See if there's a tornado warning near Hicksville," I say.

"Hicksville? Where's that?" Brady says.

I never call it that in front of anyone without Buckingham DNA. "A little abandoned community, near Batoche," I say and blush. I'm a useless liar. My mouth says one thing but my face says another.

"Yeah, I think I know the place well," Brady says, more insulted than I thought he'd be. I walk into the back porch to get a better look at the sky.

High above the pasture, coming towards the corral, huge, black, ominous clouds churn and spin, darkening the sky. "Silver! What should we do about Silver? Should we put her in the barn?" I say.

"I'll go get her," Victoria says, then struggles to jam her clumsy feet into my cowboy boots.

"Leave her in the field. She's safer out there," Brady says.

A strong gust rocks the porch.

"We should get in the basement," I say.

The thunder of feet follow me down to huddle underneath the flimsy wooden staircase.

Marx has rotten breath. He licks my bare legs nervously then farts. "Marx! Have some manners," Victoria says.

"Admit it, Brady, that was you," Mark says.

"No, that one was you, Mark. I swear, I heard her say, 'Get some manners, *Mark*'," Brady says.

"Sorry. Can't blame that one on you boys. Marx's been eating horseshit again — stop licking my legs. Off!" I say.

"Looks like there's a town down here," Brady says.

I hoped the dark corners of the basement would have held onto our secrets for tonight but no luck. After the eyes adjust to the dim lighting, Barbie Paris shines in full, mortifying illumination. I hide my smiling, red face inside my crossed legs and laugh.

"They're Lydia's," Victoria says.

"They are not! They're Victoria's. I just helped her build a few things." *Fuck off*, I mouth to her. She gives me the same back, with arm signals.

My bare leg accidently rests on Brady's bare leg. His prickly hairs tickle. His pulse thumps against my calf at the exact spot our skin connects. The porch door bangs and smacks violently against the side of the house. "You made sure the fire was out, right, Mark?" I say.

"Yeah, absolutely," he says, with his eyes half open, as though drifting into a drunk slumber.

"The dessert!" Victoria says.

"I'll get it. Where is it?" Brady says.

"In the fridge."

Brady pushes aside my legs as he crawls out from under the stairs.

We eat, hunkered around the plate, scooping up the thick, undercooked, gooey chocolate mess, like one gluttonous mouth with four hands, until Mark's finger slurping sounds are too revolting for me to continue.

"What was it like up there?' I ask Brady.

"Quiet."

"What does that mean?"

"We're either in the eye of the twister or the storm has passed," he says.

We walk towards the massive poplar bluff where my family spent Christmas morning. Silver is on the other side of the corral, eating peacefully beside the cows.

"Doesn't look like it touched down."

"Probably not — I think we're being followed," Brady says.

"Ignore them. You can't shake them. Wherever I go, Marx follows, wherever Marx goes, Silver follows, and wherever Silver goes, the cattle follow."

"When are your parents due back?" Brady says.

"Not until tomorrow. They're driving so I don't expect them until afternoon sometime."

"Your dad's pretty strict, isn't he?" Brady says.

"Yeah, why?"

"No reason. I just thought that he might be — why does he drive such an old truck? Isn't he a university professor?"

"What does it matter what he drives? He's insanely frugal — he's a communist, okay?"

"Sorry, it's just that I thought you'd be rich, your dad being a professor."

"Well, we're not."

I sit on a fallen poplar. Brady sits beside me, the log teeters under his weight. "I don't know anything about my father," he says.

"What do you mean? Is Bill cold and standoffish?"

"No, he's fine. He's great. He's my dad. But Bill isn't my biological father."

"I had no idea."

"I don't even know who my real father is. Only that it was someone my mom went to high school with in Saskatoon."

"That explains your dark eyes. Everyone else's eyes in your family are blue."

"Really, you noticed that?" he says. I nod. I bet his real dad was handsome and tall like Brady.

"It's probably because I'm half Indian," he says.

"Really?"

"Cree."

"How?"

"My real dad, I think. My mom won't tell me anything, but my grandpa always says stuff and then she shuts him up."

"What kind of stuff?"

"He wouldn't let me have a beer last summer, even though he gave one to my cousin who's a year younger. He said I couldn't handle it — because of the Indian in me."

"Weird — your grandpa sounds racist."

"I don't know — probably."

I lean forward and kiss his cheek unconsciously. The bold move doesn't even register until my lips leave his warm skin.

I take hold of his hand and attempt to lead him from the trees. He stops, our arms extended. "Stay," he says.

"I've got to get back and check on Victoria. Mark is just a little too into her boobs for me."

"You can't be serious," he says.

"Sort of. Come on."

Victoria and Mark sit side by side on the sofa, not even holding hands.

"What's on?" I say.

"*The Craw*," Victoria says.

"A horror," Mark says, seeming much more sober than he was an hour ago.

"What kind of a stupid name is that?" I say.

"It's Japanese — dubbed," Victoria says.

"None of it makes sense," Mark says and reaches above his head, stretches, and yawns.

"Let's just say English isn't the translator's first language. Mark has to take off after the show. What about Brady? When does he have to go?" Victoria says.

I shrug my shoulders and go back into the kitchen where Brady waits at the table. I take his hand. "Come on up to my room."

"Did you do that?" he says, pointing at my black and white fashion wall.

"Who else?"

"What's with the pictures?" he says.

"They inspire me. If you look closely, you'll find a few common themes."

He lies back on my pillow to get a better view of the wall. "Sex?" he says. I slap him playfully. "She's thinking about the sex she just had with that guy," he says, pointing to a male model in a Ralph Lauren advertisement.

"Shut up. It's obvious what the themes are."

He narrows his eyes, appearing to be deep in thought.

"Okay, if you must be told, the themes are nature, fashion, and travel," I say.

"I believe you, but I don't see it. How is this nature, travel, or fashion?" He touches a black and white photo of a shirtless male model in a cologne advertisement.

"Okay, you win. It's sex, pure, unadulterated sex — but only that picture. The rest fit the themes." He rolls onto his back and stares at the ceiling. I touch his arm. "Not bad," I say, exploring his bicep.

He grasps my toothpick arm. "Not bad," he says.

"I haven't filled out yet. Just wait, the muscles will come," I say. He leans over and plants a kiss on my bicep, then on my mouth. I'm lust-drunk or beer-drunk or both. It's as though the last month never happened. We pull off each other's clothes until I'm in bikini panties and he's in blue briefs underneath Holly Hobbie sheets.

"Don't," Brady says into my ear.

"Don't?"

"Don't fuck with me again."

I want to say, *never again — I'm your love slave forever.* "Yes, well — I was a little screwed up back then," I say.

I sleep soundly and wake up thinking it's Victoria beside me, but it's Brady. He opens his eyes, and his lips break into a sleepy smile. He's enraptured by me, like Bowie, in the song. He wants to pick up where we left off last night, finish what we started. I hate to break it to him, but morning or night, it's not happening. I push him off me and jump onto the floor. "You've got to get out of here. My parents are coming home today."

He sits up. "My parents don't know where I am. They know nothing except that I went dirt biking with Mark — yesterday, after lunch," he says, struggling into his T-shirt and shorts.

"They've probably called the cops looking for you," I say.

He flies down the stairs, missing the landing completely, then out the front door. Marx trots over in greeting. Brady ignores him, jumping on his bike and starting it up. He races down our driveway. Gone, without so much as a wave.

Victoria is still asleep in her bed, and Mark is long gone. I count four empties in the back porch and six outside by the firepit: ten beers. Plus two on the floor by the chesterfield, make that twelve. We are dead.

I have the sudden urge to barf. I make it upstairs just in time. As I lie on the cold bathroom floor, my head starts to ache. I crawl back into bed.

"Lydia?" Victoria's hoarse voice calls out.

"What?" my hoarse voice answers.

"Did you just vomit?"

"Yeah, I'm sick."

"Me too. I can't get out of bed."

Mary Jane and Alex arrive late afternoon. Victoria and I are still in bed. The hot truck cab messed with their moods. I hear them in the kitchen, bitching back and forth. I won't tell them we got stuck in the slough. Going near a slough, never mind wading into one, is so off limits that it's never even been discussed.

"What happened to my beer?" I hear Alex say. That happened way faster than I could have ever predicted. He's like a bloodhound.

"Victoria?" I rasp.

"What?"

"Let me do the talking — say nothing. Got it?"

"Okay — Lydia?"

"What?"

"I'm scared."

Mary Jane calls our names. We are silent. She ascends the staircase and walks into my room. She stands beside my bed. I don't turn over. "Lydia? What's wrong? Where's your sister?"

"She's in her room. She's sick. Me too. Too much sun yesterday."

She places her hand on my forehead.

"Where were you?"

"In the field — we had a picnic on the Mexican blanket — stayed out too long."

"You're probably dehydrated. I'll bring you something to drink after I check on your sister."

Victoria sticks to her promise. She says nothing but moans on about her dizziness.

My drink, ginger ale with ice, arrives after about half an hour. Alex drove into town to get it. Unfortunately, he accompanies Mary Jane to my room to deliver it to me. He sits on my bed. "I had a case of beer cooling in the fridge when I left for Edmonton. It appears to be missing. Do you know anything about that?" His voice is quiet, inquisitive. I've heard him argue with colleagues at parties with the very same voice. He uses it to draw out information he knows will incriminate his victim before he goes in for the kill.

"Your light beer?" I have no idea why I said that. I keep my covers pulled up to just under my chin. I stare straight ahead at my dresser.

"No, as a matter of fact, it wasn't light beer. Not that that's important," he says.

"Well — I don't know exactly, but we had visitors while you were away, Mark and Mark's cousins from Saskatoon — and Brady. They stopped by yesterday afternoon, totally unexpected. It was so hot out and we had nothing to offer them. They asked for beer. The cousins drank most of the beer. I didn't know how to stop them. I didn't want to be rude."

Alex stops me, holding up his hand.

"You had boys in the house while we were away?" The inquisitive voice has turned less solicitous, more cold and serious. He's ready to pounce.

Shit. I had forgotten about that minor detail.

Victoria's raspy voice comes to my rescue. "No, we sat outside. We tried to have a bonfire in the pit."

· "You had a fire?" Mary Jane says, alarm rising in her throat.

"I'm going to shut up now! I suggest you do the same," I yell to Victoria.

⚡

The ginger ale must have cured Victoria. She's been in the basement with the Barbies for over an hour. The parents are in the living room discussing our punishment. I don't want to know what it is, but I'm so bored I might puke again, just from boredom.

The discussion is over. Alex is attempting to get it on with Mary Jane in front of the piano. He has his hands down the back of her pants, cupping her butt. The loving butt-cup is something Victoria and I virulently avoid. It's get-a-room material. I attempt to dart past, low and fast, like a prairie badger. "Back to good old UBC. Better you than me," Alex says.

I freeze in the door frame. "What are you talking about? Who's going back to UBC?"

"I'm going back to school. I only need a semester to finish my degree. Then I can work here at the university hospital. We could use another income," Mary Jane says.

"You're moving to Vancouver without us? How can you do this to us? You can't leave Alex in charge of this nuthouse — he'll start toking up again."

Alex, for once, shuts his mouth.

"I'm not leaving until the end of August. You'll be in school; you won't even know I'm gone," Mary Jane says, an alien coolness in her voice.

"Then take me with you."

"I'm staying with Granny and Granddad."

177

"Take us, there's room for Victoria and me."

"Alex! Tell her she can't come. I won't have time for anything but university," Mary Jane says.

Alex stays mute. He doesn't want us either.

"Why can't you stay here and finish? The U of S has nursing. You could drive in everyday with Alex."

"I'll be home for Thanksgiving and then for good at Christmas. What's three months?" Her cold calm is evaporating and her voice is getting shrill, a grim reminder of Mary Jane with the Halcion eyes. I calm my voice. If she freaks again, she'll be back in Vancouver forever.

"But December is too far away, and you know Dad's useless at taking care of things."

"Easy there," Alex says.

My calm is gone in an instant. Alex is easier to yell at than Mary Jane. "How bloody long have you been planning this? I bet you've known since the spring. You were just too chicken to tell us," I yell. "This is totally fucked up."

I run for the basement before anyone has the chance to bawl me out. Victoria is crouched behind the furnace, attempting to stuff her Barbie family into their camper (a cardboard box upholstered in purple velvet left over from my smoking jacket). "Take your time — no rush," I say.

"Why?"

"Trust me on this one. There's butt-cupping going on in the living room."

I haven't seen Brady since the morning after the storm, and it feels like forever. I'm tempted to take the truck, but Eva and Hitler are sitting in the living room with their coal tar shakes, guarding both exits.

"I am trapped. I want out of this chickenshit tower. I need to get off this fucking farm!" I scream, muffling the "fucking" part into my pillow.

"Shut the hell up, Lydia. You're giving me a headache," Victoria shouts.

"They're at the Ex right about now, watching Bryan Adams live. How about that?" I yell.

Silence. Fuck Victoria. I need to see Brady. Nothing will make it better. Nothing. I hate my parents. They want me to have no friends. They want me to be trapped in their prison every single day of my life. I dig my fingernails into my bare thighs until a drop of blood seeps beneath my nail. There is no point to it. It hurts and my legs look like shit. I think Brady has fucked with my mind. He's like Halcion. I want to jump on the back of his bike and take off to California with him. If this is love, I hate it.

I'm listening to the coyotes and waiting for the midnight train when someone calls, "Lydia," in a ghostly voice. Something hits my window. I struggle out of my twisted sheet and peer into the lit yard. Brady. I want to tell him to be quiet or he'll wake up my parents but the window is painted shut.

The front lock thuds as I open it. I step on air to get to him, tiptoeing barefoot on packed dirt towards his tall dark shadow. His big white runners seem to glow. He attempts to focus his eyes in the yard light to read the shirt that I use as a nightie. It's a too-big T-shirt from one of Alex's anti-government protests that depicts the premier as a cartoon pig.

"Grunt Devine?" he says and laughs. He's too happy. He's either drunk or high. I pull him against the house into the shadow.

"Do you get it? Grunt instead of Grant," I say.

"Cool," he says.

He's all over my face, trying to kiss me with beer breath.

"Calm down, my parents could wake up any minute! How was the Ex?" I whisper.

"It was all right."

"Who all was there? Who'd you go with?"

"Just Mark — and a few of his city friends."

"Who were the city friends? Boys or girls?"

"Ah, girls, I guess." He tries to kiss my neck.

"Who were the girls?"

"Don't worry, they were ugly girls. Mark knew them from some school dance he went to in Saskatoon."

"Ugly? Right. So relieved you like to hang out with ugly women — so, what did you and the ugly girls get up to?"

"We went to the Ex, drank a few beers back at one of the girls' places, and then I drove here."

"Are you serious? You spent the night with some other girl?"

He stops kissing me. "Not with another girl. There were some girls there but I wasn't with them."

"Don't fuck with me again," I say, throwing his line back at him.

We stay hidden in the shadow of the house, kissing until the midnight train blows its whistle. "Come on, we can't stay here," I say, taking his hand.

The barn smells of hay and chicken poop. I pull a blanket from the sleigh and lay it down on top of the prickles of hay. "What the . . . Lydia, are there fleas in here? I'm so itchy," Brady says and scratches wildly at his back.

"I doubt it, but maybe the chickens have them; they sleep in the next stall."

"Come here. If I'm going to get eaten alive I might as well be enjoying it," he says.

I have an eerie out of body sensation. It's like I am hovering above, watching us kiss for a second, then smack, I'm back inside me again. His T-shirt smells a bit like cigarette smoke and a lot like fried food. "You have an amazing chest," he says.

"Thanks." He slides his hand into my panties. His touch feels good. My hand reaches inside his rugby pants. I hold his penis, exploring it with my hand. I didn't realize guys can get it up when they're drunk. "The penis is a weird appendage," I say.

"Are you ready?" he whispers.

"For what?" I say. He's brought a condom. I'm sure I should be insulted that he thinks he can even have sex with me, in the barn, with him half drunk, but sex in general is so terrifying that it overrides my sense of self-worth. "I assure you, you'll want to be totally sober the first time we have sex."

"You're right — I will," he says.

His apathy makes me realize he's probably more than just half drunk.

I awake scratching my bare chest. Brady's passed out beside me. "You better go. We fell asleep," I whisper in his ear.

"Okay," he says with his eyes closed.

He walks back down the road to where he left his mom's car.

"Goodnight, Lydia!" he whispers too loudly.

I wave to him, slink into the house undetected, and float back up to bed — silent, like a goddess of the night.

TEN

Mary Jane leaves in two weeks. I am cold to her and a little bitchy. It's punishment for leaving me in charge of the nuthouse again. It's like she's already left me.

"Mom's taking us into Saskatoon for back-to-school shopping," Victoria says, as though she's won a shopping spree at Harrods.

"It's August, for God's sake! I don't even want to think about that hick school," I say.

"She leaves soon. It's the last chance you'll get."

I sit begrudgingly in the pickup, behind Mommy Dearest and Prissy Tits. I refuse to acknowledge that this is back-to-school shopping. "We're picking out our prison uniforms," I say, from the back seat.

Mary Jane waits until we've parked downtown to tell us her plans. "We don't have much money," she says, then leads us suspiciously close to her favourite hangout and stops in front of the revolving doors. "The flyer said they have a new shipment of fall pants."

"Have you lost it again? The effing Army and Navy?" Mary Jane ignores me. "I'm not going in. I don't wear clothes from there."

"It's this or nothing," Mary Jane says, and she means it.

I stay behind Victoria and slink into the store. We stop on the first floor, in the men's department, under a sale sign, at a table of neatly folded pants. "For God's sake, Mother, they're men's!" I shout.

"Stop it! If you can't behave, go back out to the car," Mary Jane says.

Victoria holds up a pair of army-style khakis. "What do you think, Lydia?" she says.

I admit, they do look kind of macho-girl cool. They will definitely stand out at Hicksville High. "They're different!" I say sarcastically, using one of Mary Jane's favourite lines. So, it's seriously men's pants or nothing . . . I cave.

Once we get home, Victoria and I run up to try them on. On examination in the mirror, I say, "They look sort of cool. Who would have thought?"

"You don't think they're too baggy?" Victoria says, pulling at the puffy fabric.

"They're not supposed to be fitted," I say.

She sits down on my bed. You can tell that they are men's. Victoria's crotch balloons forth like she's stuffed a couple of socks down the front. I sit beside her. My crotch balloons forth too, like a boy in heat. Victoria's eyes bulge in shock. "I've got a stiffy!" she shouts.

I become hysterical with laughter. We roll all over my bed and end up in a pile on the floor. Victoria laughs so hard she starts wheezing. "I'm going to piss my pants, move off me!" I shout. I take a few deep breaths.

The phone rings, I wait for the double and then the single. Yup, it's for us.

"Telephone for you, Lydia!" Mary Jane shouts.

Victoria eavesdrops from the landing on the stairs, watching with curious eyes. I keep my voice low and turn my back to her.

"I started playing for the Blades," Brady says.

"What are you talking about? The hockey team?"

"Yeah, the Saskatoon Blades."

"How?"

"I'm an AP for the Blades. I replace a defenceman if he gets hurt — he got hurt."

"What does it mean? Are you moving to Saskatoon? Will you have to quit school?"

"I'll finish grade twelve in Saskatoon — Evan Hardy. I'll board with my aunt."

"Wow — congratulations — I guess. When do you start?"

"I'm moving into my aunt's place this weekend. I started practice with the Blades yesterday."

"Yesterday?" I shout accidentally then regain my composure. "What happens when the guy gets better?"

"I'll go back to Junior A — he's off for awhile though. He's hurt pretty bad."

"What happened to him?"

"Broken neck."

"Jesus!" I say with far too much emotion. I subdue my voice and say, "Okay, thanks for the update — I gotta go. Bye."

My composure is all for nothing though, because as soon as I hang up the phone, I burst into tears. It is so unlike me, full out crying. I run up to my room, slam the door, and cry for about two minutes, then I get angry. The huge balloon crotch of my Army and Navy specials sums up my empty life. I punch the fabric flat with my fists. "Brady is a liar! A big fat fucking liar!" I shout. The world is full of big fat fucking liars. He can join the long line of losers leaving me. Hockey's all that matters to him.

I immediately start to separate from him. It's a mental process ice queens excel at. I tell Victoria to say I am out when he calls back.

Alex loads Mary Jane's bags into the back of the truck. We say goodbye in the front yard. I hug Mary Jane and hold on to her. I cannot speak. My throat is tight. I don't know why I cannot see past our parting. Intellectually, I know she'll be back in four months and in just two for a visit. But my body doesn't get it.

Mary Jane waves, until I can't see her anymore. I sit on the top of the dirt pile, left over from when they dug the new well. The cloud of dust disappears as the truck turns onto the main road. I climb the mountain of stairs to the tower, my mind feels heavy, like it's soaked in grey goop.

Victoria — she's startled me. She stands at my bedroom door, an angel in pink frills and cocoa dust. "I thought you could use these," she says. She presents me with a pan of double chocolate brownies. She leaves me with the entire pan, pink floating away. I cry muted, wet tears. They splash onto the white chocolate ganache, leaving shiny polka dots. The ache inside of me has eaten a hole too big to ever be filled. But I am going to try, starting with the brownies.

Alex is on the back porch. I smell him, though only the red glow of his cigar is visible. I sit outside on the back steps and listen to the crickets. A flock of moths and insects fight in the yard light, trying to get closer. I feel the same way about the summer. Please don't leave me, sun; stay near and keep me warm. I cannot endure being frozen away in ice again. One moth is fantastically huge. Its wingspan is as wide as a robin's, as magnificent as a bird's. But the poor thing is not a bird. Its beautiful wings have let it down. It will not fly away and follow the sun. It will die here. The cold will freeze it solid. I don't want to be a moth, destined to die here. I am a bird. Wait for me, crows. I need to follow the sun.

I can't even think about starting school. It's all too tragic.

Alex has left his lair. I pull open the screen door. He's in the kitchen concocting a coal tar shake and singing "Hotel California" in a voice as flat as Saskatchewan.

"Is it true, Dad? Did your grandfather really disappear in a blizzard?"

"I don't know — where did you hear that?"

"How'd he die then?"

"I don't know. Heart, I think. They might have found him in the winter. I can't remember. It would have been his heart though. If there were livestock missing, he would have been out there looking for them, blizzard or no blizzard — why?"

"Just trying to sort out the ghosts around here."

"There are no ghosts here," he says and takes his drink into the family room. "I have good news," he says from his La-Z-Boy.

"What?"

"I start teaching at the University of Regina next week."

"How? You live here."

"I teach two night classes, Tuesday and Thursday. I'll overnight in Regina for three nights and be back in Saskatoon to teach the Friday course at the U of S."

"You're leaving us alone?"

"For three nights. Your mother and I will only be a phone call away."

"What? I'm supposed to look after Greaseball all by myself?"

"Settle down, Lydia — it's not Victoria we're worried about."

"Yeah, well — you should be," I say.

Victoria and I trapped alone on the land . . . he'll take the truck. "I'll be turning sixteen soon. I want to get my license right away."

"I won't have time to take you until the Christmas break."

"That's impossible! I'll need a car before that if we're going to be left alone on this fucking land four days a week."

"Watch your language — we can't afford it, not with your mother's tuition. Why do you think I'm taking this job in Regina?"

"How in the hell are Victoria and I going to survive?" I slump over the kitchen table and bury my head in my arms.

"I thought you might be interested in this," Alex says and thrusts a newspaper in front of me: yesterday's *StarPhoenix* — an article about the Blades with a photograph of the new lineup. Brady. Tears sting my eyes. I don't look up from the paper until Alex has left the kitchen.

ELEVEN

Victoria's parted her hair straight down the middle. It hangs down the sides of her serious face. She stopped washing it the day Mary Jane left. Mary Jane would be calling her Oil Can Harry by now. She doesn't get it. Fashion is about protest; you make a statement with your clothes, not your hygiene. I hold my tongue and try not to catch a whiff of the little street urchin. I'm too lonely to piss off my only confidante. She's decided to give the new Army and Navy pants a try. I'm not as brave. I wear black jeans and a black T-shirt.

The bus makes its way down the gravel road towards the house, like a giant yellow beast, spewing dust across the fields, looking for teens to inhale — a rerun of a horror movie I don't want to star in anymore.

I shut down all my emotions and walk into the school like a zombie. It is the only way to survive. My biggest, most horrible nightmare is a reality: Mr. Kent is gone and Pervert Pants Polinski is back. First Mary Jane, then Brady, and now Mr. Kent. Polinski is murdering *Macbeth*: "out, damned spot!" Shakespeare is painful without Mr. Kent.

I eat lunch with Michelle on the sidewalk in front of the school. The schoolyard is lower than the sidewalk so we hang our legs over the edge. I eat the peanut butter sandwich that Victoria made while Michelle smokes. "Must be nice to live in town," I lie. "Don't you ever feel like going home for lunch?" Michelle takes one long drag and lets it out slowly. "What? What are you smiling about?"

"I'm seeing someone," she says, pressing the end of her cigarette into the sidewalk.

"Who?" I say, afraid to know what pimply-faced farm geek she's stooped low enough to make out with.

"You wouldn't know him. He's older."

"Come on! Spill it." A sudden wave of panic surges through me. Has she somehow managed to hook up with Mr. Kent?

"Clint. Clint Dyck."

"Who is he?"

"He graduated about five years ago. He works at the gas station on the highway."

"Any relation?" She gives me a nasty look. I guess it is rude of me, but in this town it's a viable question.

"Only very distantly," she says after lighting up another cigarette. "Like fourth cousins once removed or something."

Victoria's eyes are fixed out the bus window. I know that look. Her day must have topped mine. As soon as the bus stops at our place, she bolts off the bus and heads to the basement. I follow out of curiosity. She's in the middle of an aggressive strip down: kicking off her new Army and Navy pants. She opens the furnace and stuffs them inside as though to burn them, but it is only September and Alex hasn't started the fire.

"What's up?"

"Some asshole made a crack about these fucking pants," she says, stuffing them further into the furnace ashes.

"Who?"

"Some shithead in my class — he said I look lik Polinski — in track pants — with a stiffy!"

I try hard to stifle a laugh but I can't. My snorts send Victoria into a rage and she stomps up the stairs, half sobbing, half screaming, leaving her "cool" new pants lying at the bottom of the furnace, covered in ashes, waiting for the first flames of winter.

I decide to sit on the back porch. Oddly, as the only mature person left in the house, I'm drawn to the orange chair to ponder. Our Barbies still sit in the corner where we last left them. We haven't played in ages. They sit, frozen in time, staring out the camper windows, waiting to get the hell out of here.

Victoria stays barricaded in her room. Somehow she's taken my laughing at the pants comment as an even bigger slight than the original comment made by the pervert. As soon as she spots the truck from her bedroom window, she charges down the stairs and meets Alex at the entrance before he even has a chance to take off his shoes. "I need money. I'm joining 4-H. Twyla's mom said she'll pick me up and take me with them each week. The first meeting is tomorrow. From then on we meet Wednesday evenings."

"Slow down. Repeat yourself slowly — enunciate," he says.

I haven't figured out his listening glitch yet. Is he really too stupid to understand what we say the first time, or is it his way of torturing us?

"Forget it. All you need to know is that I need thirty-five dollars by tomorrow," she says, slamming her bony hand on the kitchen table.

Alex is a little afraid of her. I can tell by the clueless look that washes over his tired face. If he agrees to it, it means on Wednesdays, Marx and I will be totally alone on the farm. We hear things when we're alone — ghosts — the murdered and the messed up.

Deirdre phones after supper. She's one of Alex's colleagues, a communist like him. The one Mary Jane doesn't like. He's out in the barn working in his office, with strict instructions not to bother him or risk death. I kind of guess that her phone call might be important to him, but I take it upon myself to filter out any unwanted distractions. "He's indisposed," I say, deadpan. She won't leave a message but I know it's her.

Victoria is drawing horses in her bedroom. She seems content, as though 4-H is a done deal. "Victoria, urgent meeting under the captain's bed," I say. We meet under her bed now, whenever we need to spill our guts. It muffles the sound so no one can over hear us through the big heat vent.

"Give me a minute," she says, then drops her pencil into its case and tucks her stringy hair behind her ears, almost in slow motion.

"She better not be sniffing around, now that Mary Jane is temporarily out of the picture — she has this seriously sexy woman's voice. Maybe it works on Alex, but it leaves me cold."

"He's having an affair. I know it. Just wait until Mom finds out," she spits in anger.

"Victoria! You can't tell her. You don't even know if it's true. Some chick from work phones Alex. That's all we know for sure." She pushes out the bed with force. I've unwittingly unleashed the wrath of Victoria.

As soon as Alex walks in from the barn, she's on him. "Deirdre called tonight. Are you having an affair?" she demands, like his wife.

Alex laughs. His face flushes as he pulls off his toque and rubs at the red rim around his forehead. "Hit the sack. It's past your bed time," he says. He walks past me and down the basement stairs. I notice he didn't deny it.

⚡

I regret supporting the 4-H aspirations. 4-H takes Victoria away from me every bloody night of the week and weekends too. If it isn't a meeting, it's a show or practicing and prepping for the show. Victoria is either out in the barn or out in the field, riding. Without Mary Jane here to take me into Saskatoon to buy the occasional piece of fabric, I can't even sew. It's bad enough being bored out of my mind, but I look pathetic too. I either have to wear all of last year's outfits or look like a transvestite with a perpetual stiffy in the men's army pants.

I am alone, alone in a haunted house. That's what Mark called it. Mark, the guy won't even look at me in the halls since Brady left. Coward. Too afraid to be seen talking to the ice princess. Brady's gone the way of Mary Jane and Mr. Kent — gone, gone, gone — everyone, except me. Tears drop into the peanut butter jar. I wipe my runny nose with my hand as I prepare supper. I don't wash my hands. I'm the only one eating tonight.

The orange chair looks macabre without Alex sitting in it. I never thought I'd miss him. I wish he were home tonight, blowing smoke rings in front of the hockey game. "Marx! Hurry boy, get your ass in here and quick!" I yell into the black night. I pull shut the screen door and wait for him inside the safety of the back porch. Marx's floppy face bangs on the screen unexpectedly. I let him in fast and lock the screen door, the inside door, and the back porch door before breathing again.

Twyla's mom's truck deposits Victoria under the yard light just as *Family Ties* is ending. I watch the last few minutes, waiting for my lovely shit-ster. After ten minutes I realize she's not coming in. The barn light is on.

Silver is tied in the first barn stall. Her coat is silky, smooth. "She smells like Mom."

"I used Mom's conditioner on her," Victoria says.

"When is the monumental event?" I say and watch her comb the knots out of Silver's long tail.

"Saturday morning, early. Alex's renting the horse trailer and will bring it home tomorrow night," she says.

It's ironic how much energy she puts into grooming Silver, and yet her own hair remains an oily helmet. She combs it daily, yes, but why she bothers, I'll never understand. It continues to hang, parted in the middle, in flat, oily strands. "What are you going to wear?"

"I borrowed a cowgirl outfit from Twyla."

"That brown polyester thing?" I say, unable to hide my distaste.

"I hate it but I get points off unless I dress Western — did you see Napoleon's saddle? Over there, on Alex's desk. He's lending me his best one and the blanket too," Victoria says.

"The suit's not so bad — looks nineteen fifties cowgirl — Patsy Cline," I say and stroke the gleaming leather knob on Napoleon's saddle. "But this — this is amazing — so posh. The black will look good on Silver. I can help you with your hair. If you wash it, I'll French braid it — weave black ribbon through the braids to match the saddle."

I open the barn door to leave. "Okay," she says to my back.

⚡

Victoria's pacing. She's wearing the brown polyester suit with the bold white stitching and oversized lapels. The suit screams, "I'm a seventies rhinestone cowgirl, but I don't let on." I don't know who's better groomed, Silver or Victoria with her fresh-washed, French braided, golden hair. The get up is only a test run. I'll have to braid her hair again in the morning.

At 10:00 PM Victoria spots headlights on our road. It's Alex, sans the horse trailer. Victoria runs to greet him. His hair is a mess and he has grease marks all up his sleeves. "The truck died on University Drive. I had it towed to Canadian Tire," he says, then rubs his forehead with his dirty hand. "The rental place was closed by the time I got there. I'll try first thing in the morning." He drops a stack of papers and a filthy car part onto the kitchen counter.

"It doesn't open until ten. My first event is at nine thirty," Victoria says.

"I'll have it here as soon as I can. You might have to miss the first event." Alex says and disappears down to the dungeon.

If he can't pick the trailer up until ten, it means he'll first have to swing by here and load Silver. That will take at least an hour. Victoria won't arrive at the arena until almost noon. Victoria's obviously done the same math. She looks about to cry but instead she bolts to the barn where beautiful Silver waits in her stall.

I call Mary Jane. She shouts into the phone, "I don't know what you expect me to do about it from here!"

Granddad gets on the line, "Is this Lydia again? I want you to quit calling your mother with every little problem out there in Saskatchewan. You're upsetting her!" He hangs up the phone. I don't even get to say goodbye to Mary Jane.

Victoria's back from the barn. She dials Twyla's number.

"Don't do it, Victoria. I'll think of some way we can get Silver there."

"Sorry. My dad couldn't get a trailer. I can't make the show — bye," she says and hangs up the phone. "It's too late. I let her go. She's out in the pasture rolling by now," she says.

⚡

Victoria comes down for breakfast in her housecoat over jeans. She's unbraided her hair and it sticks out wildly all over her head. She won't talk to me, won't even make eye contact. "What is this? Why is it suddenly my fault?"

She ignores me. I used to feel sorry for her, but now she deserves what she gets. She leaves to ride Silver.

It is her longest ride ever. She doesn't come home until suppertime. She almost had me worried.

⚡

I awake suddenly to a horn blasting outside of my window. I jump out of bed and run into the sewing room to look out the front window. "Holy shit. It's the bus. We slept in, Victoria — what time is it?" The horn blasts again. I lie down on her bedroom floor. "Get down!" I hiss as Victoria steps from her bed. "Don't let Jim see you."

"Okay, I'm down, I'm down," she whispers.

We wait, paralyzed on the floor. Jim blasts the horn one more time and then the bus drives away. I wait a few minutes before I have the nerve to get up and check. The bus pulls onto the main road. Victoria grins like she just devoured Alex's secret stash of candy bars.

TWELVE

The three nauseating flypapers hanging in the kitchen are completely covered in dead flies. No one has changed them since before Mary Jane left. The flies moved inside about a month ago, hoping to get another month of life. Fools.

I've had nothing to eat all day and it's almost noon. Alex forgot to pick up groceries before he took off. He gave me cash to pick up a few necessities during noon hour at the overpriced mini-market in Hicksville; however, as I no longer ride the school bus into Hicksville, it has yet to happen. There are sacrifices to be made to remain home-schooled. If food must be that sacrifice, then so be it. Victoria and I manage to get by on scraps from the cupboards and freezer. Peanuts fried with a little canola oil, sprinkled over white rice with soy sauce on top is my latest supper specialty. I open the freezer again, mainly out of habit. Victoria slams it shut. "Don't bother. I already checked. There's nothing."

"Orange juice?"

"Nope. It's empty."

She whirls around as fast as lightening and smacks the window behind me. "Yes! Got him. That's number twenty-six already today and all before breakfast." Victoria holds up her hand, and I give her a high five.

"Way to go, cowgirl. You beat Mary Jane's record, twenty-four before breakfast — fuck, I am starving."

"You swear a lot," Victoria says.

"Yeah? I don't know why, I just do."

"Wait here; I have an idea," she says, then runs down to check out Alex's closet stash.

I rummage through the baking cupboard beside the stove. The cupboard holds all the usual inedibles: flour, salt, baking soda, sugar. Hiding behind Alex's giant no-name coffee can is a box of white Bakers Chocolate and a tin of cocoa. How could we have missed them?

Victoria barrels up the stairs, excited and out of breath. "Lydia, I have a surprise for you," she sings. She holds up two cans of beer, Alex's light beer.

"You're brilliant!" I say, and snatch the beers and place them in the freezer.

I hold up the chocolate.

Her smile says she's about to trump the chocolate. She lifts a big fat Cuban cigar from the back pocket of her cut-offs.

"You're not going to rip it up, then?" I say.

She shakes her head. "Not this baby. It has our names on it."

"Where's my *Seventeen* magazine? I need the recipe in there for double chocolate brownies." The phone rings — our ring. "Don't answer it!"

"What if it's Mom?"

"It's not. She thinks we're at school — it's gotta be Horney Forney — or Binstead. New rule, no one answers that phone unless Alex is home — then one of us has to get to it first — got it?"

"Got it."

Grasshoppers leap diagonally from each step. I am Moses, parting a sea of gold. We walk the Carleton Trail, our trail. The sky is brilliant, not even a wisp of a cloud, an ocean-deep hue. Victoria's long toffee-coloured hair shines and her skinny arms are still freckled from the prairie summer. My tanned legs stick out beneath my cut-offs, looking lean and strong. I toss my long blonde hair, hoping to catch it shining in the sun.

"We need to go to Japan," I say.

"Why?"

"We could make big money there. They love blondes. We could be models."

We walk along in silence for a few minutes. "Okay, I'll go with you," Victoria says. I break into an enthusiastic skip. Maybe we will get off this wretched land one day. We skip awkwardly in our cowboy boots to the far eastern corner of our section. Victoria throws the Mexican blanket onto the grass. The cold, bitter beer quenches the sweet chocolate brownie rush. We dig in with abandon, giddy and crazed, alcohol and sugar sending our brains into drug-induced mania. I stuff an empty beer can in my shorts.

"Dear little Victoria, let me be your father figure; you can call me Mr. P. P. Polinski. Oh my, there's a crumb of chocolate on your booby. Let me brush it off," I say with a lecherous laugh and chase Victoria all around the blanket. I've never laughed so hard. I've never eaten nearly an entire pan of brownies in one sitting before either. Everything is amusing. Even the smile on Victoria's face is rapturously silly. Her mouth is filthy, chocolate oozing out from between her teeth.

"We are here, and we are amazing!" shouts Victoria. She's all arms and legs, bouncing around the field.

"We are the centre of the universe!" I yell.

Marx leaps and barks, circling us, wanting so badly for us to chase his big crazy arse all over the pasture. The cattle have found us, all lined up, our audience of peers. I feel their energy, like true friends. Victoria makes a T with her hands. "Time out — I think I'm going to puke — okay, which one of you hates Alex?" she says.

"That would be Cleopatra. She's the one who charges him every time he walks into the corral — the one with the broad forehead and big ears."

Victoria studies the row of brown and white faces, square snouts, and wide foreheads. "That would be all of them," she says.

"That's her. See? Big forehead girl," I say, pointing to the cow with extra big ears. Hiding behind her is the smallest steer. "She's Caesar's mom."

We lie on the blanket. Victoria pulls out the Cuban cigar and tries to light it when suddenly the cows spook, bolting from view instantly. A huge shadow darkens the blanket, followed by an unearthly roar, like a dragon spitting fire. Armageddon is upon us. Above, hovering like a mythical beast in the sky, is a giant hot-air balloon. Inside stands a lone man.

"Who the fuck is that?" Victoria says as she shields her eyes from the sun's glare.

"Why the fuck is he flying so low? He nearly hit us."

The balloon gains altitude and floats across the pasture without so much as a wave from the lone occupant. "Maybe it's a sign. Maybe he's God. Maybe, in some weird way, we are the centre of the universe." Victoria says.

"No. God's a woman — but you're right. We are the centre. Like the centre of a tornado is a vacuum — nothing there."

"We are nothing?" Victoria says.

"Perhaps — thank you, who ever the hell you are, for bloody well pointing out the obvious!" I shout.

"You're flying lower than the balloon," Victoria says, then points to my crotch.

I zip up my cut-offs. The zipper separates instantly. The beer can must have blown it out while I was dancing.

We walk back as the sun begins to set.

"That was weird. Wasn't it?" Victoria says.

"Yeah — a parallel universe — I changed my mind, by the way."

"About what?"

"God's no woman."

"Okay."

"No woman would have created such a fucked-up world."

Alex, the control freak, is home. He mistakenly thinks that he is still in charge. However, I run the farm all week, which counts for four out of seven days. He is only home for three. It only makes sense that I am in charge, at the very least, of myself.

"You are not staying up past nine thirty and that's an order. As long as you're living under my roof, you'll do what I tell you to." He parks his ass smack in front of the TV with a beer in hand and a toque on his head.

"Your food? *What* food is more like it. You have us on soldier's rations. There's nothing in this house but dog food." I sprint to my room and lock the door. I let him think that he's won, then I sneak around and do what I want. There's nothing to do down there anyway. All night long it's hockey and beer, then a Cuban cigar will be unveiled sometime during first period. I hope to God he doesn't notice one's missing; I'll blame it on the anti-smoking crusader if he does. I turn my ghetto blaster on low. Bowie to the rescue.

Alex is shouting at someone — either Marx, Victoria, or the phone. I turn down Bowie and listen. It sounds like Mary Jane and Alex are at it again down there but they're not. It's the pink-robed goddess and Alex. Their fighting is perversely comforting. "I hate you! You can't tell me what to do. I'm watching my show — now! Get out of my way," Victoria shouts.

"Hey, stop it! That hurts," Alex says.

I'm sure she's punching him. She's done it before. She's nuts. It's quiet for about five minutes then the front door slams shut and the truck starts. I run to the sewing room window. Our truck pulls onto the main road. *The Facts of Life* is on the TV. She's won. He's taken off to Regina early and left me here to deal with the little bitch. He saves himself and lets me burn. I don't know who makes me more ill, Alex or Victoria. They're both tyrants. I'd like to be Alex right now, driving off, down the road, away from Victoria, the house, and the land.

Prissy Tits is back with a vengeance and she thinks she's going back to school.

"Who are you trying to kid? You've been enjoying home schooling as much as I have."

"Stay home if you want. I'm going," she says.

I don't want to be the only delinquent in the family. I pull on black jeans, which are now too loose, and a black turtleneck.

Polinski calls me to his desk just as first period starts.

"What's this?" he says, pointing to Alex's scribbled signature. It's a form for some field trip. I don't even remember filling it out, though I recognize my fake attempt at Alex's hairball signature.

"What? It's my dad's signature."

"You're telling me that this is your father's actual signature?" He raises his thin brows at me. "Well?"

"I already told you that it is," I say flatly.

"That's all. You're dismissed," he says.

When he says "dismissed", my brain hears "suspended". I glance up, hopeful.

"Sit down, Lydia," he says, annoyed.

As third period ends, the classroom intercom orders me down to Binstead's office.

My stomach knots into a tight fist. I squirm in the chair to alleviate the pain. "Sit still, Miss Buckingham, and listen to what I'm telling you," Binstead says. My mouth starts to tremble. I cannot stop it. "Both you and your sister have missed far too much school this term, and I have been unable to reach either of your parents to discuss the problem. Why are you not attending classes?" He pushes up his glasses with his middle finger and leans across his desk. "And how might I reach your parents?"

Damn, I guess Lydie and Vic from the parallel universe haven't been attending classes for us while we've been away. "I've had appointments."

"Appointments?"

"I'm getting braces."

"How does one miss an entire month of school over braces?"

"It hasn't been a month," I say defensively. "I go to the orthodontist in Saskatoon — a lot."

He sighs, pushing his belly out until it touches the front of his desk. The white skin and black hairs on his belly poke out between his shirt buttons. "How can I get in touch with your parents?"

"My dad teaches at the U of S and the U of R. He travels a lot, back and forth, but he's home every night, late."

"What about your mother? Does she work outside the home?"

"My mom's out of town for a few weeks — visiting family."

His nasal breathing is peculiarly audible, and the black hairs on his belly are disturbing. I want to bolt.

"That doesn't explain Victoria's absences," he says calmly.

"Her teeth are crooked too."

He sits back in his chair, taking his black belly hairs with him. He drops his voice and leans forward abruptly. This time his chest hits the desk. "Miss Buckingham, Lydia — you and your sister are not yet sixteen. It is unlawful for either of you to deliberately miss school. I want you to realize the gravity of your situation. If you don't start attending classes regularly, I'll have to notify social services. I'll be mailing a letter to your parents to set up a meeting."

The hall is empty. I take a deep breath and focus on the fire escape door. Why did I ever let Victoria trick me into coming back? Alex cannot find out about this. I must remain vigilant about checking the mail. I'll wait until the letter arrives, then I'll officially phone Jim and tell him no we'll no longer be riding the bus.

Victoria walks down the hall towards Binstead's office. "Tell him we've been at the orthodontist," I whisper as she passes. "Whatever you do, don't tell him that Alex is away all week." She nods and steps into his office.

I wake up to Bowie crooning "Let's Dance" and get ready for school for one reason; it's my ticket out of Hicksville for one precious day. We're finally going on a field trip to Saskatoon. I pull on a jean miniskirt and tie-dyed tights for the occasion.

Michelle is back. She's hardly ever at school anymore either. I wonder if they give her the third degree? I haven't talked to her in ages — obviously, because we're never at school on the same day, except today. Maybe she doesn't want to miss a chance to go to the university to see *Macbeth* either. I sit beside her on the bus. I don't ask why she's never at school for fear she'll reciprocate the question. No one can know about Victoria and me. Like Binstead said, social services might start sniffing around.

The yellow school bus, bursting with dweebs, pulls onto the campus. Sophisticated college people are everywhere, and I have to be lumped in with the Hicksville High gang.

Some hick behind me cracks a loud burp, probably Nathan Dyck; he's the one laughing hysterically. Polinski's "Enough!" shuts him up momentarily. The scent of dry ice spreads through the seating area. Stage lights suddenly illuminate three hunchback witches gathered around a caldron of dry ice, chanting, "By the pricking of my thumbs, something wicked this way comes."

I sit through the next scene of average looking guys and boring soldier chit-chat until the witches come back. Dancing witches are awesome. Suddenly, one buff Macbeth walks on stage. "Macbeth is hot," I whisper to Michelle.

"He's all right," she says, trying to appear uninterested.

We walk through the campus to the cafeteria. It's Friday, so there is a possibility I might run into Alex. He teaches here on Fridays. I order fries and Hawaiian pizza. It is delicious, my first real meal in weeks. All the guys in my class are acting like total morons, trying to draw attention to themselves. "Hey, party tonight on Strawberry Hill," Nathan Dyck shouts to every female within ear range. He has fries stuck to his braces. I actually feel pity for the guy. Braces and zits, yet he has the clueless confidence to try and chat up university girls.

"Some of these college guys are really hot," I say.

"You're funny — you should come to Strawberry Hill on the weekend. You might get along with Clint's older brother — but you have to like to party. I mean, *really* party," Michelle says. She hasn't eaten a thing. She holds an unlit cigarette under the table, like she's waiting to light it any minute.

"Maybe I will," I say, highly doubting it. Clint's got to be at least twenty-three, and if his brother is older than that and hanging out at high school bush parties . . . loser! Polinski announces it's time to walk back to the bus. I slow down my pace, trying to distance myself from the class. We walk past Louis', the campus bar (named for my hero). I bet it's full of interesting people, not just a bunch of boring old communists like Alex, as he's tried to convince me. I glance through the glass doors, trying to see inside. I stop. Michelle stops. Alex, my father, stands just inside the glass doors. "It's my dad," I say. "I'll catch up with you in a bit. I want to go in and say hello."

I walk to the doors, nervous to even open them, as I'm not legally allowed into a bar for three more years, plus a few weeks. Alex is talking to someone, a woman only a few years older than me. His hand holds her arm as they talk and slides its way down to her hand before letting her go. She walks towards the doors, towards me, as Alex disappears down a staircase inside.

I run fast, catching up with the class, and hide amongst them. I look back, catching a glimpse of her shoulder length brown hair and tan mini skirt. I might puke. The pizza and fries were too rich for my stomach. I take the empty seat at the front of the bus not realizing until it's too late that Polinski's across from me. His shiny brown loafers with their black rubber mudguards look like clown shoes on him. I cross my arms over my chest and stare out the window at the elegant stone buildings. Our stones, our rocks, our godforsaken land built this university. For once, I just want to get back to those rocks and stones and hide inside our godforsaken house.

Fuck that father of mine. He's a pervert like the rest of them. If he doesn't come home this weekend, I'll know what he's up to. I can't tell Victoria; she'll go ballistic.

I try to avoid Alex all weekend. He is a stranger to me. And the weirdest thing is that he seems to be enjoying our estrangement. He is perversely jolly hanging out by himself. He whistles to himself as he makes his coffee and tells himself jokes as he butters stale toast. "That's for sure Alexi — for sure — for Shirley — no, for Betty!" I smile secretly at that one. It's so stupid, it's funny.

Victoria can't stand the quiet dissonance. She marches into the kitchen to wash dishes, as though she's some kind of a neat freak. It's a joke because the house is a pigsty. No one has vacuumed or washed a floor since Mary Jane left. It's only an excuse for her to bang the pots and pans around and break a couple of dishes by slamming them down on the counter to annoy Alex as he tries to eat his breakfast. "Easy, easy," he says, then scurries into the back porch with his toast and coffee.

THIRTEEN

Happy Birthday to me! I'm sexy and sixteen. Mary Jane phones after school, not that we even went. She' s bringing my present with her when she comes home for Thanksgiving. She sounds like the Mary Jane I've been missing since we moved here. Vancouver Mary Jane is back. She seems to exist in yet another parallel universe: a universe that is happening at the same time as the one I'm moving through, but one I can't access.

"Is Victoria helping you with the cake?" she asks.

She obviously has no idea about the grocery situation around here. I'd be eating air if Victoria and I hadn't sacrificed our freedom and made a shopping trip into Hicksville during lunch hour yesterday, spending the last of Alex's grocery money on baking supplies. "Yep, she's starting it now," I say, omitting the details. I don't want to endure the wrath of Granddad again, telling me to quit burdening my fragile mother with all of my problems. I don't hear from Alex. He's not good with birthdays.

"It's the most fantastic cake I've ever seen. It's almost too beautiful to eat," I say.

"Forget that! I'm eating this thing. I spent the last of our grocery money on the food colouring," Victoria says.

I sit down at the kitchen table, "We have a cake. Boy do we have a cake — but no place to go. Piss pockets, I'm bored already."

Victoria pulls out a chair and sits beside me. My words seem to have had a sobering effect on both of us. "You never give up that easy," she says.

"You're right, this is my sweet sixteenth. If I allow it to suck, I'll remember this depressing day for the rest of my life. It will bring my entire life down — I just thought of the perfect guest list."

"Who?"

Victoria looks so excited, I almost don't have the heart to follow through with my cruel joke. "Oh, just a couple of cuties — Nathan Dyck and the guy you kicked in the nuts, Balls McSquishy."

"Don't be an asshole. Come on, I thought you were serious," she says.

"Okay, let's just say, the sky's the limit. Where's the most bizarre setting you can think of to have a party?"

"That's a hard one — in the corral? Cow-pies and all," Victoria says.

I'm a little disappointed with her imagination, but beggars can't be choosers. We carry the kitchen table out to the corral, unscrewing the front legs to get it out the back porch door. It's awkward and heavy.

I take a rust-stained sheet from the linen closet and pull down the attic ladder. I reach for the light cord with my hand, refusing to even look up until the bulb turns on.

"Vic! Get up here, quick!" I yell.

Victoria arrives with her arms loaded with candles. "I found quite a few — for the table," she says.

"Come on, let's find something cool to put on," I say and open Mary Jane's trunk.

"Bring back any memories?" Victoria says, holding up the wide legged pants Mary Jane wore on the night she checked herself into the psych ward.

"Don't. I don't want to ruin my birthday."

Victoria picks out Mary Jane's old psychedelic, circle print minidress then holds up the silver platform sandals from the infamous Ziggy Stardust night.

"Go for it," I say and pull on jeans (with legs are so wide they look like a long denim skirt), a snakeskin belt, sequined halter top, and the only other shoes in the trunk — white patent leather, zipper go-go boots with the mother of all heels.

I plop my bag of makeup on the kitchen table. "No Ziggy tonight — just to be safe. I'm going for macabre," I say, then begin the delicate task of surrounding each of Victoria's eyes with black and orange eyeshadow. Victoria backcombs my hair into a lion's mane and then I backcomb her hair into a foot-high rat's nest and stick in yellow Post-it notes from the nothing drawer. "Lovely little butterflies."

We teeter through the spongy corral towards the elegantly set table and sit at opposite ends. The wind is just strong enough to extinguish every one of the candles. "To Lydia, on her sweet sixteenth. May this year bring you lots of cool times, happiness, and maybe even sex," Victoria says, raising a coal tar shake.

"Shut up! I'm too young for sex."

"You mean, you and Brady never did it?"

"I'm not saying."

"Guilty! Lydia had sex with Brady!" Victoria shouts for all the cattle to hear.

"Victoria groped McSquishy's balls!" I shout.

"Shut up, girl! Marx and I have a song for you." She howls like a wolf and that starts Marx. Silver and the cows gather closer to investigate. "Speech! Speech!" Victoria bangs her heels on the edge of the table.

"Thank you, thank you, my esteemed guests. Being a mature woman of sixteen, I have gathered a lot of wisdom in these past years, " I say, raising my shake in the direction of the cattle. I can't think of anything witty to say. Deep inside, the hole of nothingness is growing and threatens to extinguish my spirit of adventure. I stall for time, swinging my glass. Brady and those perfect teeth of his flash inside my mind. "Stay out of sloughs, they only lead to trouble," I say.

A chunk of cake lands on my parka. "Heads up, birthday girl," Victoria says. I dig into the tower of cake and hurl a wad of it at her. "Hey, no fair, you're messing my hair!" She plucks another chunk, tosses it but misses me.

"Hey, hot chick, you look good but you can't throw," I say.

She chases me like a deranged psych patient. The cattle spook, stampeding out of the corral. I hurl a chunk of cake at her face. She turns and the cake hits the back of Mary Jane's fringed jacket. "Careful with the suede! It's dry clean only," I say and snatch what's left of the cake as I sprint past the table.

"You be careful! You're the one throwing cake at it!" Victoria says and attempts to duck behind the water trough but slips and falls forward into the mud that surrounds it. She stands, covered in fresh cow-pie.

"Stay away from me!" I shout.

"I can't decide if it's cow or horse. It tastes like moldy salad," she says.

"You must be drunk on coal tar. That is so disgusting. Mary Jane's going to kill you. Her suede jacket is covered in shit."

The wind blasts through the corral. The tablecloth threatens to take flight. Victoria wipes her face on the edge of the sheet. "I'm going in," she says.

⚡

"Why won't Marx come in?" Victoria says, stepping into the kitchen from the back porch.

"Come on, it's your turn — forget Marx. He's still in the corral, vacuuming up all the cake he can find," I say, then laugh at the sight of Victoria.

"What's wrong? Do I still have some on me? Where's the crap?" she says.

"No, you're clean. You just look insane, iced like a cake."

"So do you. It looks like birds pooped icing all over your head — Puke! I keep tasting turd no matter how many times I brush my teeth."

"Okay — Victoria — the truth, remember? So, just how far have you gone with Mark?"

"Not very far. We only necked, not even any major boob touching."

"Well, that's good. You're too young for booby touching. Although, trust me, that guy wanted to touch your boobs and how."

"Shut up. Now your turn, truth or dare, birthday babe?"

Victoria's eyes are wild. "Dare," I say, knowing I'll regret it.

"I dare you to walk out to the cow cemetery — alone — no Marx," she says.

"Now?"

"March it."

The moon is nearly full so there is a little light. Bugger, I'm going to have to do this. "I'll need my parka." I pull off the platform boots and pull on my cowboy boots.

Victoria hands me the parka. "Hurry up. I'm going to watch you from the back porch — all the way there and back, no cheating. Come, Marx! Here boy!"

There must be no more cake crumbs because he bolts inside, nearly knocking me over. Stepping from the porch steps is difficult; it's dark and windy. Walking through the corral is easy enough, but once I hit the Carleton Trail fear crawls in. I walk in the tracks of the dead, soldiers heading into battle, never to return. I should have insisted on Marx. I walk fast, focused on the goal. After the big rock pile, it's only about a ten-minute walk. Focus on the rocks. Please, don't let the rocks be occupied by a family of coyotes. It's too dark. I want to turn up the moon.

I watch myself walk into the night. It's surreal, as though walking through a spooky dream. My breath sounds in my ears, my heart beats fast, and my nose drips. What if there's an entire pack of coyotes chewing on bones? They'll see me as a threat. Keep walking, girl, one eye open. I pass the rock pile. The rocks look like a pile of giant black horse turds. I don't stop to listen for coyotes.

Dark shapes protrude from the ground, far in the distance. The shapes become more defined, like delicate sculptures. I have arrived. I don't want to look at the alabaster bones glowing in the moonlight but I can't help myself. The top of the shape resembles a skull with horns. Our cattle have never had horns. Thunder sounds, or a freight train with no horn. I can't see them, but they're coming fast, thousands of hooves, pounding the earth — the buffalo. It's just my imagination . . . it's just my imagination. Breathe in and hold. Three, two, one, exhale . . . repeat. I run. I ran as fast as my legs will move. Their breath snorts on the back of my neck. I head for the dim yard light ahead. Damn Victoria! Damn myself! Why'd I ever let her talk me into this? I can't let go of the image, the glowing pile of bones, the pointed horns. It becomes a disturbing memory reel, and my mind derives some perverse satisfaction from replaying it over and over again as I run.

A ghostly apparition floats down the trail towards me. Could it be him, my elusive ghost date? The wind slides under my flared pants. I have to pee. As it drifts closer I see that it's not Louis Riel. It's Victoria with her housecoat, billowing behind her. She is out of breath by the time we meet. I slap her. "How dare you scare me like that! I thought you were a ghost."

"It's Brady," she says, between gasps. "He's waiting for you at the house."

"What? Brady's here? Why?"

Victoria is already running back to the house. I see she ditched the spiked sandals and is running in cowboy boots. My heart pounds in my head. He's come for my birthday. Oh God, he must still like me. I can't believe it.

"Help me, Vic! Get this icing out of my hair!" I yell.

We stop just outside the back porch. Victoria tries her best to pick out the large chunks of cake and icing, but I know I look a fright in my seventies clothes, frizzed hair, and icing makeup. I step into the porch, a nervous smile frozen on my lips. Victoria grabs my arm hard. It hurts. I glare at her, confused.

"You've been out feeding the chickens," she whispers. I nod. I pat my hair in a vain attempt to calm the electrocuted look. I throw the parka in the corner, on top of the Barbie camper.

Brady stands in the kitchen, trying not to laugh. "I like your new look," he says. His hair is shorter, straighter, his face a little thinner, his legs a little longer.

"Yes, well, I've been out with the chickens." I say in a prissy librarian voice.

"Happy birthday," he says, pulling a present from behind his back and handing it to me.

I blush. Victoria beams. "Open it, Lydia!" she says.

I feel a million eyes on me. My hands shake as I open it. It's a book, a big heavy book, *Paris The 1950s* — black and white photographs. "Thank you, I love it," I say. I peek up at him. Damn, our eyes connect. I feel like he can see right through me, to my hollow core. "Come and sit down — how's hockey?" I say as I walk into the living room and sit on the chesterfield.

"Good," he says, then sits down beside me.

There is enough awkward energy in the room to ignite us all. My billowing flared jeans touch his jeans at the knee. I try to catch a whiff of him, for old times sake, but all I smell is the chemical scent of food colouring from the icing squished in my hair.

"Where's your dad?"

"Regina — he teaches there all week."

"Lydia and I run the place now," Victoria says triumphantly, "and no one gets in our way," she adds.

"Victoria, why don't you run down and check if Alex left any beer."

"You know there's nothing down there."

She clasps her hands together and firmly plants them on her lap. She's not going to budge.

"Would you like to go for a drive?" Brady says, looking at me.

Victoria's mouth drops open.

"Sure, I guess so. I'll be back in a little while, okay, Vic?"

She flies from the winged chair and up the stairs.

"Did I do that?"

"Don't worry about her, she's moody," I say.

Guilt wriggles in; it's been our private party until now then I go and dump her. "Be back in five, Victoria!" I yell up the stairs.

Brady drives an almost brand new truck. The heater is divine. I crank it up full blast and aim all the vents at myself. "When did you get the truck?"

"September — my mom and Bill helped me out a little." He turns off the main road towards the river, stopping on the bank.

"Don't cut the engine. I'm addicted to the heat," I say.

"How have you been?" he says.

"Good — and you?"

He stares ahead, out the front window at the black river. The moonlight reflects off the dark river, reminding me of the Van Gogh painting, *Starry Night over the Rhone.*

"I've missed you," he says.

I can't speak. The words are trapped in my throat. I reach for his hand and hold it. I can't help myself. I need to touch his skin. He leans towards me. His nose presses against my head, smelling my hair. It must stink with all the hair spray and icing. I turn my face towards his. "I wouldn't do that if I were you, " I say. He kisses me. I kiss him back.

"Do what?" he says and kisses me again.

"Touch my hair. It's full of stuff," I say.

"I noticed," he says.

His hands slide under the halter top. He is in luck because I'm not wearing a bra. He pulls down the sequined top. I watch him, kissing my breasts. It is as though it's happening to some other girl and I am the watcher. Everything is in continual motion. He pulls at the waist of the flared jeans. They are too big for me and slide off easily. He unzips his jeans. I am too young for this. But it is my birthday and if anything will make my sixteenth memorable this is it. My underwear is the next to go. "I don't want to be naked alone," I say, pulling at his jeans. "Come on, get rid of them."

His skin is soft and prickly at the same time. We flow in and out of each other. His skin becomes smoother and warmer until I no longer feel anything prickly, only silky skin on skin. "Maybe we should cut the engine. I don't want to die of carbon monoxide poisoning," I say.

"Are you sure?" he says and opens the glove box and pulls out a condom.

I'm not certain if he means sure of the condom or sure of turning off the engine.

"Yes — I'm sure. But do it now before I change my mind." I watch him in his nervousness. He sits up and turns off the ignition. His naked body looks comical behind the wheel in the moonlight. His penis sticks out from a messy nest of black hair like a bald, pink creature that's so homely it's embarrassing.

It occurs to me that I'm the one deciding to do all of this. At this moment, I am the calm, he is the storm. I almost laugh as he struggles with the condom. But once it is on, it suddenly doesn't seem that funny anymore. Where did the girl I was watching a while ago go? Come back. I liked when all of this was happening to her and not me. Real is unsettling. Even though all of the kissing and touching feels beautiful, like a

magical ride, I can't completely get my mind around the penis.
God only knows what I am even doing in this truck with it.

After a while, his fingers are nice but I crave more.

I am the storm. I am doing this. Happy birthday to me.

Something is not right. He is not getting inside my body.
"Maybe you're too big for me. Is that possible?"

"I don't know. I don't think so."

"Well, keep trying then."

I'm not in my body anymore. I'm outside, observing
myself, listening to my breathing. Is it me that I am listening
to? He's inside. I know that much. It doesn't even hurt. My
body reacts without me even trying. It's instinctual. It starts
to feel cool, beautiful even. How does something so ugly on
the outside feel unbelievably good when it's inside? Brady sort
of collapses on top of me, unexpectedly. He lays on me for
what seems like too long. I need to breathe.

"You okay?" he mumbles.

I kiss his neck. "Get off," I say. He rolls to his side, his body
still pressed tightly against mine. I am suddenly cold. "Turn
on the heat again — please." My legs start to vibrate with
gentle shaking and my teeth chatter. Tears start to fall. I don't
know why, but they won't stop pouring out of me.

"Lydia, what's wrong? Did I hurt you? Did I do
something wrong?"

"No. I'm just cold," I say.

"I love you," he whispers in my ear then sits up to start
the truck.

I pull on my underwear and seventies flared jeans. I want
to say that I love him too but I can't. We drive back to my
house. He looks stressed.

"Do you want to come in?" I say.

The words are what he needed me to say. His face becomes soft and animated. He looks happier than I think I have ever seen him. It is contagious. The night feels right for the first time.

Victoria is in her room, the door's shut with a crack of light shining out beneath it. We head for my bedroom. He sits on my bed. I have lost my modesty and strip naked before pulling on my Grunt Devine T-shirt. "Come, take off your jeans and get under the covers," I say.

"You're okay?" he says.

I don't know the answer to that question. On what level am I okay? In what universe am I okay? "Let's just go to sleep," I say, wrapping my arms around his chest. We fall asleep, all twisted together.

Brady wakes up at six. He has to get back to school in Saskatoon. I don't want him to go. I'm lost without him. But I retain my dignity and I say nothing.

"I've got a game in Medicine Hat this week but I'll call you as soon as I get back."

"I'll miss you." Whoops, that flew out of my mouth without my permission.

He leans down to kiss me. I remember his breath in my ear last night — he loves me.

I watch his truck disappear down the road, the sun peeking above the horizon. I can't tell Victoria what has happened. I left her on my birthday, and she holds grudges.

FOURTEEN

The school tracked down Alex and mailed him a letter at his U of S office. Friday night the fireworks start. "If your mother has to give up her degree to come back here and babysit you two, you'll be begging me to let you go back to school. I'll send you two to the most right-wing, Christian fundamentalist, military boarding school I can find. If I have to send you to the States, I will," he shouts.

We return to school like dutiful daughters. Polinski's pervy eyes are all over Mary Jane's sequined halter top. I'm wearing a black cardigan over it and only leave the front open but he just can't keep his perverted peepers off my navel. I am this close to losing it and telling the creep to fuck off. As soon as I sit down in my desk, Nathan slides into the empty desk in front of me and says, "What'd you do, Fuckingham?"

"Shut it, Pencil Dyck," I say. I have no idea where those words came from. I've never called anyone a Pencil Dyck before in my life.

"In your seat, Mr. Dyck!" Polinski hisses, then his voice softens into a self-satisfied tone. "Lydia, Mr. Binstead wishes to have a word with you in his office. Leave your books."

I move, in slow motion, down the shining tile hall, towards the office. It's not me walking, it's parallel universe Lydia. She walks towards Binstead as I drift away. Binstead motions parallel Lydia into his office. Her mouth turns down. She cannot force the edges of her lips up, they tremble in defiance. "Relax — this isn't about you," Binstead says.

I leap back into my body. "Has something happened to my sister — to Victoria?"

"No, she's fine. You're a friend of Michelle Dyck's, is that right?" he says.

"Yeah, I guess," I say.

"Do you happen to know where she might be today?" he says.

"No — is she in trouble?"

"Her parents have been to the school this morning. Michelle never returned home last night or the night before that. She's been missing for two days — are you sure you don't know anything about her whereabouts? Maybe the name of a new friend she might be staying with?"

"No, not really — she has a boyfriend, Clint Dyck. He used to go this school."

He stares into my eyes. I stare back, unflinching, forcing my lips to be still. "That will be all for today," he says, then stretches back in the chair, exposing a whole lot of white belly, protruding from underneath untucked shirttails.

I hope I haven't said too much, gotten Michelle into trouble, but she has been weirder than ever this term. I want to shout out to the class, *it wasn't about me!* Instead, I sit in my desk and ignore the looks.

Six days since my birthday and I haven't heard a word from Brady. I don't get him. I was cruel last summer, but he seemed to forget that. So what game is he playing? I have constant butterflies in my stomach but I suffer in silence. No one could possibly understand what I am going through, and they wouldn't even want to know.

Thanksgiving is like old times inside the casket of the farmhouse. Victoria and her satin lining have been chained to the stove all day, smack beside Mary Jane and loving it. Alex is acting like a sulky baby. He's holed up in the back porch, sitting in the orange chair with his toque on and a cup of coffee. I can tell he's jealous that Mary Jane's spending time with us, her daughters. He wants her all to himself. Strange, you'd think he'd act different in some way, like the guilty bugger that he is. She obviously has no idea. He's acting exactly like the same old Alex. He rises out of his chair to put on his workboots and parka, chopping wood again. I bet he's going to try and chop through Thanksgiving supper.

As predicted, Alex won't come in and eat with us. "How dare you! I'm home for three days! Three bloody days and you can't be bothered to sit down with me for a meal. The girls and I have slaved for four hours to prepare this feast," Mary Jane yells, sliding a piece of Victoria's undercooked pumpkin cheesecake across the table. She stands up and jerks open the utensil drawer. The spoon, why didn't I have the brains to throw that out long ago? She whips Alex on the arm then moves up to his shoulders. He's still wearing his ripped parka so I don't think she's really hurting him.

"Easy, Mary Jane, easy," he says between smiles that turn to grimaces.

The wooden spoon smacks his skull. Even all of his thick hair is no match for the spoon. I jump up from the table and push Alex hard, away from her and that spoon.

"Stop it! Stop it, you two. This is Thanksgiving, for fuck sake!" I yell.

Victoria uses the situation to exercise her pent-up aggression. She bolts from her chair and pushes Alex with much more force than I did. "You're an asshole!" she says. He stumbles back, hitting the wall.

"Stop it! Fuck, Victoria. What are you doing? Leave him alone!" My mouth is dry and my throat raw.

Mary Jane throws the spoon across the kitchen. It takes out an ancient flypaper before hitting the wall behind Alex's head. She storms down to pack. She flies out tomorrow morning anyway, so it is no dramatic move.

"What's her problem?" Alex says with wide, innocent eyes.

I roll mine and say, "Don't involve me."

"You're an idiot. That's what's wrong," Victoria says.

Alex slinks down to the basement like a nervous puppy, his hands clutched to his chest protectively.

Brady calls from a restaurant somewhere in Montana. He has no privacy so it's hard for him to talk. He sounds sex starved. I can almost taste his lips through the receiver. My face blushes. "I'm aching to be with you tonight. I'm in pain," he says.

"Are you drunk?" I whisper, holding my hand over the receiver.

"No. Why would you say that?'"

"Sorry, just wanted to make sure."

⚡

Reality hits on Tuesday. Everyone's gone. Victoria and I are left to struggle on the land. It is becoming more difficult with winter approaching. Soon the chickens will have to be in the barn day and night. Thank God the trough is automatic and heated, so we won't have to worry about water for Silver and the cattle. The biggest burden is the basement beast. Alex has, most unfortunately, decided we are finally mature enough to feed her solid food. I was hoping he'd never come to that conclusion. A liquid diet of oil is so much easier, for everyone involved, and it helps with the beast's digestion; she doesn't belch thick smoke through the vents all day long.

"I don't know what we'll do when it snows," I say to Victoria.

"We could carry in all of the wood and store it down here. Then, when it gets really cold, we won't have to go outside at all." Victoria looks like Charlie Chaplin. She has a black charcoal mustache from rubbing her face, and black smudges on the arms of her pink goddess robe from rearranging the furnace logs.

"We could. It might be hard to chop it up though," I say.

"When we swing the axe up it will go right through the ceiling," she says.

"I'd like to try that. The image intrigues me," I say and crouch down to watch the beast's solid meal burst into flames. My Barbie bungalow is illuminated in the warm firelight. It looks cozy, like a real miniature house. I close the furnace and turn the heavy metal handle with my sleeve over my hand. "What's that fabric, in the corner, beside my Barbie house?"

Victoria picks it up. "My army pants! Damn, Alex must have found them and taken them out."

"Burn them. I want to see them burn — hold on, I want to burn mine too," I say and race up to the tower. I pull the khaki pants from the bottom dresser drawer.

"Here," I say, handing them to Victoria.

Her face is serious in the firelight. "Are you sure?"

"Forget them. Burn all, burn everything. Fire is bright and fire is clean," I say, quoting Beatty.

I watch Nathan as he saunters towards his seat. He catches my eye as he walks back from where he hung up his jacket. Like clockwork, he slides into the empty chair in front of me.

"Hey, Fuckingham, I saw you checking me out," he says.

"Whatever, Dyck Head," I say and toss my head in annoyance. "Have you heard any news about your cousin Michelle? Did they find her?"

"Yeah," he says, jerking his shaggy mop to the side.

"Where was she?"

"Shacked up with some old man," he says, pinching his nose and inhaling.

"Pleasant," I say sarcastically. "Was she with Clint?"

"Nah. They broke up. She was living with his older brother. Why so concerned — missing your lesbian lover?" He stands up to leave, pulling up his jeans in the process and exposing sockless ankles.

"Where is she now?"

"Why do you want to know?" he says.

"Because I miss my lesbian lover, idiot — you don't even know where she is, do you?"

"Her parents sent her to Prince Albert to live with her sister — satisfied?" he says, then struts his small, awkward body across the room to his desk. Our classmates are watching, curious as hell. Let them wonder. For once, the Dyck has been a useful informant — looks like Michelle is gone for good.

The pleasant calm brought on by satisfied curiosity doesn't last long. Polinski's eyes have been upon us the entire time.

"Lydia, I want to see you after class. Please stay behind," he says.

What does the loser want now? I'm only staying if the door is left open. If he makes one move to close it, I am outta here. Everyone leaves the room, even slimy little Nathan Dyck, although he spends a couple of minutes stalling at his locker before Polinski boots him out. The door is open. Drat, I wanted to bolt.

"I haven't noticed any significant improvement in your attendance, though I see you still aren't wearing braces. Will there be anymore absences in the future that I should know about?"

"No one can predict the future, sir. We're all equally ignorant in that area — I need to get to chemistry," I say, then stand up and walk towards the door.

"I'm not finished with you yet. Sit back down, Lydia."

I keep on walking. "I can't. I'm not feeling well." I say and exit the room. I sprint across the hall, never so happy to see Mrs. Proctor in my life.

As soon as the noon bell rings, I run to the post office. I walk through the door into the familiar warm air that smells of wet socks and cardboard.

"Vic? What are you doing in here?"

"I needed a walk," she says and darts outside before I have the chance to ask her what her fucking problem is. Everything is hopeless. Michelle is gone, Brady is gone, Mary Jane is gone, Alex is gone — everyone has fucked off the hell away from Hicksville and this miserable land. It is so unfair. I hate this place more than anyone, yet I remain.

I refuse to look at Victoria when she gets on the bus. My blurry eyes attempt to focus on the grey outside. I could be on a bus to anywhere. Victoria slides into the seat next to me. I don't flinch. The bitch just wants to chew on any grim gossip I might hold.

"What happened?" she finally says.

"Nothing."

"Pervert Pants?" she says. I ignore her. "I can't stand that fucker either. He was all over me today, trying to scrape out any nasty details about our life at home."

My head jerks around to meet her red eyes. "What? He's harassing you too?"

"Yeah. He's infatuated with anything Buckingham," she says, then wipes her nose with her mitten.

In the distance I can see the top of our house and the attic window peeking above the poplars. It looks lonely and sad, as though waiting for us to return. "I don't know what to do. If we don't go to school they'll phone social services and Alex will ship us off to military school in the States — at least you still have Twyla."

"No, I don't."

"What? Why not? I thought you guys were inseparable."

"Not anymore — religious differences. I'm not ready to be baptized into her church. She took it as a personal insult."

"That's crazy! They can't force you to convert — you should have told her your dad's an atheist."

"I did. She thinks you're a bad influence."

"What? I'm a bad influence?"

"All of you. Let's just say she's praying for all the Buckinghams."

"That snot-nosed, bible-thumping — Twyla's a twat," I say.

Victoria laughs. She looks down at the ratty tote bag in her lap, clutching the dirty straps. "We're fucked," she says.

I call Jim to tell him we no longer require his bus services. I say we're going on a family vacation to Vancouver for the next month and I'll phone him when we return. Victoria paces back and forth in front of the stove, her housecoat pulled tightly around her, listening to my every word. He asks to speak to Mary Jane or Alex. I tell him that they're working late. I accidentally scratch a line through the hall wallpaper with my fingernail as we talk. We are finally free.

"We can't just hang out here anymore. The school will send a letter. It's only a matter of time before the letter reaches Alex and then it's military school in the States. We're going to have to figure things out and fast. Alex will be home Friday night. We have to make our move by Friday morning at the latest."

"What are we going to do? Go to Vancouver?" Victoria says.

"I wish. Mary Jane would just ship us right back to Alex's waiting arms."

"What then?"

"I don't know. Not yet anyway. I'll think of something."

I call Brady, to at least say goodbye, but his aunt says he's gone to Alberta to play the Calgary Wranglers.

He has no time for a mixed-up chick like me.

I'm wide awake. The midnight train sounds. Alex's voice speaks from inside my head. It says, *disappear!* He's right, to disappear is our only option. I strip off my covers and tiptoe into Victoria's room to see if she's asleep. I have no clue as to why I am on tippy toes. The folks aren't going to hear me all the way in Regina and Vancouver. In the moonlight she looks sweet and innocent, younger than her fifteen years. I rock her shoulder. "Victoria, are you awake?" I whisper harshly. "Victoria, wake up!" She opens her eyes and lifts her head.

"What time is it?" she says.

"Midnight."

"What's up?" she says sleepily.

"I have an idea. It can't wait until morning."

"Why are you whispering?" she says.

"I don't know, habit maybe. Do you want to hear the plan or not?"

"Do I have a choice?"

"No." I hoist myself up to sit on the end of her captain's bed. "This is serious stuff, so you have to shut up and listen — the secret sanctuary."

"What? Are you kidding? The place has no insulation, we'll freeze." She pulls herself up into sitting position and fluffs up the pillow to rest against her headboard.

"We have a wood stove. The place is tiny. That stove throws a lot of heat, remember? We'll be safe there — no school, no Polinski, and no Alex. It borders reserve land on one side and an empty field on the other. There are no homesteads for acres and across the river is a massive Hutterite farm. They don't work the fields in the winter, so no one will see our chimney smoke."

"We have to take Silver."

"There's no way. We can't tether her night after night, and what if it snows? She's safer here. We'll leave her hay and Alex will be home on the weekend. Same with the chickens, we'll leave them in the barn with tons of water and food. But we can't leave Marx. He's coming with us."

"What will we eat?"

"For once the cupboards are full — thanks to Mary Jane. We'll take everything."

FIFTEEN

Morning comes slowly; I sense Victoria's awake too but I don't call out. We lie awake in silence.

We load up the toboggan and a plastic sleigh with a thirty-pound bag of dog kibble, cords of firewood, Alex's axe, matches, candles, a can opener, a newspaper to burn, toilet paper, pots to cook with, cans of frozen orange juice, a bag of apples, two bags of flour, oatmeal, a sack of rice, cans of meat and veggies, peanut butter, carrots, a box of macaroni noodles, grated parmesan cheese, one sharp knife, two forks and two spoons, two metal bowls, two metal camping mugs, tooth-brushes, paste and floss, a bar of soap, deodorant, tampons, and two bags of chocolate chips. We pack three sleeping bags, two pillows, and all of our cold weather gear.

"This is more food than we've eaten all fall. It should last us a couple of months at least," I say. Marx sticks his big head into one of the food boxes, looking for a snack. I knee him in the chest and push him off. "No!"

"How long are you planning on us staying there?" Victoria asks, sitting on top of the pillows and blankets on the sleigh.

"I don't know." This is where my plan gets shaky. But Victoria needs clear-cut plans or she has a tendency to go catatonic. "Until Christmas holidays. Mary Jane will be back then, and we can convince her to take us into school in Saskatoon. She wants to get a job at one of the hospitals. We can drive in with her everyday."

"That would be amazing. I just hope she gets a job." Victoria says. Her hair hangs in greasy globs on the sides of her pretty freckled face. Her eyes shine turquoise, reminding me of our mother's. I'm stabbed with an abysmal loneliness for Mary Jane, just Mary Jane and none of the crazy people she's been known to impersonate.

"Come on, Vic, finish packing. It's going to be an exhausting walk, at least four to five hours. Thank God it hasn't snowed here yet," I say, then look beyond the corral at the grey pasture and sky.

"I'm tired. Can't we stay one more night and leave tomorrow? It's past noon and we haven't even packed our clothes or fed the animals."

I pick up a cardboard box filled with food from the toboggan and walk towards the house with it. "Help me get the food back inside — the coyotes — and wash your hair. You won't get another chance for awhile."

I can't sleep. My biggest fear is that Victoria will jam out on me. I drift in and out of dreams all night until I hear the sound of Jim's bus. The clock says 8:10 AM. I've over slept. I rush to the front window in time to see Victoria riding away on the big yellow bus. She waves to me from inside the bus, a smug smile on her face.

I wake up, covered in sweat. The clock says 6:23 AM. Morning has come.

I feel like I have to leave Alex a note. To let him know we haven't been kidnapped, or worse. I write: *We're together and we're okay. We'll be home for Christmas.* I sign it: *Lydie, Vic & Marx. P.S. Please feed the chickens, Silver, and the cattle.*

We leave early, before the sun's fully up. Fear of the unknown burns inside my stomach until I must concentrate to suppress the urge to vomit. The toboggan is heavy. Even though it slides fairly easily over the frost-covered grass, it's hard to pull as things keep falling off. The wind is cold but we're overdressed with layers upon layers so we don't have to carry them. Marx is nervous. He knows something is up. He keeps glancing at the pasture, trying to find Silver. The house stands tall and silent. I want to run back and hide within its protective walls. But the walls won't protect me tonight if Alex has received the latest letter.

A thin slice of green on the horizon reassures me that the sun will rise today. We follow the Carleton Trail. We know the way by heart even though we've never walked the entire way before. We stop at a familiar pile of rocks to rest, circling the pile until we find the perfect spot, the side protected from the wind. I sit on the edge of a large round, sand-coloured rock. The cold from the rock seeps through my snow pants and jeans. Victoria packed us cheese buns. "I smell snow. It's coming," she says as she clutches a fake cheese bun, seemingly uninterested in even trying a bite of it.

"I smell it too — we'll make it before it hits — are you okay?"

"I don't know." She takes a gentle bite of her bun and stares at the grey fields, patting the top of Marx's hungry head. Maybe Victoria is even more lost than I am. At least I've had Brady to distract me.

It starts to snow, the odd flake in the cold wind. Maybe I've miscalculated. The trip was so much shorter when I drove part of the way. We walk until we reach the river. The water near the shore is frozen, though there is still an open stream down the centre. "Soon it will be so thick we could drive a car across it if we had one," I shout.

"That will be good. We can maybe raid the Hutterite's supplies if we have to."

The landscape is not as I remember: golden, dry, and warm with sprinklings of new green amongst the bluffs. It is black and grey, monochromatic and dull. I walk focused on my feet, occasionally glancing behind to make sure the toboggan hasn't spilled any supplies.

The dark landscape has become white with snow. My nose drips. I open my mouth to breathe and inhale sharp, icy flakes that feel as though they're attacking my lungs.

A dark box appears, partially hidden amongst the blur of white and streaks of scraggly grey willow branches and poplar trunks. Victoria breaks into a run with Marx, the plastic sleigh threatens to dump its load with her abrupt movements. She stands frozen, blocking the doorway to the sanctuary. "Move," I say, pushing her out of the way. It remains just as we left it: stark, clean, and drafty.

I remove the wood from the orange sleigh and stack it beside the stove as Victoria blows on a single pathetic flame. "That's a lot of smoke," I say.

"I think it's going to hold — hand me more wood — smaller stuff," she says.

Marx whines. "I know you want water, but it's too dark to go down to the river tonight. This will have to do." I pour some pop bottle orange juice into the smallest enamel dish.

He laps it up as Victoria and I unload the food and place it up on the attic ledge so Marx won't eat it all tonight.

I unroll the sleeping bags and smooth them out onto the bed. Victoria finds two apples, sits down cross-legged on the freshly made bed, and pulls off her jacket. I unzip my parka, sit down beside her, and pull off my Sasquatch boots. We sit, side by side on the bed, crunching. The firelight spreads a soft glow throughout the shack. The warmth from the stove moves up, onto the bed. The hot fire has tricked my mind into thinking I have come home, that I am safe. My eyelids are heavy and chewing is work. "It's actually kind of cozy." Victoria says, whittling down the apple core with her teeth, like a hamster.

"Yep, small but civilized." I deliberately take large, aggressive bites in contrast to her annoying nibbling. The wind howls at the window and the pane shakes. "For now — oh-oh, the orange juice is going to melt." I stand on the bed, reaching for the attic shelf.

"Outside. Store them outside. It's got to be minus twenty out there."

I don't bother to put on my boots. My shoulder pushes open the door, against considerable resistance. The wind catches it and it snaps open. Icy grains blow into my face. It's coming down hard and furious, not exactly snow, but miniature flecks of ice. I push the bag of orange juice cans under the toboggan, against the cottage, and step back inside, pulling the door closed.

Victoria pulls off her socks to examine her blisters. My head is heavy but my mind is swirling. Snow changes everything. People die in blizzards all the time — people with cars, central heating, telephones. Victoria has moved up from her feet to pick her ears. If Victoria thinks she can sit on the bed all night picking at herself like an oblivious idiot, she is dead wrong. "We have to keep the fire going, all night. I only packed enough wood for three days tops. I thought there'd be plenty of time to gather wood. We should be out there right now, before the snow buries all the good wood."

Victoria pulls her finger from her ear. "Hail Alex."

"Call me whatever you want, but I am sure of only one thing," I say.

"What?"

"He'll never forgive us. He'll lock us away, send us to some crazy American boarding school. And you know Mary Jane will go along with whatever he decides. We'll have ruined her chances to finish her degree."

"Are you saying we should go back?" In firelight, her face looks about twelve.

"It's too late for that. We'd die in this blizzard. We're screwed, either way."

The wind howls and the snow falls in solid, vertical sheets. The moon is hidden.

The cottage is dark except for the flicker of flame shining through the burners. The three of us lie side by side in bed, one sleeping bag underneath us and two on top. I'm wearing my grey tracksuit but Victoria remains fully dressed in jeans, a T-shirt, and the pink robe. She's done up every button. The robe is tightly fitted right up to under her chin. She looks regal in the firelight, like she is some sort of prince charming from a fairy tale with the long thick ponytail flowing down her back.

The night is long, eternal . . . no midnight train to ground me to the present. I am lost in the wilderness. I watch the window glass shake and I wait, as though I'm in an opera house watching a climactic scene — I must be quiet and patient.

We take turns stacking the fire through the night, drifting in and out of sleep. At four in the morning I nearly lose the flame. "We were so lucky to make it here before the blizzard hit," Victoria whispers from the bed as I blow my lungs out, trying to get the grey embers to flash red and to light the newspaper. I place a log on the fast-burning paper and close the stove door. "Do you think it will hold?" she says.

"The fire?"

"This cottage."

"It's held for over fifty years as far as we know. It's probably way older than that. Even without upkeep, it's held since the thirties."

"Lydie," Victoria whispers. I open my eyes to her sleepy smile. "I didn't know where I was when I first woke up. It was weird."

"Are you sick?"

"No, why?"

"Your voice."

"It must be the smoke, or maybe my allergies to Marx are acting up," Victoria says, wiping her nose with the sleeve of her robe.

"With all your snoring, I think I must have slept for about five minutes tops," I say, then push off the heavy sleeping bags and step onto the icy floor. Something squishes between my toes. "Marx! What did you do? You bad dog — bad dog."

"Get a grip. It's not his fault. I couldn't get the door open."

"Stupid beast," I mumble, limping towards the door. I push against it, but it won't budge.

"The snow's blown against the door. It's impossible to open."

"But I haven't peed since yesterday." I shake from the cold and the urge to pee combined. I wipe the bottom of my foot on newspaper. Marx whines and scratches at the door.

"Me too," Victoria says.

We rush the door. We have ten feet of floor space to run and we use every inch of it. It takes us six turns but we finally manage to budge the door open about a foot. Marx pushes his head through but chickens out and tries to back his way in again. Victoria and I push his hips through. He resists. We shove him out again. He lifts his leg and pees on the side of the cottage, splashing most of it in the direction of my grey sweatpants. Finally, he's done and I pull him in. I edge through sideways and pull down my sweatpants. I can't go. My butt is on fire and the wind sucks away my breath. It's no use. I pull up my pants and squeeze back inside.

"It's too fucking cold out there," I say and reach for the big enamel basin.

"The smell in here is making me sick!" Victoria says as she squats.

"It's only a bed pan. What do you think they used last century?"

"You dump it then," she says and pulls up her jeans.

"Get the door, quickly!" I shout, reminding myself of my father. I carefully carry the basin, holding my breath, and crouch down to tip it so the pee drains into the snow. The wind threatens to blow it all back onto me. I gasp for breath and smell the strong, warm scent of fresh urine. I gag and dry heave before throwing the entire basin into the snow. I pull the door closed, silencing the low moans of the wind.

"What if it blows away?" she says.

"Who cares? " I say. I am suddenly filled with intense anger and despair combined. I feel the urge to shout at someone.

"Come on, get in. I'm cold." Victoria says, holding open the sleeping bag. "Wait. Did you wash your hands? I smell pee."

"Yes, in the sink over there, and I used that pretty rose scented soap. Want to smell?" I say, omitting the detail of Marx's pee spraying on my pants. My attempt at dry humour erases a little of the despair. "Move over. Beggars can't be choosers." I pull at the sleeping bag.

"Gross. Get those disgusting hands away from me!"

"Don't worry about drinking the river water, Vic."

"Why?"

"Look outside. We've got snow. There's more water out there than we could possibly need."

"This is where it happened, you know," I say and step from the bed for the first time in four hours.

"What happened?" Victoria says, joining me at the window.

"The final fight, the last stand at Batoche — the end of the Wild West."

"I thought the battle was fought in town."

"It was. But this is where the navy attacked. The steam wheeler packed with government soldiers, that creep Major Middleton, and his posse unloaded here. I blame Queen Victoria." I whirl around and point an accusing finger at Victoria. "Did you know she knighted him for that? I bet he had a beard — never trust a man with a beard, Victoria, remember that."

"Now I know you're bullshitting me. Grand'Mère never said that stuff — the beard theory gave you away."

Victoria fills Marx's basin with snow and melts it on the stove. She knows she has me. If I complain about her choice of baking dish, she won't make the food. She scoops up a fist of flour, and adds it to the melting snow. She mixes the mess with her bare hands (hands that pick her nose, scratch her greasy head, pat Marx, and pick her orange teeth). Then, she forms the mess into two balls and flattens the balls into mini pizzas. She throws the flatbreads right on the stovetop and flips each one with a fork as soon as they're brown. Marx lazily hops from the bed and presses his nose against Victoria's hand. His tongue licks the back of her hand as she tries to spread peanut butter around with a spoon.

"Fuck off, dog," she says as her knee nudges his chest.

She hands me a dog-licked flatbread. I eat while tucked in bed. The warm peanut butter fills my mouth. Food is love. "You're a genius, Victoria."

Three long days and nights we've been trapped in the shoebox. If Marx's breath doesn't kill me, Victoria's will. We're burning the last of the wood we took from the barn. The storm has to let up today; we have to find more wood or we'll freeze to death. No one will ever find us here; the blizzard's erased any trace of us.

"What's for supper?" I ask, mentally tracing the paisley-shaped frost designs covering the window. Prissy little paisleys, the kind you'd see on Pervert Pants' tie.

"Guess," Victoria says, picking her nose.

That's the way things are in the shit shack.

"Vieners?" I say in a German accent.

"In your dreams."

"Found anything yet?" I add sarcastically. Victoria's finger drops from her nose.

"Shut it, or you'll get a nasty little surprise in your rice."

"Rice, what a surprise! I wish it were brown rice — I need fibre. I haven't gone since we left the ranch," I say.

"Me neither — do you smell that?"

"What? I don't smell anything."

"Marx farted again."

"You didn't fart, did you, my handsome Prince Marcus? I say, then look deep into his anxious eyes and kiss the cold wet tip of his black nose. He licks my face.

"He knows he did," Victoria says. I wait for her to put him out. I know she won't, but I wait just the same. To date, he's shit three big piles as wake up presents for me. I've cleaned up every one: the first two because I stepped right in them and they smooshed all over, and the last one I cleaned up out of pure joy; I was so happy that I saw it before I stepped in it.

"Okay, I'll put him out. But then I won't cook tonight, and I don't think I'll feel like getting the water tomorrow morning either," Victoria says.

She has me. I rip off the sleeping bag and stand on the cold floor. Whispers of movement swirl around my feet. Mice. I jump back in bed.

"My boots, I need my winter boots," I say, then stretch across Victoria, trying to reach the boots tucked under the bed.

"Lydia! Get off me. What the hell are you doing?"

"The boarders. They're everywhere." I pull on my boots and stomp across the floor to the stove. The mice scatter, all except one.

"I killed it — shit." I lift my boot.

Victoria leans over the bed to look. "It's a baby."

"It's not my fault — I waited for them to scatter."

"Look at this." Victoria holds up an empty plastic bag. They ate the peanut butter flatbread I was saving for lunch.

"I'm a murderer."

"You murdered a baby."

"Shut up. I cover my hand with a bag, pick up the baby mouse, and throw it out the door, into the snow. It disappears into the white; all that remains is an indentation in the snow. I immediately regret throwing it in the snow. I'll never find it, not until the snow melts, then I'll have to deal with its body all over again.

⚡

I can't lie to myself any longer. I want to go back. The air in the shack is smoky and fart filled. Outside is not much better, too much white with pockets of grey.

"If only I could go outside. I could breathe outside," I say. Victoria rolls her eyes. "What's that for?" She ignores me. I have a choice: punch her ugly face right on her pimply nose or return to my private internal monologue. I, the pacifist, choose the inner monologue. I want to feel the sun on my face and listen to the snow crunch beneath my feet. I know I'd feel better if I could go outside. The land, nature, I can relate to. It feels like home. This shoebox is not the perfect sanctuary I envisioned. It's a prison.

"Freaky," Victoria says. Her foot kicks my shin. "Freaky!" she shouts. She wants to start up our never-ending word association game. Today it feels as excruciatingly boring as yesterday's game.

"Sex."

"Screw."

"You."

"Suck."

"Lemons."

Marx barks. I laugh. Victoria wipes her red nose on her hand and coughs. "I don't know what's wrong with me. I feel like crap."

"Maybe it's your asthma. Sleeping with Marx can't be helping."

"And what am I supposed to do about that?" she says, then pushes Marx's head off her pillow. He looks at me with offended eyes and flops his head right back down on her pillow. Victoria coughs, Marx barks, I laugh. Repeat.

We are like the shrews in a bottle. We will freeze like they burned inside the bottles. Their enemy, fire; ours, ice. The wooden walls, like the glass bottles, are nothing more than an illusion of safety. The cold will scorch our flesh like flames, leaving our skeletons perfectly preserved inside the pristine shelter, bones, chewed clean by coyotes, bleached by the sun . . . white bones, white like the snow.

The cottage is quiet. It takes my mind a minute to realize why. "There's no wind today," I say. Victoria lifts her groggy head from the pillow. "You don't look so good. Your eyes are puffy."

"Fuck off," she says, pulling the covers over her head.

I reach for my boots, step across the mouse-infested floor, and try the door. Dog kibbles pelt my head from above. Marx jumps from the bed. His heavy limbs pounce in all directions, trying to inhale the kibble and catch the mice as they scatter at the same time. He loves his morning game of mice tag, though he's not quick enough to catch any. I kick open the stiff door. "Shit! It's gotta be minus sixty today!" The air is death: frigid, stiff, and calm. I inhale, filling my lungs with sub-zero air. My chest contracts in shock. I push Marx out and watch him from the window. He lifts his leg against the shack and looks longingly towards the river. He snaps at his paws like something's bit him and cries at the door to be let back in.

Victoria hasn't moved from under the sleeping bag. I pull on my parka, toque, mittens and pick up the axe. "Come with me, big boy," I say. Marx makes no move to follow me; instead, he turns and leaps back onto the bed. "Suit yourself, lazy boy."

One small piece of wood, lying near the roots of a poplar, doesn't even need chopping, which is good because my hands are too cold to grip the axe. I return to the prison, stick in hand. The beasts are both up, sitting on the bed together. Marx's eyes follow my every move. Victoria doesn't even bother to look up. Her nose is purple and puffy against a flour-white face. "Whoever decided that hell was hot never lived through a Saskatchewan winter," she says.

I feel disgustingly filthy. My skin is crawling with zits and my teeth are probably orange like Victoria's. I scoop snow into the large pee basin until it's over flowing. "I'm going to sterilize it. Then we can wash our hair." Victoria is about to object. "A shampoo would do you good. You're no babe yourself." She lifts her hand out from beneath the sleeping bags and holds up her middle finger. I catch my reflection in the corner of the window that remains frost-free. It isn't me, it's a wild bush woman, one crazy-ugly, skinny woman. "I think I've aged. I look like shit on wheels," I say.

The wind isn't howling and the windows are still. I use the end of the deodorant stick to scrape frost from the window. The northern lights are spectacular: green, orange, pink, and blue — dancing, swirling, the colours blending into the next, climbing upwards. "We could be at the North Pole or on the edge of the earth," I say.

Victoria unwraps her hair from damp sweatpants. "It's Jacob's Ladder — souls climbing upwards towards heaven."

I look away from the lights. "That was weird. For a minute, it felt like I was home, watching a movie," I say.

We sit on the bed, staring at each other by candlelight. Victoria's hair sticks out in all directions. She let it dry however it came out of the sweatpants. I make a grotesque face, bulge my eyes and make my chin vanish. Victoria tries to copy me. Her face is thin, bony, and frightening in the candle's glow.

"Attractive — a chinless scarecrow."

"You're a zombie. Only uglier than a zombie," Victoria says. I push up my nose and pull my cheeks down. Victoria snorts, "Oh my God, you are so butt ugly I think I'm going to cry!"

I laugh. It's the truth. I am butt ugly. My stomach aches, my cheeks too.

Marx's ears stand up. He's heard something. A deep, slow, low growl sounds inside the shack.

"Who growled?" I whisper.

"Who do you think, idiot? There's something out there," Victoria whispers.

Marx continues an almost inaudible growl, so low and deep that I feel it more than I hear it. If Marx senses danger, I believe him. All the possible suspects enter my mind: coyote, a lost drunk weirdo, Hutterite, a trapper from the reserve, a neighbouring farmer, the police, Mary Jane and Alex — Louis Riel in ghost form. Marx jumps from the bed to the floor. The sudden movement sends fear through my spine. He growls as he walks warily to the door.

"Put something against the door," Victoria whispers.

"Quiet! I thought I heard a coyote," I whisper.

"Did you hear any yips?"

"Shh!"

"Do you hear any barking?" Victoria says.

A deep howl cuts through the cold night. It's loud. It's close. Another deep howl, followed, in turn, by more howls, some deeper and louder than others. Their song surrounds the cottage.

"I don't hear any yips," Victoria says.

"So what?"

Victoria slides towards the frosted windowpane in sticky socks. "It's a wolf!" Victoria whispers.

I push her face from the peephole. All I can see are shadows of bodies in shades of black and grey. A shadow moves closer; it has four long legs.

"It's huge. Listen to their song," I say.

"I didn't think there were wolves this far south," Victoria whispers.

Marx's deep resonating growl shakes the window.

"Help me. Push the bed against the door!"

Their serenade surrounds the cottage, threatening to burst through the door and push the princess bed across the room. I can't be sure how many there are. Marx leaps back onto the bed with us. His silence frightens me more than his growl.

"Should we blow out the candle?" Victoria whispers.

"Why? They know we're in here."

Silence. We listen to the silence for too long. We let the fire die.

Victoria's asleep, sitting up at the opposite end of the bed. I shut my eyes as a trial. Maybe it will be okay to shut them a short while before I have go out and get some more wood.

I find it too painful to open them again, and my body is too heavy to move. I fall asleep, hard and fast, sitting up, my arm wrapped tightly around Marx and my back resting on the scrolled princess footboard opposite Victoria.

Victoria's screams awaken me. Whatever was out there must be in here, attacking. "What is it? What do you need?" I scream, in sleep-drugged terror.

"Help me! There's something on me. Get it off! It's on my arm," Victoria jumps up and stands on the bed. A big mouse runs across the mattress and off the bed.

"It's all right. It's only the big Mama mouse. She's run onto the floor. You're safe — get up. We have to move the bed back. I have to pee." My words hang in the air in a thick fog.

Victoria stands up robotically. "Holy shit it's cold!" she says and her teeth begin to chatter.

We push the bed back from the door, feeling every ounce of Marx's nearly two hundred pounds. I stare at the closed door, afraid to open it. "Come on, open it," Victoria says.

"You."

Marx squats on the floor, about to poop. I grasp his collar and push open the door. The yard has changed. The familiar paths we have made to and from the poplar bluff and river are hard to distinguish amongst the newly flattened snow: paw prints, hundreds, maybe thousands, some right up to the door. They are bigger than Marx's. Wolves.

Victoria draws a horse on the wall beside the bed with charcoal from the stove. She won't talk to me, for some real or imagined reason. I brush Marx with our only hairbrush. I part his hair down the middle of his forehead and smooth it gently towards his flat ears. "There now, aren't you the most handsome lad in my queendom?" I say and kiss the top of his silky head. I stand with my back to the stove, absorbing all its fiery heat, my arm dramatically following the length of Marx's long back.

Victoria jumps from the bed, her foot getting momentarily stuck inside the sleeping bag. "That's my brush!" she shouts. Her hand cuts through the cold air, connecting with my cheek. I instinctively slap her with the back with the hairbrush. It smacks the side of her jaw. "I hate you!" she shouts, her jaw clenched and her eyes growing more transparent, as though she's fading away.

"I hate you more."

She snatches her jacket and opens the door. "Come on boy. Marx, come!" she orders. He follows her out before I can restrain him.

The door remains open. After a minute I decide to close it. "Good riddance, you fucking little bitch!" I shout.

I wait for over twenty minutes. They might be heading home. She'll never make it. It's too cold. I put on my boots and parka and follow their tracks that lead to the river. They're nearly half way across the river, which appears to be completely frozen over. "Victoria!" I yell. She doesn't turn around. I run onto the ice and catch up to her. Marx is far ahead, nearing a small stream of open water, close to the other shore. Why'd she let him get so far ahead? "Marx!" I yell. He stops, turns his head to look back at me, then bends down to drink from the open stream of river. I know the ice is going to break before I hear the crack. It's a vision in my head that I cannot stop. "Bickie, bickie, Marx! Come, Marx!" I scream and then run, passing Victoria. He turns again, to look back at me. In that instant I hear another crack. Marx loses his footing. His body crashes into the river. He lurches ahead, his front legs and

chest straining to pull up his hind end. He struggles, panic
in his eyes. I cannot get there fast enough. It happens in slow
motion. "Marx! Come on, boy! Come, Marx!" I shout. He
tries to pull up his hind end, his eyes bulging. He disappears.
"Where is he? Where is he? For fuck sake, where is my dog?
Marx — Marx — Marx!" I lie on my belly and slide as close
to the edge as I dare. "Marx! Marx! Marx! My boy! Where are
you, my baby?"

SIXTEEN

The temperature outside must be dropping. I cannot get warm. I lie still beside Victoria, dressed in my parka under the sleeping bags. The fire is blazing. Victoria has taken it over and she likes a big fire. "This place. This is where Mayor Middleton attacked Batoche," I say. Victoria rolls onto her side, farther away from me. "Evil never dies. It only sleeps."

It is cold, bitterly cold. My chest is tight, full of peanut brittle. I don't cough but it hurts to breathe. The fire burns. Victoria must be getting out of bed once in awhile to tend it, though I never see her leave the shack to get wood. I haven't been out of bed in a couple of days, I think. I have been up to pee in the basin on the floor.

The window shakes and howls, a sound more comforting than silence. I pull myself up into a sitting position, like a crippled old lady. The interior walls of the cabin are covered in charcoal drawings. They are horrible. I cannot escape the images of Silver and Marx, Marx and Silver, all over the walls. Victoria puts down her charcoal and watches me with renewed interest. "Finally, you're up — there's wood to chop," she says.

I cough and taste blood. I slide my legs from under the blankets, placing them on the cold floor, and attempt to look out the window . . . nothing but ice designs. "There is too much art in this shack — I need to see outside," I say.

I don't know how long we've been in the shack, or how long I've been in bed. Everything is surreal, blured, as though I'm lying inside a green skeleton bottle on the museum shelf. I am hot. Victoria stands by the fire.

"Could you turn down the heat?" I say.

Her hand is on my head. "Have some water," she says. It tastes good but I only want a sip. A wet tongue methodically wipes my face, over and over. Marx. His breath stinks.

"Off, Marx," I whisper.

"Your lips are white. I wiped them with your sock."

It must be morning. It's bright in the shack. Victoria and Marx are gone. The fire is low. I feel a little better. I can think again. Maybe my fever has broken. I sit up and slide my legs from under the blankets and let my feet touch the floor. My legs shake. I hold onto the headboard and lower myself onto the basin. How long have I been wearing this nightgown? Mary Jane made it for me. It reminds me of her, her love. It stinks. I stink. I don't think my pits have ever smelled this bad. My mouth feels rough and dry inside. I pull myself up and collapse back on the bed. The burst of wellness has faded. I am cold.

The sound of the door opening awakes me. Victoria's been crying. Her eyes are bloodshot and swollen. "I think I'm getting better," I say. I close my eyes. "I think my fever's breaking."

"Good — I can't do this anymore."

"Where's Marx?" She doesn't answer me. "Where is he?"

"Marx is gone — for God's sake, Lydia, how could you forget that?" she shouts.

Darkness crawls inside, cooling my bones. I shake under the sleeping bag, until it's wet from the sweat pouring off my feet. I don't want to go to that place Mary Jane told me about, that dark place that awaits the living and the dead. But I fear it has found me. It knocks on the shack window, threatening to break inside. Too much blood has been spilled outside. The walls can't keep it out any longer. At first I believed Mary Jane, evil is hiding in the earth, the soil — the poisoned land. But now I know different. Evil is not hiding in the land; it is in the wind, the wind that shakes the window and howls day and night. It is a desperate wind that blows across the prairie. The wind is home to the ghosts of the dispossessed, the malcontented, and the murdered: the buffalo, Métis, and Cree, floundering amongst the ghosts are Middleton's dead soldiers. They roam inside the wind, eternally displaced. The wicked wind poisons the living, seeping inside our bodies, howling inside our heads. This land belongs to the dead.

Victoria opens a can of tomatoes. I know it's the last can. Canned tomatoes poured over macaroni noodles with Parmesan cheese shaken on top: the best meal she's made since we arrived at the cottage. The smell makes me nauseous. I take a bite but cannot swallow.

"Tomorrow, if you feel well enough, we should take a walk to Batoche. It's gotta be closer than our place."

I nod and close my eyes.

I wake in the dark, suffocating. I dig myself out of layers and layers. I don't know where I am or what I'm doing. I've never been more confused. Someone sits up beside me. I know her; she is Victoria, my sister. I am supposed to be doing something but can't remember what it is.

"What's my goal?" I whisper. Victoria doesn't answer me. I try again, "What am I working on?"

"What? You're trying to get better."

"What am I fighting?"

"You've got a bad cold," she says. Her voice is calm and quiet. She doesn't sound at all like Victoria

"I can't breathe," I say.

I can think again, and I got my period. I am too weak to put in a tampon. I'll lie here and bleed. The blood will feel warm. I'll wreck the sleeping bags. Victoria will be mad. "Can you hand me the roll of toilet paper?" I don't recognize my own voice. I sound like an old woman with emphysema.

"How much?"

I can't understand the concept. What is wrong with my brain? Tears well up in my eyes. "I don't know." She throws the entire roll at me. I carefully wad it into a big pile, moving in delicate jerks and slow motion. I stuff the wad into my underpants. I don't know how long I've been wearing this pair. They have to be over a week old. I hope the toilet paper works because I am too tired to care if it doesn't.

Victoria does nothing but cry. I watch her with weighted eyes. "You need drugs. You're getting worse. I have to find some antibiotics." She puts on her parka and boots over top of her grey gown. I don't recognize the gown. When did she go shopping without me?

"Please stay. Don't leave me," I say. She folds her arms across her chest and begins to pace. I'm too tired to keep watching her pace but I am afraid to close my eyes. I disappear into blackness, emptiness. Not sleep, but blankness.

I am alive, my eyes are open. Victoria stands at the window, scraping the frost with a stick. She scratches the word *help*. She throws the stick onto the floor and opens the door to a frigid blast of wind. It blows snow into the shack, covering the bed in a fine powder. "We're trapped — another fucking blizzard."

I don't want to die in the shack. Death is watching me from behind. When I black out it is like death catches me and holds me for a moment before letting me go. It is dark and empty down there. I have to will myself better. If I can take hold of the nausea, make it mine, own it, then maybe I can conquer the weakness next. I focus on the nausea. I hold on to it like a little hard ball inside me. I can will myself better. I want to live. I am too young to die.

Night finally comes and the fire is low. Victoria stands in front of the freshly scraped window as though it is a mirror reflection, smoothing her straw hair. A man's face appears beside hers. It is a face that has known death. I pull my arm from under the heavy blankets.

"Why are you pointing?" Victoria spins around from the window, her voice alarmed.

"There, behind you," I say through raspy whispers.

Victoria turns back to the dark windowpane, startled. "What? What is it?" she says in hushed terror.

"That man, that man in the window," I say.

"Where?" she whispers, jumping onto the bed beside me.

"There," I say, pointing to the window.

"What man?" her voice breaks into a cry. Her hands grip my stick-like arm. They are heavy and tight. It hurts.

"That man, there in the window — he's going to hurt me."

"Stop it! Stop it, Lydia. There is no one out there. I can't see anyone!" Victoria screams. She stands on the bed and runs her hands through the straw on her head. "I can't do this anymore. I can't fucking do this anymore. I hate you. I hate you!" She says it over and over, too many times to count.

I place cold, boney hands over my ears and close my eyes. Go away, bad man. Shut up, Victoria.

I cannot hold on to the weakness, it escapes my grasp. Marx never leaves his place on top of me. He is a heavy weight paralyzing me. *Don't leave me, Marx. I love you.*

Our cottage is transformed into a French salon of carpets and velvet. The air is thick and heavy, the lighting dim. Everyone is smoking. The French and their cigarettes — it's hard to breathe. I want to fight my way from beneath the throws on the sofa but I am too drugged. Why is Marx talking so much? He doesn't even speak French. I need to get away from Paris. I drift away, across the ocean. It is cool up there, above the icy water, cool but dark. I am on a very dark journey, but I live. Angels pull me by sleigh. They can't be real angels; they look like Marx and Victoria. The buffalo are close. The steam from their nostrils covers my face; their hooves plow through the snow. They stay with us, just behind. They force us on. Run faster, angels.

I slide through the corral like a curling rock. Silver. Is she real? This is not home; it is a castle of ice. I am in Russia. It is so beautiful, everything glitters. My angels pull me inside the castle. Victoria is going to a party at Grand'Mère's. It must be *la fête des Métis*. I want to go too. Napoleon said he'd take us someday.

"Don't." I mouth the word.

"I'll come right back, promise."

Marx stays with me. He licks my mouth and nose. I can't breathe. I try to yell, *off*, but nothing comes out. It is cold. The ice castle needs a fireplace.

SEVENTEEN

Alex stands at the end of my bed. I see him for the first time: my beautiful father, the misplaced Viking. I am afraid. I don't feel like me. I am disgusting: teeth thick with plaque, tangled hair, smelling of sweat, smoke, grease, and dandruff. I'm sure my face is covered in zits, but I'm too tired to get out of bed and hobble to the bathroom mirror to check. The only thing clean is the pale yellow hospital gown. The Royal University Hospital — first Mary Jane, then Alex, and now I am the patient. I've never liked pale yellow. It looks faded and old, like plastic roses placed on a gravestone.

"I'm your angel, but there were no buffalo," Victoria says. "I rode Silver to Grand'Mère's. Napoleon took us to Saskatoon in his truck."

"Mother?"

"She's on her way. Her flight arrives in an hour."

"Vancouver?"

"She came home to look for us and then went back. She put up the most mortifying posters on earth — all over Vancouver."

"No — do we look like freaks?"

"Worse."

Robson Street in the grey and pouring rain fills my mind. Mary Jane stands on the street corner. Cars and buses spray water as they pass, and floppy wet posters fall from her arms. Dark tire tracks erase my ugly face.

"They thought we were hiding — either in Saskatoon or making our way to Vancouver. They questioned everyone about us, everyone."

"I'm going to be sick."

"Seriously?"

I shut my eyes.

"Look," Victoria says. She's smuggled in one of the posters — my grade ten school picture. My expression is stone cold verging on crying. I belong in Hicksville.

"I'm hideous."

"Look at me," Victoria says. Her hair is dark and greasy, pulled back in two tight French braids. Her eyes are bloodshot, as though the photographer interrupted her during a good crying session.

"I can't face them. They must despise me."

"I don't think so. Alex has been unusually calm and quiet about everything. He spends all of his time on the phone."

"Calm? Not bloody likely. He's simmering, waiting for Mary Jane to arrive before he explodes — what should we do?"

"You're asking me? Now?" Victoria slides off my bed and walks towards the door.

"Victoria?"

"What?"

"Do they know — about Marx?" She opens the heavy door, hesitates, and disappears into the hall without answering.

Mary Jane arrives late, long after they've cleared away my supper tray. I was beginning to think she might not come at all. The smell of the gloppy brown gravy and rice still lingers in the room. I am grateful for the stink of hospital food. The pathetic smell might make Mary Jane feel sorry for me, see me as the victim in all of this. I pretend to be asleep. I want to open my eyes, to see her beautiful face again, but they remain closed in fear.

"Your father's down in emergency. They're monitoring his heart," she says in greeting. I open my eyes. "He's had chest pains all morning, "she adds. She is not the mother who left at Thanksgiving. Her face is thinner. It makes her look older and somehow wiser. Her eyes are turquoise but not sad, maybe dried out from the flight. She smells cold, like the prairie winter.

"What's wrong with his heart?" I say.

"He spent last night on the back porch with the vodka."

"That explains it — coal tar shakes," I say and look out the window. The blinds are open, exposing a black sky with swirls of white blowing in the wind. I wonder if it's been blizzarding straight through since we left the cottage?

"He knows he can't drink like that. His heart beats irregularly." The coldness in her voice drifts deep inside me. I want to touch her thin hand, the blue veins on top somehow making it look fragile. I wish she still loved me. But I am pretty sure I killed that love just like I'm killing my father.

"I'm sorry," I say.

"You can tell that to your father when he gets out."

She hates me but no more than I hate myself.

Victoria thinks I might be sent away. I've read about "behavioral modification" boarding schools in the States.

They lock you in your room at night. I don't want to go to prison. I've been there already. The world is a mess, my mess. Victoria somehow seems blameless in all of it. I thought having double pneumonia would somehow soften their opinions of me. But no, all blame is on me, the devil child. I've never felt more alone on earth. Everyone has the potential to turn into an enemy. I've been shut out, rejected, hated by all; all, that is, except the chrysalis. The tall, gloomy house opens up its black cloak and welcomes me inside once again, the return of its progeny, the dark child who carries out its sinister desires.

I sleep for days, in and out of mass boredom and coughing fits. Aside from meal trays, the only visitor to the tower has been Victoria.

"Alex was offered a position at Simon Fraser," she says.

"Did he take it?"

"No. Mom said he turned it down because we were missing at the time."

"You've been talking to her?"

"Who? Mom?"

"It's just that she's been so bitchy to me. I'm surprised she's talking to you."

"She's back on tranquilizers, you know."

"I know—that's our fault too—I just hope it's not Halcion."

"She was going to fail her courses. She missed finals."

"I know, my fault — she's not going to fail anymore?"

"I heard Alex say that the dean saved her ass — she pissed off the entire faculty, but she let Mom write her finals late."

"Thank God. The dean has no idea she saved our asses too."

There is lightness inside my ribs. Breathing doesn't hurt. Even the sound of my parents arguing sounds different, comforting. "Why didn't you tell me they were skipping school? Why didn't you let me know before things got out of control? Why are you treating me like a child? How can you treat me this way?" Mary Jane yells.

Shut the hell up, Mother. Alex could have a heart attack.

The phone rings. Alex answers. "No comment," he says. I hear the knock of the receiver back on the wall. "The media's picked up on their weeks in the bush. They want to know how they survived the elements."

I push the pile of used Kleenex and toilet paper wads onto the floor and swing my knobby legs over the bed's edge. The place where I've slept for over a week is suddenly revoltingly warm and the sheets full of itchy crumbs.

"Who was that?" I call out.

"No one," Alex says.

"Did they want to talk to me or Victoria?"

"I said no one you need to know about, " Alex shouts. The phone rings again. "No one is to answer that phone, do you understand?"

Someone is at the front door. Alex's booming voice greets them. Victoria runs up the stairs and into my room. "It's Brady," she says, slightly out of breath.

My face flushes before the fear even hits my brain. My stomach falls. I can't see him. I don't want to see him. I'm not ready. I shake my head. "It can't be good. I haven't heard from him since we got back. That was ten days ago," I whisper.

"Well, he's downstairs now. That's a fact you can't change."

"What should I do? Tell him I'm asleep," I whisper.

Victoria shakes her head. "Here, put on my pink robe."

"It's not pink. It's rotting flesh grey," I say to the silky pile she thrusts onto my lap. The robe is warm and unusually lightweight, it seems to have lost most of its fibres during its shit shack vacation. I reluctantly pull the rag over my week-old flannel nightie. "My pits stink."

"He's not interested in your pits."

I don't bother to look in the mirror. I know I look worse than horrible.

"Just don't breathe on him," Victoria says.

I give her the finger and tiptoe down the stairs, never wanting to reach the bottom. Mary Jane is smiling, treating Brady like a long lost friend. Even Alex is wearing a smile. They've forged a silent bond with him; someone else did in by me. I stop on the bottom stair and look at his feet — white leather gym shoes with snow on the toes.

"We can talk on the back porch," I say, not making eye contact with anyone.

"That's not a good idea. It's too cold back there. Your lungs aren't healed," Mary Jane says.

I stand in the hall, my back towards him, stopped mid-flight to the back porch. I want to bolt down the basement stairs and hide underneath them until he leaves. "I'll be in the living room then," I say.

"I heard you have pneumonia," he says from behind me.

"No. Not anymore — I did, but I'm better now."

I sit on the sofa. He stands beside the coffee table. He forgot to take off his runners. That's not like him. My eyes crawl up to his blue jean knees. "I tried to call you but you were in BC," I say.

"The police talked to my coach while I was in Calgary — he wasn't impressed." His hands push deep inside the front pockets of his jeans in frustration. "They came close to accusing me of knowing . . . something. I might have to find a new place to live. My aunt doesn't want the responsibility of me — the police came to her house three times. I've fallen even farther behind at school because of everything." I long to kick his butt, super hard, so hard that he shuts the fuck up. "I thought I knew you — guess I don't."

I feel words slipping out of my mouth. Even as I hear them, I am embarrassed. "I bet your mother's happy." I glance at his face.

His eyes are like black ice. "She was part of your volunteer search team. So yeah, you're right." He walks towards the front door and lets himself out.

The motor of his truck coughs a few times and then rumbles. My face burns with shame. I drag myself up the stairs and shut my bedroom door. The filth is suddenly revolting. Snot rags, crunchy sheets, and the oily smell of eucalyptus hanging in the air. I hate all the pathetic pictures of Paris. I couldn't be farther from Paris if I lived on Elephant Island in Antarctica.

Victoria opens my door with the idiotic confidence of an insensitive clod. She stares at me with a self-satisfied smirk. "Are you done with my robe yet?"

I glance down at the ugly thing. "Oh, yeah. I forgot I had it on." I rip it from my shoulders and throw it at her.

"You're welcome," she says and adds, "Bitch," as she slams my bedroom door.

I am naked, stripped to my evil core. The house wraps its cloaked arms firmly around me, the prodigal daughter. It is of little comfort. The fabric is made of thick, grey guilt.

I still don't know if and when they're sending me to Lockdown High: Boarding School for Devil Children. But for starters, they're sending us back to Hicksville High. Every cell in my body resists. I do not want to go back. No one knows about Polinski except Victoria. I know they'll all think it's my fault that he hates me, because I wrote the Pervert Pants poem.

Mary Jane is flying to Vancouver after our first day back at school. Apparently she has to graduate. Alex can't take any more time off but we're finally getting some parental supervision. Granny is coming to stay. She's never been to the prairies. It will be a shock to her system. Her dyed dark brown hair will turn black or orange, and no amount of hair dye will keep it brown. It'll match either a coal tar shake or the chair on the back porch.

My sole focus is to survive the first day back at school. I am Gabriel Dumont. I return, unnoticed, to the place of my defeat. I drag my body into school, void of emotion. I talk to no one. No one talks to me. There are the looks, whispers, all of it. But at least no one actually speaks to me. Nathan Dyck can't keep his peepers off me, but he physically avoids me. It seems the slimy toad is suddenly frightened of Fuckingham.

Polinski's shirt is the colour of plastic yellow roses and his brown too-wide tie hangs down the centre like a long turd. He stands at the front of the class with his hands in his front pant pockets, rocking back and forth on his heels, smiling a self-satisfied grimace behind the prissy mustache. He seems to be ignoring me, not one question so far. Maybe some good will come out of this. "Class — grade eleven — quiet please — we have a guest this morning. A representative from Child Find is here to talk to you about teenage runaways." He won't let me go. Swallow me, desk and all, deep into the earth.

Granny looks out of place in her long, fur-trimmed coat, hat, and high-heeled winter boots, the Russian Queen from St. Petersburg inspecting our humble Siberian peasant treasures. Her first royal duty is a visit to the natural history museum. The thermometer says it is minus thirty-one degrees Celsius inside the front porch. The steam from my breath makes it hard to see the specimens. Granny's glasses are nothing but fog. It's a joke holding the shrew bottle up for her to see. Her presence is surreal, almost like having Mary Jane home but more work. I have to make an effort. It is easier with Mary Jane. I can ignore her without guilt.

So far Gran's hair dye is holding up, but it's only a matter of time. Sooner or later her white roots will show up and she'll try to dye them using her usual kit from the pharmacy. That is when things will get interesting. There is no way our well water will allow her hair to remain brunette. I know it seems mean-spirited to secretly delight in the possibility of my grandmother's hair turning a godawful unnatural shade, but I can't help myself. I guess I want her to share in my misery, living on the land of the malcontented. Perhaps then I'll see pity in her eyes rather than doubt and the determined conviction to set me straight.

"I feel a nasty draft," Gran says and walks into the hall to turn up the thermostat. I wait for the purr of the furnace before heading for the living room to sit down on the vent. I untuck my T-shirt and lean against the wall, letting the warm air touch my back. Alex blows through the front door with the wind. He doesn't even bother to take off his snow boots. I know he's looking at the thermostat. He walks into the living room and tries to solicit me with pantomime.

"Sorry, Alex. I can't understand what you're trying to say."

He holds his finger to his lips to shush me. "Did she turn up the heat again?" he whispers. I nod. Granny is killing him and I love it. It's a cold war between them. Alex is too afraid to take her on overtly. She's never liked my dad, never trusted him to look after her precious Mary Jane. I do believe he has fucked up on that account. If Mary Jane's stories about what he was like when I was a baby are even slightly accurate, he was a total ass. Maybe that's why I feel the distance; I remind her too much of Alex. I'm long, lean, freckled, and blond like him.

"Who wants to go to Saskatoon tonight? I've got tickets to the hockey game," Alex says, setting a stack of university essays onto the kitchen counter. The scenario is dodgy: a hockey game in Saskatoon, and he wants to take us. His girlfriend must have backed out.

"Take the girls. There's a BBC mystery on tonight," Gran says.

Now I get it. Gran's been monopolizing the TV. He's going through *Hockey Night in Canada* withdrawal. "The Blades are playing the Regina Pats," he says. "Who's coming? I'm leaving in a half an hour."

The Blades. Brady. "I'll come," I say.

I sit, under down feathers and wool, trying hard not to inhale the scent of Victoria's candy apple body splash. As we approach the outskirts of Saskatoon, the city lights turn the horizon into an orange glow. I'm terrified that I might see Brady and terrified that I won't. I want to stay in the truck, cozy in my unisex down armour, driving into the night towards an orange glow that we never actually reach, like chasing a rainbow.

Hockey might be fun to play, but it's boring to watch whenever Brady's not on the ice. I can't help myself, my brain chants, *Brady, Brady, Brady,* each time he skates in front of where we're sitting. "How many periods are there in hockey, three or four?" I ask Alex, during the first break.

"Three," Alex says.

"What? We have to sit here two more times?" Victoria says.

"Two more periods, one more intermission," Alex says.

"Thank God," I say. The twenty minutes felt like twenty hours.

Something happens in third period. The game turns violent — elbows, pushing, jabbing, slamming into the boards, sticks stabbing. Just hit the damn puck, all you testosterone-filled losers! Number nine is helped off the rink. He leaves behind bloody splotches that stain the ice.

"Brady's in the naughty box!" Victoria shrieks.

I catch a glimpse of him as he slams his stick into the boards in a rage, just before he enters the penalty box.

"Did you see that?" Victoria says.

"Yes! He's a little cranky tonight, isn't he?"

"What did he do? Did you see?" Victoria says.

"Nothing that the other players weren't all doing," I say.

"Boarding," Alex says.

Victoria pulls off her mittens and begins to chew on her fingernails. The enormous grey pompom on top of the navy toque bobs as she pecks away, like a squirrel chewing a pine cone. "Is it over?" she asks, glancing up from bleeding nail beds.

"Where have you been? The Blades won five to three."

"Good game. Did you girls enjoy it?" Alex says.

"Yes," we say in unison. We are the unisex twins tonight.

"If you wait outside the locker room, you might see Brady," Victoria says.

"No!" I shout, far too loudly. The ice queen has made a royal ass of herself. Alex might use this bit of sensitive information to humiliate me.

"You're missing out. Boys like nothing more than a pretty girl waiting for them after the game," he says. Alex is being nice. Alex is almost never nice. Maybe he's getting carried away because he's on a high from the game. Maybe he gets how terrified I am. Everything is truth or dare in this family. I have to go and at least look like I am trying to find him. Brady, that old school chum who I don't give two shits about.

"I don't know — I guess so," I say.

"I'll bring the truck around to the front entrance, where we came in. Be there in half an hour," he says.

"What am I going to do?" Victoria says.

"Come with me. I want to pick up a newspaper," Alex says and leaves, taking Victoria with him.

I stand behind a group of little girls, waiting to meet the players. I unzip my parka and stuff the giant toque and scarf into the inside pockets. The players start to trickle out, wearing suits, their hair damp. None of them give me a second look; they walk by like royalty. Their egos are disproportionately huge. Brady — I want to bolt. My face flushes at the sight of him. His hair, wet with either sweat or a locker room shower, looks straight and nearly black. The back has grown a little longer. Hockey hair. If he were still my friend, it would be chopped off in no time. He looks almost NHL material in the suit. The cluster of little girls surround Brady before he has a chance to see me. How mortifying; he's got himself a little fan club of prepubescent groupies.

Why did I ever listen to Alex? When has he ever given me good advice? I knew this was a stupid idea. I back up, trying to disappear into a hallway behind me. Brady looks up. Our eyes lock. My face flushes a deeper shade of red, like blood on ice — pathetic groupie. I struggle for a facial expression. My face can only manage an embarrassed smile, the one I share with Alex, resembling a chimpanzee in distress. He looks down again, stopping to sign his autograph for the girls, a heartthrob to minors.

"Hi," he says.

"I came with Alex," I blurt out.

"You saw the game?"

"Yes, I did."

"Did you like it?"

"Yes, I did — good game — although . . ."

"What?" he says.

"You weren't very happy about getting a penalty. I saw you slam your stick into the boards."

"Oh, that — it happens," he says, with authority and confidence, as though I'm a locker room reporter and he's in the NHL. The crowd of minors thins and the hall suddenly becomes too quiet. "Katie said you're back at school."

"No choice. It was either that or boarding school in the States."

One of his teammates passes us. He stops to playfully hit Brady a few times. He looks back at me and then at Brady. He raises his eyebrows a few times. Brady shakes his head, slightly embarrassed by him. Two teenage girls, about my age, in tight jeans with poofed-up bangs, appear at the end of the hall. Brady's more than embarrassed, he's nervous. They're Saskatchewan girls and they're waiting for him.

"You're moving to the States?" he says, obviously too distracted to care what I just said.

I don't know what to say. He knows nothing about my real life, nothing about the weeks at the cottage. He's right, he doesn't know me. "You were right about one thing," I say.

"What?" He looks puzzled and curious.

"Nothing. Really, I should go. Good game. I'll tell Katie that I finally saw you play." My legs are wooden. I feel defeated, embarrassed — a loser. He lets me walk away.

I wait outside, as far from Brady as I can get. I can't stop the tears that fall from my chin onto the icy parking lot, salty water on ice.

"Lydia?" It's Brady, out of breath.

"Sorry. I didn't know what to say. It's been a long night, a long month," he says.

I can't read him. Does he feel pity for me? Is that it? I can't bear it, anything but pity. "I'm sorry too — I hope your aunt didn't kick you out or anything," I say, taking off my mitten and wiping under my eyes. My hand is black with mascara.

"No, still living there. Everything's cool." His hair is starting to curl ever so slightly around his forehead.

"Your mother, does she still hate me?"

He laughs a half-laugh and runs his hand through his wet hair. "No, not really. She's not your biggest fan but whatever — she was here tonight, watching the game." He swings the wet hair that settled over his left eye from his forehead.

Thank God I missed her. I feel a surge of anger. It fuels my self-confidence. "I'm okay with it. I frighten some women, mostly the boring ones."

"Katie likes you," he says.

I feel a tiny spark fly from him and land on me. "Don't forget Victoria, on a good day. That's a total of two," I say, flustered. Small headlights crunch their way through the nearly empty parking lot. "My chauffeur has arrived. I have to go." I open the truck door. Victoria refuses to look out the window and acknowledge Brady.

"Lydia? What was I right about?"

"I'll tell you some other time — see you." I slide into the black seat. I don't wave to him. I don't look back.

EIGHTEEN

Alex banishes me to the tower and Victoria to her room every night at eight thirty on school nights, nine on the weekends. It's off to the neo-Christian army we go if we dare come out before morning. Ironically, it's so boring at home with Granny and Alex keeping guard that Victoria and I banish ourselves early, just after supper.

Parisian pink my ass; the rotting flesh-coloured walls have darkened into Pepto-Bismol and, somehow, the colour is not soothing at all. It makes me nauseated, dizzy. Even the fashion photographs leave me cold. One stirs my loneliness — a woman's naked shoulders embracing a man hidden behind her. All you can see of him is his muscular arms embracing her naked back. My gut hurts.

A vision of grey frills floats past my open door and hovers at the top of the staircase as though eavesdropping on a conversation downstairs.

"What is it?" I whisper. She places one finger in front her lips and motions me to join her with her other hand. Brady's truck. The sound of his muffler is like heavenly chanting and screams from hell all at once. "Why?" I whisper, then add, "He hates me."

Alex opens the front door and lets him in. From my perch on the landing I see that he's not wearing white runners. In their place are snow-tipped, shiny black round-toed Oxfords. I follow a straight line of black right up to a freshly shaven face and slicked-back hair. "Lydia!" Alex shouts. I throw myself backwards, flat against the wall, hidden from view. I skulk into the tower, pull off my nightgown, pull on jeans, and wrap the smoking jacket tightly around my bare chest.

"Hi," I say, standing several stairs taller than him.

"Hi," he says and looks at the carpet.

The silence lasts too long. "Would you like to come in?"

"Ah — sure," he says and looks surprised, as though the thought had never occurred to him; then he bends down to unlace the sharp-looking Oxfords.

The house is quiet. Alex has retreated to his lair. The only sign of life seems to be Granny in her slippers, sipping tea at the kitchen table, gazing out of the window.

"Granny, this is my friend Brady."

She looks up from her teacup and walks to the hall entrance. Her hair has a slight florescent orange glow this evening. The water is working.

"Hello, Brady." She smiles politely but suspiciously. The no-boys-in-the-house rule seems to go way back in our family.

"We're just going to play a little chess," I say and lead him into the living room.

"Chess?" Brady says.

"Do you play?"

"A little."

I remove the chessboard from the sideboard and place it on the coffee table in front of Brady. "Who do you want to play? Blondes or brunettes?" I say.

"Never heard them called that before — brunette," he says.

"Mistake. Blondes have more fun — for real."

"We'll see," he says.

I sit beside him on the sofa and move a blond pawn two squares ahead. Brady is frozen on the sofa. He says nothing, moves nothing. "I don't have all night," I say. He moves his dark horse.

"Nice shoes — the Oxfords," I say. "Are you going British on me?"

"Maybe. Nice . . . robe?" he says.

I laugh. "Thanks — it's a vintage smoking jacket."

"You smoke?" he says.

"Only cigars — you?" I say.

"Only a pipe."

Our pawns dance in silence. My knight takes his castle. "Where are your girlfriends tonight?" I say, then immediately regret it.

He clears his throat. "Girlfriend," he corrects me.

My heart plunges unto my gut.

"You've put yourself in check," he says.

I reposition my knight to take down his queen if need be. "Why are you here?" I say.

"My girlfriend lives here — checkmate," he says.

I never go down without a fight. I lean my tall blond king to the side and shout, "Screw you!" at Brady's dark queen.

"Please."

"You're better than I expected. I only ever play with Vic and perhaps that's been my downfall."

I hear the inside back porch door open. It sounds like a decompression chamber, Alex trying to exit his sealed lair.

"I have to go soon," Brady says.

"I know," I say.

"Do you have time for a drive?"

"It's minus twenty."

"That never stopped you before."

He's quiet in the truck. I have nothing to say to him either. I put in the Bowie tape I gave him, probably the last time I saw him before we left for the shack. We drive through the dark night, along narrow, snow-packed gravel roads, not talking for two straight songs.

"If you kill the headlights it will be a black velvet world," I say.

He shuts them off.

"Speeding into the black void," I say.

The truck dips, bounces and abruptly lurches right.

"Shit — a black hole," Brady says and turns the headlights back on.

"Were you scared?" I say.

"No. Were you?"

I don't answer.

"What was it like?" he says in the ten second pause before "China Girl" begins.

"Horrible — I want to forget everything."

"You look different," he says.

"I am. I aged a hundred years in the shit shack."

"Shit shack?"

"Forget it."

"So where do you want to go?" he says.

"Anywhere but the river."

"The black velvet world has returned," I say as he cuts the engine and turns off the headlights. I stare through the windshield into a void. He's looking my way. I turn and kiss him, a solid kiss on his lips. His energy floods into me.

My smoking jacket flops open as he pulls me towards him. He leans in to kiss my naked breasts, then slides his mouth lower. I slip my hands under his T-shirt to touch his tight abs and then lower, following a narrow trail of hair, stopping to fumble with the button on his black jeans. I want him inside me. My body knows what it's doing on its own, without my mind. My hips are fluid. Everything is swollen and wet, rising and falling with the tide. I gulp in Brady like he's oxygen.

I lie across the front seat, partially undressed and tightly pressed against his warm, smooth body. Brady's eyes are closed. His breathing's changed. "No way. You're not going to sleep. We've only got twenty-eight minutes." I pull my jeans on but leave the underwear off. I stuff them into the inside pocket of the smoking jacket. "Get up. It's freezing in here." I toss him his jeans.

"Just give me a minute," he says sounding groggy. He starts the truck. The air from the engine is still warm. He pulls on his jeans. I smooth his hair and wipe the lipstick off his face but I leave his lips. They're covered in messy lipstick smudges.

"I love your lips," I say.

"Thanks." He turns on the interior light and looks at himself in the rear-view mirror. "They are lovely," he says, sitting back, not bothering to wipe his mouth.

We drive home wordlessly. I sit beside him; I need to be touching him. Once we reach the main gravel road, Brady pushes the accelerator to one hundred and forty. "Don't hit any ice," I shout over Bowie.

We arrive in our driveway at eight twenty-seven, three minutes to spare. The house is dark beneath the yard light. He stops the truck and lets it idle as I tug on my boots.

"I like your Thurston Howell the Third jacket," he says and pulls on the smoking jacket's belt.

"Shut up."

"My schedule is pretty tight until Christmas. I don't know when I'll see you again," he says.

"I'll see you again," I whisper, then lean in and bite his lip.

He rubs his bottom lip as he backs out of our driveway, then jerks the steering wheel and spins the truck around, the space between us growing until I can no longer hear his muffler.

Everyone appears to be in bed but I know they're listening to my every move. I tiptoe up to my bedroom. The air is icy behind the closed door. I flip on the light. The walls of the familiar pink tower feel slightly unfamiliar. I lie down on the bed. The night settles on my mind, and a warmth drips into my hollow core.

I sense a grey, frilly creature shuffling her way down the hall. Keep on shuffling. I don't want anyone to taint the night before I can sleep on it. "Alex took the job at Simon Fraser. They want him to start in January," the nose at my door says.

Alex is in the dungeon, toque on and newspaper in hand.

"What's going on, Alex?" I say.

"What do you mean?" he says, playing coy.

Not a good sign. It's a done deal. "Victoria says you got the SFU job," I say.

"Did she?" he says.

Don't be an ass, Father, just this once. We have to follow you around the bloody country every time you snap your fingers. "Just tell me the truth. Are we moving again?"

"The black velvet world has returned," I say as he cuts the engine and turns off the headlights. I stare through the windshield into a void. He's looking my way. I turn and kiss him, a solid kiss on his lips. His energy floods into me.

My smoking jacket flops open as he pulls me towards him. He leans in to kiss my naked breasts, then slides his mouth lower. I slip my hands under his T-shirt to touch his tight abs and then lower, following a narrow trail of hair, stopping to fumble with the button on his black jeans. I want him inside me. My body knows what it's doing on its own, without my mind. My hips are fluid. Everything is swollen and wet, rising and falling with the tide. I gulp in Brady like he's oxygen.

I lie across the front seat, partially undressed and tightly pressed against his warm, smooth body. Brady's eyes are closed. His breathing's changed. "No way. You're not going to sleep. We've only got twenty-eight minutes." I pull my jeans on but leave the underwear off. I stuff them into the inside pocket of the smoking jacket. "Get up. It's freezing in here." I toss him his jeans.

"Just give me a minute," he says sounding groggy. He starts the truck. The air from the engine is still warm. He pulls on his jeans. I smooth his hair and wipe the lipstick off his face but I leave his lips. They're covered in messy lipstick smudges.

"I love your lips," I say.

"Thanks." He turns on the interior light and looks at himself in the rear-view mirror. "They are lovely," he says, sitting back, not bothering to wipe his mouth.

We drive home wordlessly. I sit beside him; I need to be touching him. Once we reach the main gravel road, Brady pushes the accelerator to one hundred and forty. "Don't hit any ice," I shout over Bowie.

We arrive in our driveway at eight twenty-seven, three minutes to spare. The house is dark beneath the yard light. He stops the truck and lets it idle as I tug on my boots.

"I like your Thurston Howell the Third jacket," he says and pulls on the smoking jacket's belt.

"Shut up."

"My schedule is pretty tight until Christmas. I don't know when I'll see you again," he says.

"I'll see you again," I whisper, then lean in and bite his lip.

He rubs his bottom lip as he backs out of our driveway, then jerks the steering wheel and spins the truck around, the space between us growing until I can no longer hear his muffler.

Everyone appears to be in bed but I know they're listening to my every move. I tiptoe up to my bedroom. The air is icy behind the closed door. I flip on the light. The walls of the familiar pink tower feel slightly unfamiliar. I lie down on the bed. The night settles on my mind, and a warmth drips into my hollow core.

I sense a grey, frilly creature shuffling her way down the hall. Keep on shuffling. I don't want anyone to taint the night before I can sleep on it. "Alex took the job at Simon Fraser. They want him to start in January," the nose at my door says.

Alex is in the dungeon, toque on and newspaper in hand.

"What's going on, Alex?" I say.

"What do you mean?" he says, playing coy.

Not a good sign. It's a done deal. "Victoria says you got the SFU job," I say.

"Did she?" he says.

Don't be an ass, Father, just this once. We have to follow you around the bloody country every time you snap your fingers. "Just tell me the truth. Are we moving again?"

and then lead him to the kitchen. He's in sport socks. What a gentleman, removing his shoes at the door even though no one was home. He doesn't know we're moving. I don't want to tell him.

"Close your eyes," I say.

"Why?"

"It's a surprise, of course," I say, kissing his cheekbone.

Granny left us with a supply of her chocolate cinnamon buns. I take one out of the tin on the kitchen counter. Victoria swoops in beside me and muscles her hand into the tin.

"There's none left. You took the last one!"

"Brady's never tried one."

"Who cares? I helped Granny make these."

"Let Victoria have it. I'm okay," Brady says.

"Trolls first," I say and toss the bun onto the counter. "Sorry. I wanted you to try one. They are like a bite of heaven."

"It's okay — bet you taste better," he says, then clutches my waist and pulls me onto his knee.

"Not in front of the children," I whisper.

"My parents and Katie are going out tonight. Want come back to my place? We'll have the place to ourselves. We have satellite now," he says.

"Sounds okay. I'll see what Alex says — stay with me until he gets home, okay?" He nods.

We lie twisted together on my bed until the sun has set and the scent of something spicy and Italian wafts under my bedroom door. "We should go down, see what Vic's making for supper." I crawl over him, pull back on my jeans. I leave him lying on my bed.

Victoria stands at the stove in her robe, very seriously stirring Granny's spaghetti sauce.

"Want some help?"

"The menu's on the fridge," she says into the bubbling pot. "Just do what it says. Granny left us supper menus for ten days."

"Spaghetti, salad, and garlic toast," I say and open the freezer and pull out a foil-wrapped loaf. "Is the oven on?"

Brady watches us from the kitchen doorway with messy hair. I hand him the lettuce crisper. "Come. I'll put you to work. Here — rip away."

Brady systematically tears each lettuce leaf into bite-sized pieces, then slices the celery into precise slivers. I nudge Victoria to watch with me. Brady's seemingly clumsy hockey hands turn the lettuce into a salad that looks like it was prepared by a grandmother. Victoria's smile connects us. It accentuates an ache I did not even know was there, longing for my sister. We are Lydie and Vic once again.

The three of us eat by candlelight.

The sound of the front door being pushed opened startles us all — Alex. I almost forgot about him. He's wearing his wool coat. He looks dapper, the sophisticated professor. It's the image of him that I like to promote. He lays a stack of exam booklets on the kitchen counter. His face is tired. The youthful elation of the move home has left. I know what he's thinking: disappear.

Driving towards Brady's farm feels comforting, like old times. His yard is dark and still except for Duchess. She runs to greet Brady, then dashes in front of the truck and jumps on me when I open my door. I rub her back with my mittens methodically — missing what the river stole.

I survey his family room. It's weird that sometimes the tackiest of rooms are the coziest too. Brenda must have made all the giant macramé hanging plant holders. Brady passes me a can of American beer. "Sorry, I'm not up to beer tonight. Could I have a pop instead?"

I snoop through the family photo albums while Brady looks for the pop. He was an adorable baby: bald with huge brown eyes and a Buddha belly. "Your mom sure looks young. She could be my age," I shout.

Brady hands me a glass of cola. "She was," he says.

"What? She was sixteen when she had you?" I say it like I mean it, horrified.

He sits down beside me on the sofa.

"Sorry. I mean, whoa, that must have been scary for her."

Brady takes a sip of his beer. "Let's hang out in my room for awhile. You've never been on my water bed."

I can't relax into it. The wave motion makes me nauseous. I have to tell him before I chicken out. A wave propels me into him. "My dad got a job in Vancouver." I am so close to him that our lips almost touch as I form the words.

"You're moving back to Vancouver?" He sits up. His chest looks lonely naked. I attempt to hug him. "When?" He pulls my hands off him.

"After Boxing Day."

"What? That soon? Why didn't you tell me?" His voice is loud.

"It's not what I want."

He says nothing and lies back on the bed and stares at the ceiling. I study his Christie Brinkley poster on the wall. From what I can make out the dark, my guess is that her bikini is yellow. I wrap my arm around his waist. He ignores me. "You don't have to go. You're sixteen. You could stay," he says, still staring at the black ceiling.

"Yeah, well, you could go to UBC next year. We'd only have to be apart for a few months until you graduate, and then you could move to Vancouver." He doesn't say anything for a minute, then turns and rolls towards me, our bare chests meeting.

"I have a job. I'm with the Blades," he says and then kisses my neck. I melt into the water, sinking deep, where there is no light and little oxygen. "Stay," he whispers. I am lost at sea. His skin is a slow current of warm tropical water. I am reminded of my very first image of us as Romeo and Juliet, doomed young lovers. It cannot be true. I will not let it be true.

I'm startled awake. Brenda, Bill, and Katie tramp into the house. Brady's clock radio reads nine thirty. I shake him. "What should I do? Brenda will kill me," I whisper. He bolts from the bed and struggles to locate all of my clothing in the dark. He opens his closet and hands me a pile of fabric. "Get dressed in there," he whispers.

"Hello!" Brady says, his voice loud, guilty, and weird. He's not a good actor. Brenda knows I'm here, I can tell by her voice. Footsteps approach. Please, please be Brady. "It's okay. You can come out. They know you're in here." I make no move to leave the closet. I do not want to see any of them. No one opens the closet door. I finally push it open myself. Brady sits on the edge of the bed, bare-chested.

"Your shirt's inside out — and backwards too."

"You're just lucky I didn't come out naked," I say.

I stay behind Brady, trying to hide. I am Quasimodo, limping from the attic, hunched and humiliated. A kind hand reaches for mine. It is so unexpected; I am touched. I squint to see them in the bright kitchen light. They're all sitting at the kitchen table blank faced, except for Katie. She's grinning, loving that we've been caught.

"Hello," I say, to all of them shyly, holding tightly onto Brady's hand.

Bill grunts hello. Brenda says nothing, only stares at Brady. "Are you hungry, Brady? Did you get dinner?" she says.

I am invisible.

"I ate at Lydia's. She made us spaghetti — I'll be back later tonight. I'm just going to take Lydie home."

He called me Lydie. He pronounced it the German way, Lee-Dee.

"Are you sleeping here tonight?" she asks as he opens the front door.

"I don't know, probably," he says, pulling me out the door with him.

"That was scary back there," I say.

"Why? It was okay, wasn't it?" he says.

I don't disagree.

Brady stops on the road about a half a kilometre before my driveway turn off. He cuts the engine. I scratch the last bit of black polish off my fingernails. "I'm going to Banff to ski with some friends on Boxing Day," he says.

"That's convenient."

"Why?"

"You know it's my last full day here."

"I forgot — I want you to stay," he says, staring through the windshield.

I pretend to bite at my cuticles. "Why?" I say. A stupid thing to say; I don't even want an answer.

"I guess — I love you." He says it like it's a sigh.

I fixate on the door lock. Good, it is up. I want to bolt. I put my head in my hands to think.

"What? Why are you doing that?" he says, sounding defensive.

I should say something. I am out of my realm of experience. I never read about this. I glance up at him. He looks sad and alone; his jaw is tense. I slide over and whisper in his ear. "I guess — I love you too." I bite his earlobe gently.

NINETEEN

My career at Hicksville High is officially over. It is bitter-sweet. I am leaving the prairie, my queendom. I can't look at Brady's farm. I'll never ride the bus onto his property again. I stare into a blurry oblivion of tears until we pull onto our road.

Jim hands me a candy cane as I step off the bus. I feel sudden nostalgia for good old Jim and his big yellow nerd bus. I'll never ride his school bus again. "That's it. No more Polinski," Victoria says.

"Yup, that's it, I guess — boo hoo," I say.

Mary Jane has returned to the chrysalis one last time to prepare us for our final departure. She seems impressively sane as she sips a cup of poison coffee at the kitchen table in freshly applied makeup; but I know her sanity is as impermanent as her pink lipstick. I just hope it lasts until the day we pull out of here.

"Do you want to make brownies — to celebrate — Lydie? Where are the eggs, Mom?" Victoria says as she peers into the fridge.

"Still in the barn — Grand'Mère's agreed to take the chickens," Mary Jane says.

"You made her promise not to eat any of them — right?" I say. Mary Jane doesn't answer.

I crunch my way through old snow to the barn. It smells of hay, leather, and chickens. Alex's office is covered in feathers and chicken poop. The barn holds no nostalgia. Horror happened here, an ambush, complete family mutiny against me. The bad feelings overtake the brief good memories of kissing Brady. I collect all of the freshly laid eggs. They are tiny. I hold all six in my hands.

Victoria is at Twyla's for a sleepover. The lucky girl attended Twyla's church Christmas pageant in Hicksville this afternoon. I have to give Twyla Twat credit; she doesn't give up easily, one last desperate attempt to turn Victoria into a born-again Christian. The house is eerily quiet. Mary Jane and Alex are subdued and haven't seemed to move from the chesterfield all day. It's a coal tar shake kind of a moment but no one seems to be drinking.

I hold Big Momma hen against my chest. She is quiet and calm, looking ahead bravely as I carry her. She is the matriarch, a survivor, the mother of our entire flock. Snot or tears drip from the tip of my nose. I don't talk. I move like a robot. I place Big Momma beside her daughters, in the cardboard box designed for transporting live poultry.

"You promise not to eat any of them? Grand'Mère promised. She'll only eat their eggs," I say to Napoleon.

"I promise," he says and lifts the box into the back of his orange pickup.

I focus on his new ball cap. It's bright red with an emblem that says POOL. He kisses both my cheeks. "Maman is going to miss you girls," he says. His breath smells of fresh mints and his cheek is soft. I want to kiss his smooth face, wrap my arms around his broad chest, and inhale his scent. I don't look up until his truck pulls out of our driveway. I walk back into the barn. It is scattered with fresh feathers. I sit at Alex's desk. I cry for all the souls that we brought onto this land and especially for those that will not leave with us.

I tramp through the corral with blurry eyes, expecting Silver to follow. But she is uninterested in my journey today. For some reason Alex has given her oats in the cattle trough. Her eyes meet mine momentarily, then she lowers her head to inhale more oats. I walk on, through the pasture, alone. It feels unnatural, painful. Marx's absence is too strong. I walk quickly, guiding my legs into a trot then, just like Silver, I transition into a full-on gallop. I stop beside the big poplar bluff, where we spent last Christmas morning, where Brady and I entertained the cattle after the tornado. Alex and his chainsaw have pillaged any and all dead wood, and with no leaves on the living trees, the bluff is stripped naked, unrecognizable.

A painful, ice-cracking scream cuts through my brain. It is coming from downstairs. I try to shake a dead sleep from my head. Something terrible has happened. Who could be dead? Has Victoria been killed in a car accident? Has Mary Jane killed herself? Has Alex had a heart attack? Blood pounds inside my head, painfully ricocheting off my skull. God, save me from the evil truth. I move in slow motion, careful and precise, as though I am following a scripted modern dance.

I'm too late. Victoria's run out the back door. Alex and Mary Jane stand in the kitchen, zombie-faced. I study their faces, trying to extract a feel for the craziness. They are uncomfortable, guilty of something. I walk past them and onto the back porch. Victoria's robe flies through the pasture. I don't want to know.

My parents are no longer in the kitchen. They've moved into the living room, watching Victoria from the back window. My mouth is completely dry, my lips stick to my teeth in a lunatic's sneer. It is difficult to form the words, "What has happened?" Mary Jane's eyes are turquoise. She pushes past me to sit on the chesterfield. Alex runs his hands through his hair. I face Mary Jane. "Tell me, Mother. Tell me now."

"Ask your father," she says, refusing to look at me.

What bloody game are they playing? "Tell me what the fuck has happened! I'm not going to ask you again," I scream at Alex.

"Settle down. Your sister's upset, that's all."

"Why?"

"I sold Silver," he says. I watch his expression. He has to be joking. His cheek muscles twitch, exposing his teeth.

"No, Silver's coming with us to BC. Victoria's researched all the stables on the entire south coast," I say, calmly. No one responds. "Where is she? Where's Silver? Has Victoria gone to find her?"

"No. I sold her yesterday. We loaded her at noon."

"She's gone? She's not in the pasture?"

He doesn't answer me.

"Go get her — now! You lied. You tricked us. I hate you," I scream. The anger is fuel. I transition into the adult, serious and assertive. "Tell me where she is. I need to know." They are mute. I lose all composure. "I'm going to buy her back myself!"

"It's too late, Lydia. I sold her back to her previous owners. They'll give her a good life," Alex says.

"That weird bee farmer? You are evil!" I physically push him in the stomach. He nearly loses his balance.

"Stop it, Lydia!" Mary Jane yells. I push past everyone and everything, only pausing to pull on my winter boots. I need to find Victoria. I run towards the biggest rock pile. My lungs burn as I climb the ice-covered boulders. The cattle are gathered way off in the far corner. I slip as I jump from the last of the rocks, crushing my tailbone. "Fuck!" I scream and limp towards the herd. They are all alert and quiet, facing the same direction. A strange wailing radiates from inside the herd, then a streak of unnatural pink. Victoria is in the middle of the herd. I follow her movements as she wanders amongst the cattle, looking for something. I am afraid for her and for me. The rogue attack cow might strike at any time.

"Victoria!" That did it — stampede. The cattle scatter, leaving one lone pink mess standing. I run to her. She swings both fists at me.

"Where were you? You could have stopped them. The only time I've ever left this place and you let this happen!"

"Stop it! I never would have left had I known what they were planning. I hate those losers! I hate them both," I scream.

"Silver!" Victoria calls her name out in wails. I hold her bony shoulders tight to my chest. She slides through my grasp and collapses onto the ground. I fear she might go catatonic on me again.

"I know where she is. I'll drive you there. We can get her back." She looks up at me startled, hopeful, her freckles bright on her red face, the poster child for pitiful.

"Where?"

"At that grotty bee farm we bought her from."

"Take me there." She stands and breaks into a run for home. I don't know how I am going to pull it off. We have absolutely no money, and I don't know how to get to Langham. I wasn't paying attention when we bought Silver.

Victoria sits inside the truck, waiting for me. I have no choice but to get into the driver's seat. Alex pokes his bushy head out of the front door. We lock the truck. He walks towards the driver's side. "Where do you think you two are going?" he says.

"Please don't bring out the axe again," I say for only Victoria to hear.

"I've got the keys," Victoria says. She holds up the extra key from the glove compartment. Alex lifts the hood and disappears behind the blue wall. I try the key in the ignition.

"Shit. He's done something to the truck so it won't start. We're screwed."

Alex slams the hood down and walks back inside the house. I pull my arms inside my sweatshirt and pull it over my knees to keep warm. We sit for one hour, one long, cold hour, and then another. The wind grows in strength, jostling the truck around, rocking our lost souls. Snow begins to fall, small, pin prick-sized, almost invisible flakes. The temperature has dropped since I ran through the pasture this morning. Victoria sits, teeth chattering, not sharing an inch of her ratty robe with me.

The snow falls in steady sheets of white. I cannot judge how long we've been sitting inside the tin can of a truck. "Take a look in there for the emergency candle," I say.

Victoria opens the glove box and retrieves an empty silver aluminum can with a short yellow candle inside. She hands me a matchbook. "Voila," I say, placing the glowing candle on the dash between us. "This should heat things up."

My neck hurts from nodding off. The truck interior is streaked black and grey in the darkness. The grey morphs into yellow and then red. The cab's become the princess bed inside the shack. "I can't — I can't do it anymore," I say. I reach for the door handle and glance at Victoria. "Come on, let's go inside and try to figure things out." She ignores me. "It's freezing in here."

"No."

I go in alone. I walk straight up to my room, lock the door, and lay on my bed. I don't want to wait for Paris. I want to live now. I rip the photos from my wall one by one, pausing to stack them in a neat pile. Suddenly, a destructive urge pulses through my brain and my hands become claws, crumpling each photograph violently and forming them into one giant wad of grey paper. I understand Dumont and his return to Batoche. He'd lost too much to stay away. Everything, his entire existence, his love, hate, birth, and death, it was all tied to the land, his land. His only hope at redemption was to come home, to fulfill his final destiny.

Victoria left the truck a few hours ago but she hasn't come in. I suspect that she's in the barn, as the light in Alex's chicken-feathered office came on suddenly. She's either out there or hightailing it for the river. It's too quiet. The coyotes are gone. They never come near the house anymore. They left about the same time as Marx. He was the reason they came, their muse.

My Marx. I need to escape but there is no place left to run. I've already been there and there was hell.

I stare out the sewing room window, past the yard light towards the tracks, waiting for the train. Suddenly, I see a reflection in the dark window, a man in a hat . . . a muddled memory of the man in the shack window. I bolt from the house, running in sock feet on ice. I reach the midnight train as her horn cuts through the frigid night. She storms by, blowing hot sparks of greasy air up my nightgown, warming my cold soul.

Christmas morning is torture. I thought last year would have topped the charts as being one of the worst ever. But I was wrong. Hauling wood all morning is a warm family memory compared to our estrangement. We open our gifts and retreat into separate rooms. No Christmas Morning Wife Saver this year. I eat the chocolate Santa in my room, listening to my new clock radio. Victoria's received an art easel and painting supplies. She only ever likes to draw horses, so the gift's rather horrific.

Brady stops to say goodbye on his way to Banff. I don't cry. It is as though I am standing behind an invisible wall, listening and watching. His eyes are like glass, as dark as Grand'Mère's black coffee. The image of him will stay with me, frozen in my mind. It doesn't matter that I'm sixteen. I could be twenty-six or eighty-six, for that matter. When it's real, you know. I won't let myself miss him. I will hide our love deep inside, so deep that no one will ever see it. I need to be an ice queen for a while longer.

The chrysalis finally cracks open, releasing us: beautifully ugly wingless beasts. What they say isn't true, that you can never go back. You can go back easily enough; we're going back. But the bitter truth is that I don't want it anymore. Too much blood has been spilled. We are a twisted bunch, poisoned by the ill wind that blows across our land, the godforsaken. It hammers at the windows of the house, seeping into our malcontented minds.

Alex slows the truck and signals, as we're about to leave the driveway. "Stop!" I shout.

"What is it?" Mary Jane asks and then turns to look into the back seat. I lunge across the seat and grasp Victoria's dingy, makeshift travel pillow.

"No," Victoria says. Her hand clutches the ball tightly. Our eyes meet. I nod. Victoria relaxes her grip. I roll down the frost-covered window and toss out the battered, grey robe—a shadow of its former pink, silky self. The cold wind catches it and sends it sailing through the air and then suddenly rejects it, dropping it onto the fence where it catches on barbed wire and flutters like a wing-damaged moth. I roll up the window as we turn onto the gravel road for the last time.

"Don't do that again. From now on, no one says stop but me," Alex says.

We travel back the way we came, retracing our naïve tracks. We are a motley crew, two members short. George never did come home. Mary Jane was wrong about that. The house looks tall, shabby, and silent. I keep watching until it becomes no more than a pimple on the prairie.

Acknowledgements

I thank the many individuals who stuck with me to bring *Queen of the Godforsaken* to fruition: my sun, moon, and stars, my daughters, Mistaya, Tabitha, and Penelope (who knew Mist would become the Bowie-obsessed girl I wrote about?); Peter, my husband, for his unflinching support and patience with my obsessive writing habits; my friend and first editor, Robert Carlson; my editor, Kim Beach, from whom I learned much; my first dedicated readers, Theresa, Miranda, Catherine, and Kyran.

Finally, I thank my dad for hanging the Louis Riel curtains in his office so long ago. I was convinced that the bushy haired, mustached man on the curtains was my father. For a brief period of my youth, I believed Louis Riel and my dad were one and the same.